I'LL
NEVER
TELL

BOOKS BY CASEY KELLEHER

I'LL NEVER TELL

CASEY KELLEHER

bookouture

Published by Bookouture in 2021

An imprint of Storyfire Ltd.
Carmelite House
50 Victoria Embankment
London EC4Y 0DZ

www.bookouture.com

ISBN: 978-1-80019-997-2
eBook ISBN: 978-1-80019-996-5

For Marlene,
For getting through one of the hardest of years,
and for inspiring so many others on your way.

1

NOW

She turned and scanned the entire street from where she stood.

She shouldn't be here. She knew that. But she just couldn't help herself.

Curiosity had finally got the better of her and the pull of the place, today of all days, was just too hard to fight against. Because she had fought it. So hard. Every single day of her life.

Knowing what it could do to her to come back here again. Knowing how much it could cost her. But before she knew what she was doing she'd talked herself into it, justifying all of the reasons why she *should* come here. Telling herself that maybe it would help her to see the place again.

This house. That maybe, after all this time it would give her some kind of closure. Closure. Who was she kidding? She laughed at the thought of the term. There would never be any kind of closure from any of this, not really. Her life had been ruined. Ripped from beneath her. And some of that had been all her own doing.

Still, what was the harm in coming back here just this once? she had figured.

Only now that she was here, she wasn't so sure. She shivered and pulled her jacket up tightly underneath her chin in a bid to keep the cold out as day quickly turned to night.

Darkness was descending and she felt grateful for that. Because without it, she wouldn't have been so brave to come here. She wouldn't have wanted to risk being seen.

But then, who would recognise her? It had been twenty years now, after all. Twenty years to the very day, she thought as she looked up at the strobe of lights above her as the streetlamps flickered on. Giving her comfort that she could hide amongst the shadows now that the natural light was starting to fade.

And it was silly really. To not be able to shake the guilt that she felt. The guilt of coming back here. As if she had done something really bad. Something so forbidden. A passer-by wouldn't see any of that. All they'd see is someone walking down the street. Just a woman taking a casual late-evening stroll. But there was nothing casual about her being here, she reminded herself. She was back here for a reason. A purpose.

She scanned the row of houses that lined each side of the road in search of some familiarity. Unsure what it was exactly she thought she'd be seeking out that would give her some kind of clarity. Because now she was here, she already knew that there wouldn't be any peace. There was no closure here.

She felt her heartbeat quicken. Then a tightness in her chest. If anything, coming here was only going to do the opposite and upset her again. Bring back the memories that she'd spent a lifetime trying to bury.

Yet robotically she continued to walk as she placed one foot in front of the other and forced herself onwards. All the while she willed herself to remember something familiar. Anything at all. As she eyed the neat rows of pretty front gardens, the carefully tended flower beds already in full bloom. The rows of narrow driveways that twisted up the side of every house.

She stared into each window as she passed. Just a fleeting glance, hoping to catch a sign of life behind the curtains. Spot a familiar face inside. But there was probably no one here any more that she had known back then. No one who would recognise her now. And in some ways, knowing that helped too. Because the world had moved on. Thank God. People had moved on. Eventually. She'd even managed to move on too. In the end. Though it hadn't been easy.

She reached the second to last house in the street and stopped dead still. The sight of the place nearly floored her. The feeling so unexpected, so magnified that it was like a punch to her gut. Winded, she took it all in. She had expected to see the messy, overgrown front garden, the grass standing two feet taller than the other houses down the street, unkempt, unloved. The broken, rusting washing machine sitting next to the front door; the round silver door hanging from its hinges as the exposed drum collected water.

She forced herself to take a slow, deep breath to calm her rapidly beating heart. Her fists felt clammy as they hung loosely down at her sides. And suddenly she was right back there.

She stared at the wooden window frames, their paint flaking, hanging down in clumps. And she remembered how the cold had crept in so easily through each thin pane of glass. How her hair had swayed with the breeze sometimes as the draught had swept through the house. How she sometimes got neck ache from sitting so rigidly, frozen with the cold. It was often warmer outside the house than it was in.

She blinked, and the fleeting memory passed. The transition startled her as she realised that she was back in the now. The present.

The worn, tired house wasn't there any more. The peeling paintwork gone, replaced with a white speckled render. The wooden windows all been swapped out to a modern anthracite grey. The garden neat and tidy, the carefully tended flower beds in bloom and full of colour. The place looked homely and warm. And she was aware that that should comfort her. That it should bring her a feeling of relief. Yet inside, the sadness still swirled in the pit of her stomach.

She held her breath then as, upstairs, a light went on. And she watched as the silhouette of a person crossed what had once been the main bedroom. Before the light went off again and plummeted the house back into darkness.

A few painstakingly slow minutes later there was more movement downstairs. A shadow danced across the room. Another light switched on.

She thought of *her* then. As she imagined her there inside, all alone, as she festered, still, after all these years, and she wondered if she ever thought of her too? After she had cast her aside the way she had.

After she had cut her out.

Liar. Liar. Liar.

The accusation still felt so raw and sharp, even now. Like a serrated knife to her broken heart. She felt something wet on her face and realised that she was crying – she hadn't noticed the tears until they had started to fall. Her fists were clenched tightly in balls at her sides. And inside, she felt it. Her anger building, raging and wild. For everything she'd been through and all that had been done to her.

She shouldn't have come here.

2

NOW

Alessia woke abruptly to the sound of shattering glass as broken shards showered down and covered her and the sofa that she was lying on. Tiny splinters stung her face as they cut into her skin and tangled themselves in her hair. Alert now, aware of the sudden danger that loomed in the air all around her, she sat up and wiped away the remnants from her eyes so that she could see properly.

Her first thought was Jacob, who like her had been woken by the sudden eruption of noise. His frantic cries travelled down the stairs and filled the lounge. She must have dozed off, she realised, as she remembered the feeling of wanting to close her eyes just for a few minutes. To enjoy the peace and quiet of the evening after Jacob had fought her so fiercely before he'd finally exhausted himself and given in to sleep. They had both been wrenched wide awake now though.

She needed to go to Jacob, but first she needed to work out what just happened. How had the living room window behind her just exploded? It must have been an accident. There must be a reasonable explanation.

Her disorientation turned to panic as she got up and stepped carefully around the broken shards of glass as she scanned the floor for clues. Though already she was filled with a sense of dread. A dread that had been building inside of her for weeks now. No matter how hard she'd tried to force it back down it had lingered there. Waiting to pounce. She knew – even before her eyes followed the trail of sparkling glass as it shone up from the carpet like a small splay of diamonds, even before her gaze finally rested on the brick that had somehow wedged itself underneath the TV cabinet – that the window had been broken on purpose.

She held her breath, aware of the irony that it had been wrapped so neatly in brown crumpled paper and tied with a frayed piece of string, as if someone had just personally sent her a gift.

She turned back to the window and eyed the small, jagged fragments of glass that still hung there. Suspended in the air with uncertainty like icicles, as if they too might come crashing down at any second. Her arms prickled with goosebumps as she felt the rush of cool night air as it blasted freely around the room. But it wasn't the sudden drop in temperature that set her on edge. It was the fear that rapidly rose up from the pit of her stomach. The over-whelming sense of immediate menace all around her.

Why would anyone deliberately throw a brick through her window? To scare her, or worse, hurt her? Did they know she would be alone tonight? That Carl was working away? Another slice of fear cut through her then. What if they were still out there right now, watching her gutlessly from beneath the comfort of darkness? What if they were drinking in her reaction, revelling in her terror? Alessia knew that she must brave it and look. That she needed to be quick, that she might only have this one chance.

She switched off the main light and pressed herself up against the wall. She tried to keep out of view as she edged slowly towards the broken window and forced herself to peer out across the street. As she scanned the road, outside all was still: the tidy hedgerows and busy flowerbeds that edged the neat strips of lawn and twisted alongside each car-adorned driveway swayed in the gentle breeze. And she felt less alone as she eyed each neighbouring house, noting as she allowed her gaze to travel how many people were home. How the faint warm yellow hues of light beamed out from behind each closed curtain and blind, and a brighter light nearer the road spilled out from the sparsely positioned streetlamps. There was no other movement or noise. Whoever had thrown the brick had thrown it with intention and moved quickly because they would have known that they would be seen.

And a small part of her wondered if perhaps it might have been kids. That maybe she was just being paranoid and thinking the worst. Maybe this wasn't a deliberate attack? And she really wanted to believe that. But what were the chances?

Stop it Alessia, you're just being neurotic. She silently chastised herself for allowing her mind to immediately jump to the worst conclusions. Though paranoia had always been a natural instinct in her, and she'd been worse since Jacob was born. A lot worse. She knew that.

Yes. It had probably just been teenagers. Bored and having a laugh. Causing some damage at someone else's expense. Just a stupid prank or a dare gone wrong, nothing more sinister than that.

But, of course, no matter how much she tried to tell herself that, no matter how much she tried to convince herself that it was nothing, the hairs on the nape of her neck still stood to attention. Her gut told her that there was danger out there. Why this? Why now? Today of all days. What were the chances?

She clutched at the wall behind her and took a long deep breath. Only her chest was restricted now, her breathing hollow and raspy. The onslaught of a panic attack – something she'd thought she'd left behind her, way back, in her old life. She couldn't go through all of this again. *Breathe!*

She made her way back across the lounge, and as she stepped tentatively around the sharp shards of glass, she thought about the brick. Wrapped in paper and tied with a string.

The paper. It might be a note? Or a clue?

Jacob was still crying. His cries louder now, erratic. She needed to go to him. To hold him close and comfort him. And she needed him. To breathe in his familiar, warm smell. To know that he was safe. With another thrill of panic, she realised Jacob could have been right there, in the very spot where the brick landed. As he had been the night before. Giggling away to himself triumphantly that he'd got his own way as he played with his toy cars and dinosaurs, after he'd yet again fought off sleep and she'd yet again given in and let him stay up later than she knew she should. What was the harm in a few more minutes?

Tonight, the harm could have been catastrophic. Somebody could have really hurt him. They could have killed him. She needed to go to him. But first she needed to know who was behind this.

Alessia's hands trembled as she reached for the brown paper and unwrapped it from what she'd already guessed rightly was a brick. She felt the feeling of pure terror convulse inside of her. Jacob's sobs were hysterical now. She should go to him. Only she couldn't move. Her eyes were fixed to the paper. The words blurry as they swam across the page.

FOUND YOU!

A pool of dread formed in her stomach as she realised that she was right to be scared. Then the banging started. A loud pounding at the front door. A voice shouting. Instinctively, she screwed the note up and shoved it inside her pocket. She stood, her hand clutching the brick, and made her way towards the door.

3

THEN

She can hear what they are saying. Of course, she can. How could she not? It's like listening to a recording playing over and over again on repeat. They say that she's in shock. And maybe they are right. Maybe she is in shock. Because none of this feels real.

Sitting here, in a police cell. Her small body shaking violently against the cold that not even the blanket she's wrapped in is able to keep out. It's as if the freezing air has seeped down, deep into her bones.

Her hands are clasped tightly around the ragged doll that sits limply on her lap, and she clutches it to her as if it's offering her some kind of comfort. As if she believes that if she hugs it tightly enough to her, it might be able to stop the tremor that ripples so dramatically through her body. The only other sound in the room comes from her as she anxiously taps her toes rhythmically against the cold cell floor.

She stops then, dead still.

The sound is replaced by the police officer's constant questions.

'Can you tell us why you did it?'

'But I didn't do it,' she keeps saying. And she's telling the truth. But it's like they don't want to hear it. She can't seem to give them what they want, because they don't believe her. No matter how many times she tries to tell them. A hundred times, maybe? She's lost count, and her voice has gone now, as if it too has given up trying to make them believe what she is saying.

Her desperate pleas have been crushed small and drowned out by their growing accusations.

'Tell us what really happened. Tell us the truth.'

And she hears the desperation behind their words. As they float in through her ears, and her brain tries to comprehend the urgency there.

She doesn't want to get *her* in trouble. She doesn't want to blame *her*. But what choice does she have?

'We know that you did it.'

The certainty of the words floors her. It's not a question now, it's a statement.

'But I didn't do it. It wasn't me. Ask Sarah, she'll tell you,' she says softly, barely audible as her voice cracks with emotion.

And then she's left alone. Alone with her thoughts. And all the images inside her head of her mother when she'd been told the news. How the guttural, raw sound that had left her mouth was like nothing Emma-Jayne had ever heard before. She squeezes her eyes shut tightly in hope of forcing the memory out from her head. And when she opens them again, the police officer is back, a woman she doesn't recognise standing beside him.

'This is Amanda Miller. She's a social worker from Children's Services. I'm going to leave you both to speak, Emma-Jayne.'

She nods as Amanda offers her a ready smile. But there is something about the way she lets her hair hang down in front of her face, as if she is trying to compose herself. Or to hide from the fact that she's been crying. And Emma-Jayne doesn't know how she knows it, but she is sure that the woman's tears had been for her.

Once they are alone, Amanda sits down on the bed next to her. Close. So close that the woman's strong, floral perfume catches at the back of Emma-Jayne's throat. And she offers Emma-Jayne her hand. And Emma-Jayne takes it, glad of the warmth. Glad of the comfort. Of suddenly feeling not quite so alone any more.

'I want you to know that you can talk to me, Emma-Jayne. About anything. I'm here for you. Just you.'

And there's something about the way that she speaks to her now that they are alone in the cell, the way that her words are gentle and full of what sounds like compassion, that makes her almost believe her.

'Do you want to talk about what happened?'

She shakes her head, still not completely trusting Amanda. Then she sits in silence and thinks it through, biting her lip with frustration.

Because no one has believed her so far. So, what would be the point in talking? They won't listen to her anyway. They don't believe that she didn't do it.

'I just want to help you, Emma-Jayne. Anything you want to tell me, anything at all,' Amanda says softly. And Emma-Jayne sees her eyes pool with fresh tears again before she fights at forcing them back.

And Emma-Jayne guesses that she does that for her. That she doesn't want to upset her even more than she already is.

And she can still feel the warmth of her hand. It's soothing.

And somehow this feels even worse than how the police officers treated her, with their awkwardness, the lingering looks. All talking about her in hushed whispers. Making her feel like one of the frogs that she observed in her science class at school. Like she'd been shoved under a microscope and was being poked and prodded before the dissection. Amanda isn't doing any of that and somehow that unnerves her even more.

'I want to see Sarah,' she asks suddenly, trying her luck. If this woman really wants to help her, then she can prove it. Because she needs to see Sarah. She needs to know that she is all right. And she wonders if Sarah is in another room just like this one? Are they both purposely being kept apart? Played off against each other as these people try to get to the truth? Emma-Jayne wonders if Sarah feels scared too. If they are prodding and poking at Sarah, just like they are doing to her. They must be.

Only she knows that Sarah won't be as easily intimidated. She's stronger than that, and smarter. Sarah would have told them the truth, wouldn't she? But if she has, then why do the police keep asking her if she did it? It doesn't make sense. And Emma-Jayne can feel a gut-wrenching swirl of anxiety forming deep down in her stomach.

Something isn't right.

'Let's just concentrate on you, right now, Emma-Jayne.' Amanda pauses. As if she wants to say something else, something more, but suddenly she changes her mind. 'If there's anything you want to tell me, now is the time.' She sits forward on the bed, her hands still warm around Emma-Jayne's. Her eyes drawn to the tatty-looking doll.

Emma-Jayne nods.

She needs to believe so desperately that someone wants to help her. Because she feels completely and utterly alone now. And she's scared.

But now part of her suspects that perhaps she'd been right all along and this woman can't help her – and that, worse, she doesn't actually want to.

She takes a moment to glance around the cell at her surroundings, taking in the sterile white walls as she questions Amanda's motive in pretending to be so nice to her. To work out why she is here. She takes in the hard, makeshift bed and the thick brown scratchy blanket they're both sitting on; the white toilet basin in the corner of the room that she's so desperate to use only she's too scared to, in case someone is watching. Because there's a camera above it.

And if someone is watching, are they watching them right now? Is Amanda's niceness all an act she's putting on to get her to talk, to open up to her?

'Sarah didn't do it, did she, Emma-Jayne? You did it. You killed him. I just want to know why. I need you to tell me why. Then I can help you.'

Emma-Jayne's mouth drops open, her eyes wide with shock, as she strains to take in what Amanda is saying to her. Her words so certain. So sure.

As if she's already made her mind up.

As if she already has her answers.

'No. I didn't do it,' she says, but her words don't carry as much conviction now as she shuts her eyes and tries to go back there. Tries to remember.

Why do they all sound so certain, so convincing?

She didn't kill him. Did she?

She squeezes her eyes shut tightly and sees herself and Sarah standing over the pool of dark, red blood. As they both stared down at the lifeless body lying at their feet.

She's crying but Sarah is smirking.

'Sarah?' she starts to say weakly as she opens her eyes again. Wanting to explain. Only Amanda slowly shakes her head.

That feeling that there's something else Amanda's not telling her grows. Something that she isn't saying.

And then Emma-Jayne realises what's really happening here.

'She told you it was me, didn't she? Sarah is blaming me?' And she doesn't want it to be true. It can't be true. Sarah wouldn't do that to her. But she has. And she can see it on Amanda's face. They believe her. They believe Sarah.

'Why would she say that? Why would she lie? I want my mum!' she says weakly, recalling her mother's earlier screams. How she'd collapsed at the news. How she'd folded in on herself, on the floor right in front of her.

'I know you do,' Amanda says simply, nodding her head.

And Emma-Jayne sees that Amanda can't offer her that either. Not now. Maybe not ever. Instead, she feels her squeeze her hand tighter. The warmth of her palms cupping her own and for a few seconds Emma-Jayne relaxes.

As she sits there, dressed in clothes that don't belong to her. Her hair still soaked from the rain. Her body trembling with the cold and the shock of the night's events. It's all she can do not to collapse into Amanda's arms and sob her heart out to her. To let her hold her.

To beg her to make all of this horrific nightmare go away.

All she wants to do is press rewind. To go back to before. Before any of this happened. No matter how bad any of that had been. Because right now everything feels so much worse. And for a few minutes she can think of nothing else.

'I can't help you if you don't tell me the truth, Emma-Jayne. I just want you to tell me what really happened. You can trust me.'

Emma-Jayne pulls her hand away. The spell broken instantly. Trust? No. Not any more. She'd trusted Sarah too, hadn't she? And look where that had got her.

4

NOW

'Okay, I managed to tape up both sides, so it should do you just fine until the morning,' Jimmy said, his tone full of reassurance as Alessia led him back towards the front door. 'Are you sure you don't want me to give you a hand moving that box of glass before I go? It's no trouble you know.'

'No, honestly. It can wait until the morning; you've already done more than enough as it is.' Alessia smiled, grateful that her elderly neighbour from a few doors down had heard the noise of her window shattering and come to her aid. He'd done his best at boarding up the window for her, while she'd picked up all the shards of glass and hoovered the floor several times to make sure she hadn't missed any.

The last thing she wanted was for Jacob to cut himself crawling around in here.

'I'll call a glazier first thing. Thank you, Jimmy. You're a star!'

'Oh, don't thank me. I'm only too happy to help. You got me out of having to endure another of those *Midsomer Murders* programmes that Sheila always insists on watching. Bore me silly they do.'

Alessia couldn't help but laugh at that, before she turned towards the sound of the phone ringing in her lounge.

'I better get that. It will probably be Carl calling me back. Thanks again, Jimmy,' she said, waving Jimmy off before going back inside to answer the call.

She glanced at the baby monitor on the side table as she crossed the room and smiled at the sight of Jacob lying in his bed, fast asleep. To her relief, one comforting hug from her was all it had taken to ensure the night's events hadn't disrupted Jacob's sleep too much. Exhausted, he'd gone back down again in just minutes.

'Alessia? Are you okay? I got your voicemail,' Carl said breathlessly. 'The meeting is dragging on, and we're still having dinner. I'd put the damn thing on silent...'

'I'm fine, Carl.' Alessia smiled despite herself as she caught the genuine concern in his voice. It always brought her such comfort that Carl always put her and Jacob first, before anything else. And she could picture her husband right now, dressed in his smart suit with a belly full of expensive wine and indulgent food, as he paced the hotel reception like a man demented after listening to the message she'd left him. 'I didn't mean to worry you. Honestly, we're fine.'

'I'm coming home.'

'Because of a broken window?' Alessia closed her eyes, recognising the determination in his voice. She instantly regretted telling him tonight. She should have waited until the morning. Things always seem so much better then. Less sinister in the cold light of day. 'There's really no need. I promise. I'd put money on it being just a bunch of kids messing about. We've had loads of teenagers hanging about down on the green lately. You said yourself, they can be a little rowdy sometimes.' Alessia hoped she sounded convincing. The last thing she wanted to do was sabotage the business deal that Carl was currently in the middle of wrapping up. He'd been working on buttering these clients up for months, and now was not the time for him to bail on them.

'I know you're just worried about me and Jacob but, honestly, we're fine. Jimmy came over and boarded the window up for me. I've cleaned up all the glass. I'll call a glazier out first thing in the morning. There's nothing you can do here. I've got it all under control.'

'Oh, I bet you have!' Carl laughed, and Alessia could hear the tension leave his voice and almost picture him relaxing at the other end of the phone.

It had been an in-joke between them throughout their entire marriage. How together Alessia was, how she always seemed to have everything under control. How nothing ever fazed her.

'Are you sure you don't want me to come home? I can be there in just a few hours.'

Alessia paused as she heard the emotion in her husband's voice. She knew how much he cared for her and Jacob. Yet the magnitude of how much he loved her still managed to catch her off guard sometimes. If she was honest, right now, she'd give everything to have him here. To feel the warmth of him in bed tonight beside her. To feel safe. But she didn't want to worry him any more than she clearly already had.

'No. I absolutely insist that you stay right there, and that you eat as much fancy food that you can handle and that you drink copious amounts of wine. And that you sleep, sprawled out, in a huge king-size bed without Jacob crawling all over you at five thirty in the morning, trying to prise your eyelids open with his sticky fingers, while you try your hardest to squeeze them tightly shut again in the hope of getting a few extra minutes' sleep!' Alessia laughed, reciting their usual morning routine. 'Stay. Do the deal. Make the most of your rare night of freedom. I bloody would,' she said, hoping that if she sounded okay, Carl would believe it.

'Okay?'

It was Carl's turn to pause now. And she took Carl's silence as resignation. Before, finally, he spoke.

'Okay! But as soon as I'm done, tomorrow evening, I'm coming home. I don't need to stay for an extra night. They can celebrate without me. I'll get this deal done and dusted, and then I'll come home and celebrate with you.'

'Well, now who's the one who has everything under control? Everything is going well, I take it?' Alessia grinned some more, happy to hear the confidence in Carl's voice.

'Couldn't be better. I just worry about you, Alessia. You and Jacob. When I'm this far away from you both. I hate to think that something might happen.'

'Nothing has happened. I shouldn't have called you and worried you. I'm sure that it's just kids, messing about and taking things too far. Do your deal. And then get your butt home so we can do our own celebrating.'

'Now that, I like the sound of very much,' Carl said, his tone grave as he flirted with her. She'd always loved that about him. How sexy and rugged he could sound, despite being so well spoken. 'I love you, baby. I'm just a phone call away if you need me. I'll keep my phone on. See you tomorrow.'

'See you tomorrow!'

Alessia hung up the phone and stared around the low-lit lounge, before she pulled the duvet cover tightly up around her and rested her head back against the sofa.

She was exhausted but she knew she wouldn't sleep tonight so she might as well spend the evening downstairs. At least that way she could keep an eye on the place and the boarding that Jimmy had put up for her. It didn't look as secure as she'd like. It wouldn't take much for someone to break in now if they wanted to.

Though there was no way that she was going to divulge that bit of information to Carl, otherwise wild horses wouldn't have kept him away. The truth was, that she was worried that whoever had done this might come back.

Remembering the note that she'd pushed into her pocket earlier, Alessia pulled out the piece of paper that had been wrapped around the brick and stared at the scrawled letters.

FOUND YOU!

It couldn't be just a coincidence, could it? Alessia had spent years building a new life for herself. A life a million miles away from the one she'd left behind. But somehow, after all this time, she had found her.

THEN

She's sitting on the floor of the cottage, her legs stretched out in front of her as she scans the room. Her eyes settle on the hole in the cottage's wall as the grey, darkened skies outside peek through where the window used to be. The dark clouds loom high above them, heavy and threatening. It's always raining lately. It's always so grey and miserable. And she can hear the rain lashing down outside. The big, fat drops hitting the roof above her. At least in here it's dry.

They'd stumbled upon the cottage by chance, she and Sarah, as they'd wandered through the dense woodlands at the back of her house after school one day. They'd been in search of the infamous rope swing that sat above 'the swamp' – as the older kids at school had nicknamed the large boggy area of wasteland. Only they couldn't find it, and they'd walked for what felt like miles, trekking through the woods, their bare legs scratched and bleeding from thorns and stinging nettles.

They must have taken a wrong turn somewhere along the way, because after what had felt like hours of walking, there had been no sign of the swamp, or anybody else for that matter.

But Sarah being Sarah had refused to give up. She'd insisted that they keep going. It was almost as if, even back then, this old cottage had had some kind of pull on her. Because minutes after that they saw the small building peeking out through a gap in the trees. Sarah had almost run to it.

'Whoa, look at this place, Emma-Jayne! We can make it into our den and come here all the time,' she'd said excitedly as they crept cautiously inside the old building and explored the place. Traipsing carefully from room to room, their feet slapping on the bare concrete floors, their bodies huddled together apprehensively in case they disturbed something or someone.

Because even though there was no one else there but them, it sometimes felt like they weren't really alone. That someone else was there too. Watching them.

Though that hadn't deterred Sarah from becoming obsessed with the place, and they'd both been back almost every day since.

The place had become like a sanctuary to her.

A place to hide and make-believe.

A place all of their own, deep in the woods, where no one could find them.

'This can be our secret place,' Sarah said as she begged and pleaded with Emma-Jayne to come with her again each time. 'A place of our own. We can say and do whatever we like. Just you and me.'

And of course, Emma-Jayne had given in every time. Just as she always did. Sarah had a way of being persuasive, and Emma-Jayne had learned long ago that sometimes it was just easier if she went along with her friend's wild ideas.

'Come on, EJ. Let's play something fun. We can do Simon Says again.' Sarah's voice pulls her out of her trance, but Emma-Jayne shakes her head, her eyes going to the shimmer of light that hits on a piece of green jagged glass next to her, making it sparkle like a rare emerald gemstone. Emma-Jayne picks it up and runs her fingers over it. The glass is cold and smooth to her touch, and she feels the sharpness of its serrated edge before she slides it into her pocket. Her eyes go to the small movement at her feet then. She stares in fascination as a woodlouse makes its way slowly over the tip of her scuffed black school shoe.

'Nah! I'm bored of playing Simon Says, we play that game every time we come here.'

'Okay then, how about... Hide-n-seek?' Sarah squeals excitedly, grinning at the suggestion. And Emma-Jayne sees her friend's posture immediately change, how she's twisted her body towards the doorway, eager to be the one who gets to run and hide first.

'And where will we hide?' Emma-Jayne laughs, unable to hide her affection for her friend. Because she knows Sarah is only trying to fill these voids with something fun to do. And she reminds herself that Sarah is two years younger than her. Ten is so much more childlike than twelve. She forgets that, sometimes, how immature and innocent Sarah can be. Because Sarah is also strong – much stronger than her anyway. And she's braver than her too. Sarah doesn't seem like she's scared of anything.

'The rooms are all bare and empty. There's nowhere to hide. I'd find you in seconds,' Emma-Jayne says with a shrug. Though the truth is she can't bear to sneak around this dark cottage on her own, knowing that Sarah might jump out and scare her any minute. Or worse, that someone else might jump out. Emma-Jayne shivers at the thought.

'Why don't we play hairdressers again?' she says, knowing how much Sarah loves playing with her long, flowing hair.

She's tired. And she just wants to sit here for a while, on the floor, with Sarah at her side, and let the whole world melt away around them.

Sarah nods her head enthusiastically and squeezes down close beside her, pulling her fingers in downward motions, her hand shaped like a makeshift comb as it rakes its way through Emma-Jayne's long, blonde hair. Her small, delicate fingers jutting against the thick tangle of knots as she painstakingly unravels each one with her fingertips.

'It's raining, it's pouring, the old man is snoring, he bumped his head when he fell out of bed and he couldn't get up in the morning,' Sarah sings softly. Her words like a ritual. And Emma-Jayne smiles to herself as she drinks in Sarah's sweet singing voice, closing her eyes as Sarah twists and plaits her hair into two long wavy trails that slide down either side of her face.

And she wonders if this is the only song that Sarah knows. Because it's the only one she always sings. But Emma-Jayne doesn't mind. In fact, she quite likes it.

And there's something soothing about her voice. About her gentle, warm touch. About them both huddled so closely together in their own secret den. That makes Emma-Jayne give in and join her for the second verse, just as Sarah knew she would.

'It's snowing, it's blowing, the old man is growing. He ate so much one day for lunch, every part of him was showing.'

And now they're both singing together, in unison. Their voices get louder, almost shouting to hear themselves over the rain as it comes down heavier. Pelting against the tin roof and splattering down the open fireplace beside them.

'It's warm out and sunny, the old man loves honey...'

And both know what's coming. Their favourite bit. The bit that they were building up to all along. The grand finale.

'He tried to seize a batch from the bees, and they didn't find it funny.' They both erupt with laughter, lunging at each other as they tickle one another, pretending to be angry little worker bees protecting their honey.

And Emma-Jayne thinks to herself that Sarah might be right, that this place isn't so bad after all. And then she stares back at the window sadly, at the dark skies outside that continue to threaten above them. They can't stay here forever.

A bad storm is coming.

NOW

'Well, this is really lovely, Alessia, I must get the recipe from you. You'd love me to cook this for you, wouldn't you, Andrew?' Harriet smiled at her husband as the four friends all sat around Alessia and Carl's dining table and tucked into the incredible dinner that Alessia had spent the entire day slaving over.

'Chance would be a fine thing!' Andrew quipped, taking another mouthful of food and swallowing it down before he spoke again. 'We're lucky if we get a chance to sling a Waitrose Finest ready meal in the microwave these days. We're just both never home. Though I have to say, Alessia, Harriet is right, this is lovely. You have outdone yourself this time.'

'She's not just a pretty face, huh,' Carl said teasingly.

'Oh, stop it!' Alessia said, rolling her eyes. Knowing that Carl was only messing with her and purposely winding her up with his tongue-in-cheek sexist comment. 'And I try!' she fired back with a grin as she watched Carl take another mouthful of his food.

And judging by the way he'd wolfed the food down, his plate already almost clean, she could afford to be a little smug. She was relieved, because it was no secret to any of them what a terrible cook she was. But this time she'd really tried her hardest to get it right, painstakingly following the recipe with such perfect precision. And her efforts had clearly paid off. As much as Carl enjoyed teasing her, she knew that he was just as secretly impressed as she was.

'I'll get the recipe for you, Harriet. It's a simple one though, really,' Alessia said, playing down the fact that the meat had been doused in a homemade marinade overnight before being slow cooked for hours today, in order for it to fall so effortlessly off the bone.

'Seriously, it's perfect. Just like you.' Carl squeezed her hand, and Alessia squeezed back tighter, grateful that Carl didn't let on how perfect she had wanted everything to be tonight. How she'd spent hours meticulously preparing every little detail.

'Honestly, you two!' Harriet said, shaking her head. 'I'm in awe at how much you guys always seem like a couple of love-struck teenagers!'

'Oi! Rather than an old married couple, like us you mean?' Andrew joked.

'We can't help it!' Alessia said, making no excuses for how affectionate they were. 'Besides, Carl needed reminding that I can actually cook now and then. I don't want him getting used to the high standards that he's become accustomed to in all those fancy hotel restaurants he's been eating at lately. You might not want to come home and slum it with me otherwise, huh, Carl?' Alessia grinned playfully.

'Slum it? Not a chance,' Carl said, drinking back the rest of the wine in his glass. 'Besides, nothing could keep me away after what happened the other night. I'm just glad you're safe.'

'Safe?' Andrew said before he narrowed his eyes. 'That sounds ominous.'

'Carl, stop...' Alessia murmured, uncomfortable now that Andrew had picked up on the undercurrent in Carl's words. She knew exactly where the conversion was going. And she didn't want to go over it all again, not with Harriet and Andrew here, which was why she'd specifically asked Carl not to bring it up in the first place.

'Has something happened?' Harriet said as she caught the fleeting look that her two friends both exchanged.

The tension in the air was palpable. They could all feel it.

'You could say that... I'm sorry, Alessia. I know you didn't want me to say anything. But maybe it would be good to see what Harriet and Andrew think?' Carl said with an apologetic shrug. 'While I was away, someone threw a brick through the lounge window.'

'What? A brick. So it was done intentionally?' Harriet said, staring past Carl to the newly replaced window in the lounge.

Carl nodded.

'Alessia had a glazier come out and replace the window yesterday morning, and luckily no one got hurt.'

'What did the police say?' Harriet asked.

'Nothing. Alessia refused to call them.'

Alessia caught the tightness in Carl's tone and diverted her eyes away from Harriet's stare, knowing how her friend would pick up on it too: that small bone of contention that stood between them both over Alessia's decision not to call the police.

And even without voicing it, Alessia knew that Harriet would automatically side with Carl on this.

Carl had been friends with Andrew since university, and he'd told Alessia that when Andrew had met Harriet, he couldn't have been happier for his friend. The fact that they'd then become best friends had been the added bonus, and Carl had often referred to Harriet over the years as the little sister he'd never had. When he'd later met Alessia, she had known how important it was for Carl that they got on too.

They were close.

And luckily for Carl, Alessia and Harriet genuinely hit it off right from the start. They'd become such firm friends. All four of them.

And as far as Carl was concerned, there weren't any secrets between them.

And Carl didn't want to create any now.

'Why on Earth didn't you report it?' Harriet said, placing down her cutlery and trying to read Alessia's expression as her friend tried to busy herself by picking up the large dish of lamb and offering her guests seconds.

'Any more?' She was desperate to change the subject – why did Carl have to cause such a fuss?

'No, thanks.' Harriet shook her head, before bringing the conversation back on track, not falling for Alessia's diversion tactics. 'Why didn't you report it?'

'Because... as I said to Carl,' Alessia said pointedly, annoyed with him now. She knew her friend would have this reaction. Harriet had worked as a police officer for the past eight years, and she lived and breathed her job. Of course, she'd say that Alessia should have reported the incident, which was exactly why Alessia hadn't wanted to tell Harriet in the first place. 'It was probably just kids messing about.' She couldn't hide her defensive tone as she tried to justify herself. 'I didn't want to waste anyone's time. You're always saying how busy you are. How there are so many time-wasters out there. Calling you out for stupid reasons,' Alessia said, using her friend's direct words as reference to why she hadn't wanted to involve the police.

'Yeah, stupid reasons being silly little petty squabbles between neighbours about stolen pot plants or trimming a hedge that isn't technically theirs. That's stupid shit. Not having a brick intentionally thrown through your window, Alessia. Christ. Even if it was "just kids" someone could have been seriously hurt. Jacob? Was he here? Is he okay?' Harriet said.

'Jacob was fine. He was in bed.'

'Thankfully!' Carl added as Alessia nodded. Unable to hide her emotion once Harriet mentioned Jacob, she bit down on her lip and shook her head.

That was the bit that really got to her. Though she wasn't going to admit that right now. She dreaded to think what could have happened if he'd done his usual to fight his bedtime routine and she'd done her usual and given in and let him stay up and play with his toys. Right there on the floor. Right where the brick and glass had landed.

'Did you see them? Did you manage to catch a look at them?'

'No, I didn't see anyone. It all happened so fast,' Alessia said, knowing full well that Harriet's mind would be whirling. Despite her having the night off, she was never really off duty. Her job was her life, and she was good at it too.

Which was another reason Alessia hadn't wanted Carl to bring it up tonight. She could do without all the questions.

'Did they say anything? Did they threaten you? Was there a note of some sort?'

'Jesus, Harriet. Alessia is the victim here. This isn't an interrogation,' Andrew said, picking up on Alessia's discomfort and shaking his head apologetically towards his friend. They all knew just how stubborn and direct Harriet could be once she got an idea in her head. She was like a dog with a bone when something riled her.

'Seriously, it was probably just kids. It's not a big deal, I mean, we were all kids once too. Weren't we? Albeit a long time ago for some of us,' Alessia said, nudging Carl and nodding over at Andrew and making light of the fact that the two men were the eldest here.

Though no one was laughing and her attempt at lightening the mood failed miserably.

'It was probably just a prank or a stupid dare, and as soon as they threw the brick, they must have got scared and ran off. In fact, they were probably more scared than I was,' Alessia said, not admitting how she had scanned the empty street outside for ages after it had happened, convinced that someone had been there. Someone from her past. *Her.* Lurking there, beneath the shadows. Watching her. And how she hadn't been able to sleep afterwards.

'Well, it's either kids like you say, or you've severely pissed someone off,' Andrew said with a chuckle, playfully goading Alessia until he caught the warning look that Harriet shot him.

'Oh, that's great, very reassuring, Andrew!'

'I'm kidding, I'm kidding,' Andrew said, flinging his hands in the air and feigning innocence. 'Of course, it was kids. Jesus, I mean come on. This is the "golden couple" we're talking about. You two aren't capable of having enemies.'

'Alessia did get quite a scare,' Carl said, and again Alessia picked up on his annoyance at Andrew's flippant comment. And she knew why he was reacting this way. Because he wanted her to take this more seriously, but equally, he didn't want her to be scared that someone had a grudge and wanted to purposely harm them.

'Of course, she got a scare!' Harriet said, nodding in understanding as she shot her friend a compassionate look. 'You were here on your own and you didn't know for sure what the motive behind the attack was. Anyone would be frightened. That's only natural.'

'"Attack" is a bit strong,' Alessia said with a laugh, pushing the uneaten food around on her plate, her appetite gone. She was done with the half-finished meal now.

'Alessia, someone damaged your property. They violated you. They could have seriously hurt yourself or Jacob. It was an attack. And even if, IF, it was just kids messing about, they acted with malicious intent. You should have reported it, in case something happens again. Sometimes these aren't isolated incidents.'

'Oh Christ!' Andrew rolled his eyes. 'And now who's scaring her, Harriet?' He tutted loudly but kept his tone playful.

'Honestly, I'm fine. It's really not a big deal.' Alessia got up. 'And to be honest, I was more annoyed than scared. And whoever it was, I'm sure that they won't come back. It was probably just a prank. A joke gone wrong. Some kids egging each other on. Now if you excuse me for a minute, I'm just going to pop the dessert in the oven.'

Shooting a stern look at her husband to let him know that she was less than impressed by him purposely putting this out there, and that they'd be having words later when their guests were gone, Alessia excused herself from the dining room.

Retreating into the peaceful escape of the kitchen, she scraped the leftover food into the bin, before rinsing her plate under the tap. Daydreaming now as she stood in front of the sink. Because Harriet did have a point, didn't she? There was a chance that whoever threw the brick might come back. That it wasn't an isolated incident.

It was possible, wasn't it? More than possible.

And she couldn't help but feel the pool of dread forming in the pit of her stomach that everything she'd worked so hard to conceal, so hard to leave back there in the past, was coming back to haunt her.

That her world was about to be abruptly shaken wide open.

That Carl would find out the truth about her.

She felt real fear, lurking, as her chest started to pull tight. The oxygen going from her lungs, making it hard for her to breathe.

'Ouch!'

The scalding hot water caught her unaware, pulling her back from her dark thoughts and the brink of a panic attack. She wrenched her sore red hands out from under the water's flow before wrapping them in a nearby tea towel. Grateful for the heat, for the burn. For the sharp jolt of pain. It enabled her to breathe once more.

She hadn't had a panic attack for years. But she recognised the onslaught of one threatening her again. Taunting her.

Breathe.

She steadied her shaking hands and fought back the urge to cry. Because this wasn't what was supposed to happen. She wasn't supposed to be found. She had been promised a new life. A chance to start again and leave her past behind her, for good.

'Alessia? Are you okay in there? Do you need a hand?'

Hearing Carl's voice call out from the lounge, Alessia took a deep breath to steady her nerves before she placed the pudding dish in the oven and made her way back into the dining room, a forced smile fixed to her face.

She still had the rest of the evening to get through. She couldn't think about any of this right now.

7

NOW

'Talk about not being able to handle their drinks. Can you hear them both? Giggling like a couple of schoolboys in there. And they say that us women are bad at holding our wine! I'd drink the pair of them under the table,' Harriet said, chuckling to herself as she moved across the kitchen to scrape the last of the plates into the bin, before passing them to Alessia who was filling the dishwasher.

'I know! I think Carl got a bit carried away with the celebrations. But he's worked hard for it. Plus, it's nice to see him unwind a bit. He's become a workaholic lately. It's nice to see him relax and enjoy himself.'

'Oh, well trust me, Andrew doesn't need the excuse of helping Carl celebrate.' Harriet smiled, rolling her eyes. 'He loves a drink, which is why I always end up as designated driver. He can't seem to say no.' Harriet glanced at Alessia, realising that she was babbling on and Alessia was no longer paying attention, as she caught her friend staring absently at her reflection in the kitchen window.

'Earth to Alessia!' Harriet said, breaking the spell, convinced now that her hunch was right and Alessia had seemed distracted this evening. 'Alessia? Are you really okay?' she said, carefully, wondering if the attack the other night had affected Alessia more than she was letting on, and her friend was just putting on a brave face. Because she hadn't seemed herself all evening, and Harriet knew her well enough to know when there was something playing on her friend's mind.

'You got a scare, didn't you?' Harriet said, softly, wanting Alessia to know that it was okay to be scared. That she understood.

'I guess,' Alessia said tightly, though she hadn't wanted to get back on this train of conversation. She knew that this would be how Harriet reacted to the news. In truth, she'd been expecting it. Which was why she'd even suggested cancelling tonight, but Carl, still in celebration mode after closing his deal at work and wanting to share the news with his two closest friends, had brushed over her hint at rescheduling.

'Then what is it?' Harriet pushed. 'Because you don't need to play things down for me. You're allowed to feel scared. It's normal. This is your home, it's where you're supposed to feel safe. Someone overstepped the mark and invaded that. They left you feeling vulnerable. Just as anyone else would feel too. There's no shame in that.'

'Look, can you just drop it?' Alessia said with more force than she intended. 'Stop psychoanalysing how you *think* I'm feeling. You don't know...' Seeing the crestfallen look on Harriet's face, she realised how rude she must sound, when all Harriet was doing was just being a good, caring friend. Alessia pulled out one of the kitchen chairs and slumped down on to it.

'Shit! I'm sorry, Harriet,' she said in earnest before she placed her elbows down on the small wooden table and held her head in her hands. She took another deep breath. Aware that the rare strain of emotion was written all over her face as she fought back her tears. 'You're right. It did give me a scare. And I do feel stupid. But I just keep thinking how any other night, Jacob could have there. Sitting right there where the brick landed, and he could have been badly hurt.' Alessia shrugged as she finally admitted what had really upset her. 'Or worse. God, I can't even think about it, and yet, it just keeps playing on in my mind. Over and over again.'

'I understand, Alessia. You don't need to apologise to me,' Harriet said. 'Alessia, none of this was your fault. You are a great mother; you dote on Jacob. Anyone who knows you, knows that he is your whole world. And he's safe, Alessia. Thank God, he is safe. That's all that matters.'

Harriet was right, she needed to focus on that. Jacob was safe.

'I'm sorry I haven't been myself tonight.' Alessia shook her head. She knew that Harriet had been observing her behaviour carefully. How she'd watched as Alessia had drunk more wine than she normally did. How she'd come across so on edge and defensive. Harriet was the only one out of them all not drinking and, like always, there was very little that got past her. She noted everything.

'I just didn't want to do this tonight. Not on Carl's night. I didn't want to make a fuss, and make it seem bigger and more all-consuming than it really was. And I'm just so tired. Like exhausted. Carl has been working every hour lately because of the deal, and I've been looking after Jacob all by myself. And I haven't slept well the past couple of nights.'

'Well, why don't you let me help?' Harriet said, placing her hand on Alessia's and holding it there, wanting her to know that she would help any way she could. 'I'd love to look after Jacob for a few hours. I could take him to the park so that you could get a few hours' sleep. Or I could just stay here with him and play with his toys. I hear that a bit of retail therapy can do wonders for your mental health. Very therapeutic!' Harriet laughed, raising her eyebrow, knowing how much Alessia loved to shop.

It was something that the two friends had very much in common and had become a running joke between their husbands.

'Thank you, that's really kind of you,' Alessia said, grateful for the gesture but about to decline, though Harriet was already prepared for that it seemed.

'Oh, I'm not offering. I'm insisting. I've got a couple of days off next week, and I'm not taking no for an answer. Tuesday or Friday works, what day is good for you?'

'Okay, okay. Jeez! I forget how stubborn you can be!' Recognising the stern look on Harriet's face and realising that she wouldn't be budging on this, Alessia laughed and finally gave in.

'Okay, how about Tuesday?' she said, grateful for the break. 'A few hours off sounds like a dream. I could hit the shops and maybe even have a coffee in a café without having to mop up spilled hot chocolate and cake crumbs the entire time.' She paused, feeling bad now for shutting Harriet out when she was just concerned, like any friend would be. 'Thank you, Harriet. I really do appreciate it.'

'Oh, trust me, the pleasure is all mine. That boy of yours is an angel. I can't wait to spend some proper time with him. You know how much I adore him.'

'Oh, you won't be saying that when he's got you playing dinosaurs from out of space for the millionth time. Trust me.'

Alessia followed Harriet back through to the lounge and smiled as her friends thanked her for a lovely evening and started getting ready to leave.

But even as she sank down into her warm bed later that night, her body snuggled into her already soundly snoring husband, Alessia knew exactly where she was going to go on Tuesday. Because if she was right about who she suspected had thrown that brick, then she couldn't deal with all of this on her own.

8

THEN

'I think we should go...' Emma-Jayne says uneasily, her body shivering violently, though she isn't sure if it is the sudden drop in temperature that causes it or if this place is just giving her the creeps today. Scanning the small, dingy room she searches for where the sudden cold blast of air has rushed in. 'It's getting late.'

It's the second time that she's pleaded with Sarah to leave. Though she knows that Sarah isn't listening. She never wants to leave once they come here.

'Shhh! Can you hear them?' Sarah says, waving her hand dismissively as she pretends not to hear her friend's pleas.

She crouches down on her hands and knees before twisting her neck around so that she can look up into the dusty remains of the crumbling chimney breast, her eyes following the nasal whining sound that echoes out from above.

'Bingo!' Sarah says, satisfied that her hunch about where the loud chirping was coming from was right. 'We've got babies, EJ. Lots of them by the sound of it. The nest is huge.'

Emma-Jayne bites her lip and tries her hardest not to cry. Because she knows that Sarah has no intentions of leaving anytime soon. Not now she's found a nest of baby birds.

She doesn't want to seem like a baby, but she doesn't like it here.

And she has no idea why Sarah has become so fascinated with the place. It's as if she can't see the thick green mould that stretches out across the ceilings and the black damp patches that rise up the walls. Or the way that the floors creak and groan as if physically in pain as they both carefully tread through the place, as if one wrong heavy footstep could bring the whole crumbling building tumbling down around them. Emma-Jayne hadn't really noticed it before either. But she can see it now. Clearly. How cold and decrepit the place is. How the cottage doesn't seem like such a nice place any more. And she just wants to leave. Unable to shake the fizzing sensation in the pit of her stomach. She has a bad feeling.

'Please, Sarah. Let's just go. We can come back another day. It's getting dark. My mum will be worried.'

Only Sarah continues to ignore her as she crawls back out of the small space and scans the room as if in search of something, her gaze finally resting on an old, jagged piece of what looks like a rotten edge of wooden window frame.

She picks it up.

'What are you doing with that?'

'I was going to see if we can unwedge the nest, so we can take a closer look at the babies.'

'No, you can't do that,' Emma-Jayne says, horrified at Sarah's suggestion. Her eyes wide with panic. 'You can't disturb a bird's nest. The mother will fly off and the babies will all die.'

'Not if we look after them,' Sarah says, screwing her mouth up to show she isn't bothered, before getting back down on to her knees and guiding the stick carefully up the chimney breast. 'We can be their new mum.'

Emma-Jayne stands back, helpless, as she hears Sarah slamming the wooden pole against the bricks inside the chimney breast.

A few seconds later she jumps, startled by the sudden loud squawking that echoes down the chimney. 'What was that?' She squeezes her eyes tightly shut, fearing the worst: that Sarah has hit the nest too hard and harmed the birds. Or worse, killed one of them.

'Relax. It's just the mum, I think? She's up on the roof,' Sarah says, her voice sounds muffled as the stick clangs repeatedly against the wall once more. 'She does sounds pissed at us though!'

Emma-Jayne thinks about her own mother then and how pissed she'll be when she finds out that she's been back here again with Sarah. Because her mother doesn't like Sarah. Not one bit. She gets so angry whenever Emma-Jayne even speaks about her friend. And she won't like her being here at the cottage. That's why it has to be a secret. Derelict buildings deep in the woods weren't safe places, especially for young girls, she'd said when Emma-Jayne had tried to mention it. And Emma-Jayne hadn't argued with her about it. She'd accepted it and agreed wholeheartedly. Glad in a way that her mother had put a stop to the visits to this creepy place.

But Sarah has managed to persuade her once more to come back here. It's as if she has some kind of power over her. As if she couldn't possibly say no. Though she had to at least try.

'Sar? Can we go? Please. It's getting dark out.' Emma-Jayne tries again, not relishing the journey back through the dark wet woodlands as the light fades. If they don't leave soon there will be murders when she gets home. 'I told my mum that I wouldn't be out long. She'll be doing dinner,' Emma-Jayne says, ashamed of the whiney tone to her voice; only she is so desperate to leave, to get out of here, that part of her no longer cares how pathetic she sounds.

'All right, all right!' Sarah says, finally giving up on her pursuit of the bird's nest as the mother bird squawks loudly above her, frantic now, making Sarah's voice sound faint and muffled.

'I can't reach it anyway. The wood's not long enough.' Defeated she smacks the stick against the wall one last time. 'Ouch!'

Emma-Jayne hears a clang and watches as a small figure falls from the chimney.

'What the hell...?' Sarah says, twisting her thin frame awkwardly inside the tight, claustrophobic space before picking the small object up.

'Oh, God! Is it one of the babies?' Emma-Jayne says, barely able to get her words out as she squeezes her eyes tightly shut, not wanting to look in case the tiny bird has met a gory ending.

'No. Look. It's a doll,' Sarah says, holding it up for Emma-Jayne to see as she wipes away the black soot that covers the doll with her finger, revealing a creamy plastic face.

'It looks a bit creepy. What happened to its eyes?' Emma-Jayne asks, cautiously opening her eyes before recoiling at the sight of the thing, covered in filth, the fabric of the doll's dress frayed and damp. The eyes faded as if they'd been scratched out.

'She's not creepy. She's... different.'

'What's that?' Emma-Jayne says, stepping closer as she sees something down on the floor gleaming up at her.

An earring? Reaching down she nudges it before recoiling in horror as she realises what it is.

'It's a tooth! A child's tooth,' she shrieks, wiping her finger repeatedly against the fabric of her school jumper, as if she'd just infected herself with a nasty disease, her face twisted with disgust at the thought of what she'd just touched.

Which only makes Sarah laugh hard again.

'Chill out. So what, it's just a tooth! A teeny-tiny tooth. Relax.' She bends down and picks it up, twiddling it between her fingers, staring at the tooth as if it was a valuable jewel, mesmerised at its sight, before tucking it safely inside the doll's dress pocket. 'Shall we keep her? We could fix her up. We could make her a new dress?'

'No. We should put it back,' Emma-Jayne says, willing her friend to do just that. To put the doll back where they'd found it, hidden inside the chimney breast. Out of sight.

Because she has a bad feeling about the doll.

'Er, finders keepers! Besides, I kinda like her,' Sarah says, amused at the look of horror on her friend's face as she cups her hand firmly around the doll in a bid to keep it.

This time, Emma-Jayne is not going to give in. She is not going to let Sarah have the last word on this one.

'I mean it, Sarah. Put it back. Put it back right now...'

Seeing the genuine fear in her friend's eyes, the tears that threaten there, Sarah reluctantly agrees.

'Jeez! Okay, Okay!' she says, sinking back down on her knees and reaching to the back of the chimney breast. Rummaging for a few minutes, as if in search of the small nook from which the doll had fallen, before standing back up again and wiping the soot from her hands down her school skirt.

'Come on, then! Let's go home. Before the doll comes to life like a zombie and tries to eat our brains for its dinner,' she says, making fun of her friend as she follows her outside and they both begin to make their way home through the overgrown woodlands.

Emma-Jayne turns back and looks at the cottage one last time, still able to hear the baby birds clamouring to be fed. The mother on the roof of the house, squawking loudly down the chimney breast. And another noise too? A child crying?

'Hey, come on,' Sarah spits with a sarcastic laugh. 'I thought you wanted to get out of here? You changed your mind? You want to go back to the doll's house?'

Shaking her head vigorously, Emma-Jayne speeds up, eager to get out of the woods and as far away from the creepy cottage as possible, ignoring the sharp twigs and brambles as they tear through the skin of her shins as she walks, her mind elsewhere, numb to it. All she can think about is that creepy doll. And that small child's tooth. Stuffed back inside the chimney breast. She shivers before walking faster.

9

NOW

'Mmm! Something smells delicious!' Carl grinned, following the smell of crispy fried bacon into the kitchen and finding his wife standing at the breakfast bar, preparing one of her Sunday feasts for them all.

'Well, now, breakfast I can do! And, perfect timing, I'm just about to dish up!'

'I was talking about you, not the food!' Carl smiled, placing his arms around Alessia as he pulled her in close to him.

'Carl!' Alessia shrieked loudly as she squirmed to break free of his hold once she realised that his hair was still soaking wet from his shower, and his skin was still covered with droplets of water. 'Hey, I'm soaked!'

Carl laughed louder, continuing to hold on to Alessia tightly, nuzzling into her neck playfully as she shrieked in protest.

Wiggling out of his hold, she moved away from the breakfast counter, holding the tea towel up between them as if it was a weapon.

'Don't do it! Don't come another step closer...' Alessia warned.

Carl had no intentions of backing down. Running at Alessia and diving out of the way as she catapulted the tea towel in his direction, Carl grabbed her again as she squealed.

Which in turn only made Jacob burst into hysterical laughter at the sight of his parents playing.

'Funny, Daddy!' Jacob cooed as he watched his daddy shake the droplets of water from his hair and spray his mummy. 'Do it to me. Do it to me.'

'You want some too, buster?' Carl laughed, happy to oblige as he leaned over the chair that Jacob was sitting in and shook his head over him too.

'Oh no, Daddy! All wet!' Jacob called out dramatically, wiping the water from his face, unable to stop his contagious chuckling.

'Right, that's enough of that now, Daddy! No more messing about or you won't be able to come to the park this afternoon!' Alessia said, putting on the stern voice that she knew both Jacob and Carl expected, as she placed the large serving dish full of piping hot food down in the middle of the table.

'Breakfast is served.'

Sitting down at the table, Alessia sipped at her coffee and watched as Carl took the lead and served the food onto each plate, smiling to herself as she watched him cut Jacob's food up into smaller bite-sized pieces, just so.

'You want two sausages, Jacob?' Carl asked, hovering an extra sausage over Jacob's plate, the two of them speaking animatedly to one another.

'Yep! Two sorsegees,' Jacob insisted, nodding his head enthusiastically.

'Course you do! Almost three means that you're a big boy now, eh? Two sausages it is! And for you, madam. Eggs, bacon, one sausage and no baked beans.'

Carl passed her the plate, and Alessia smiled gratefully before taking a mouthful of the hot food and sitting back in her chair, exhausted from laughing.

She relished days like these. Sunday was without a doubt her favourite day of the week. When Carl was home and didn't have to hurry off to work. It was their day. Their one day of the week to spend together. Just the three of them. Sitting here, like this.

Enjoying a late, lazy breakfast. And Alessia was in her element right now as she drank it all in. As Carl cracked his silly jokes and Jacob squealed with delight at the affection and attention that his father was giving him.

Such a contrast to the mornings she'd spent in her claustrophobic kitchen as a child. The tension lingering like a dense cloud above the four of them as they had sat around the table. Barely able to tolerate breathing in the same air as each other.

She recalled how her mother would hover pathetically between the kitchen counter top and the table, constantly fussing and fetching for Alessia's stepfather, Robert. Treating the man as if he was some kind of king and acting as if she was beneath him. Not worthy of him. As she served him a never-ending supply of hot tea and fresh toast, while he sat there ignoring her obvious efforts at attempting to keep him happy, his head buried in the morning newspapers.

'What's this?' he would say sometimes, staring ungratefully at the mug he'd been handed. 'We ran out of milk? It looks and tastes like dish water.' And her mother would obediently swoop the cup from his hand without a word and add another drop of milk before placing it back down on the table for him. Watching nervously until he'd taken a sip and given her a curt nod of approval. And still she wouldn't sit down until he'd taken a bite of his toast and swallowed it, waiting, making sure he had no other complaints. Because he only ever really spoke to her when he was complaining. And he complained about most things.

And Alessia's mother was oblivious to it all. In denial that her husband could barely be bothered to listen to her incessant chatter. That he barely tolerated her when she tried to tell him about her day, or some pointless gossip she'd heard about one of the neighbours. 'Sandra from number five had him over again yesterday. Snuck him in the minute that David had pulled out of the drive. Dreadful carry-on that one!' she'd say. Or she'd speak about her job. Making her part-time job as a secretary in town sound far more important and interesting than it actually was.

And occasionally Alessia's stepdad would nod. Or sometimes he'd meet her mother's eye and just stare at her blankly, as if willing her to shut her thin, lined mouth. But mainly he just seemed disinterested. As if he wasn't even listening. As if his mind was elsewhere.

She couldn't stand the way that her mother pandered to him, the way she acted as if everything in their house was normal when it was anything but.

The only other real noise in the room came from Bobby. Her sweet little brother.

Too young and oblivious to pick up on the tension around him, he sat in his chair, dragging his cars across the table. Pausing every few minutes to take a spoonful of his breakfast cereal.

Alessia sat across from him, doing the exact opposite.

Trying to stay as small and quiet as she could possibly be. Not wanting to draw any kind of attention to herself. Because she didn't want any attention from any of them. Especially from him. She was always so grateful for the days he acted like that, like she was invisible. Like she wasn't even in the room. That was exactly the way that she preferred it.

She would eat her cereal as quickly as possible so that she could leave for school. Anything to get out of that godforsaken house she'd grown to hate.

'Earth to Alessia!' Carl said as Alessia zoned back in, relieved that she was sitting in their kitchen now. With a little family all of her own.

How they were nothing like them.

And the feeling of love and safety overwhelmed her suddenly. Her heart felt full of the kind of contentment she'd once wondered if she'd ever know. If she'd ever deserve to know.

'You okay?' Carl asked, trying to read her expression. 'You looked a million miles away.'

And Alessia couldn't help but smile at that. Her eyes went to Jacob as he ran his toy cars across the table's surface and she grabbed at one.

'You want Mummy to play too?' she asked as Jacob nodded excitedly, racing his car alongside hers.

'I was!' she said honestly.

Because that was how it felt sometimes when she recalled her old life. It was a million miles away from where she was now. She'd made sure of that. And that was exactly where she wanted to keep it.

NOW

'He's asleep already!' Alessia grinned as she leaned back and stared at Jacob, fast asleep in his car seat, his head lolled to one side against the window. 'And look! He sleeps just like you.' She grinned some more as Carl turned and saw Jacob with his head tilted back, his mouth wide open. 'Like an old man with no teeth, catching flies.' Alessia laughed as Carl rolled his eyes.

'It's no wonder he's out for the count already! He was like a little loon running about after all the deer. Or should I say, "Rudolphs". I've never seen him so excited.'

Even though they'd barely been in the car for ten minutes, Alessia wasn't surprised that Jacob had tired himself out.

Having spent the day at Richmond Park, exploring the trails and spotting deer, the three of them had sat beneath the shade of the trees enjoying a picnic for most of the afternoon, until Jacob had lain down on the picnic blanket and closed his eyes.

Carl had had to carry him back to the car.

'I'm just as exhausted from watching him,' Carl joked. 'It's a shame that I have to go into the office. I could have done with an early night myself.'

'Well, maybe when you get back later, we can. Seeing as we're both so exhausted.' Alessia raised her eyebrow teasingly and placed her hand on Carl's thigh for the rest of the journey as they drove through the throng of London's Sunday afternoon traffic.

'Oh, I'll probably need to go to bed as soon as I get home,' Carl quipped as they pulled up outside his office.

Alessia couldn't help but laugh at that.

'I won't be late!' Carl said, getting out of the car and blowing Alessia a kiss before he disappeared inside the building.

————

Alessia made her way home, lost in her own thoughts and grateful for the normality of today and the fact that Jacob was still sleeping soundly. She'd felt so rattled the past few days, about the brick and the note, but maybe she was just overthinking everything. Seeing things that weren't really there. It was a habit of a lifetime, she figured. Feeling paranoid. Always expecting the worst.

'All right, mate,' she muttered, her train of thought intruded on suddenly as a car pulled out behind her.

She was so close to home now, just a few streets away from the quiet residential street where they lived.

But the car behind her was coming closer.

Too close.

'Any further up my arse and you'll be in the boot,' Alessia said as she narrowed her eyes and glared into the rear-view mirror, trying to get a glimpse at the driver behind her. 'Jesus! Does no one in London know how to drive?'

She watched as the car sped up, so close now that their bumpers almost touched. It was late Sunday evening, and the roads around here were quieter. Almost desolate.

Any other time a driver tried to intimidate her like this, Alessia might have made a point and purposely hung back, forcing them to slow down. But she had Jacob to think about, and she didn't want to spoil the lovely afternoon they'd just had by getting into an argument with an incompetent idiot driver. Nor did she want to wake Jacob up.

Seeing the driver was clearly in a hurry, Alessia pulled to the left of the single lane to allow them to overtake while the road was still clear, before anything else came the other way.

But the car moved with her. Dangerously close behind them now. Mirroring her movement.

As if they were doing it on purpose.

'What on earth?' She suddenly realised that they didn't want to go past her. She gripped the steering wheel tightly, aware that if she didn't want to get rammed, she had no choice but to speed up. Her eyes flitted frantically from the road to the mirror as she did so.

'What is this arsehole playing at?' she spat through gritted teeth, taking a chance as she turned awkwardly in her seat and peered past Jacob and out through the rear window, trying to get a better look at the driver.

Only her vision was limited. The other car was filthy. A sheet of dirt blocked most of the windscreen like a mask, shielding whoever it was behind the wheel of the car.

All she could make out was a puffy black coat. A black baseball cap. No face. No features.

Closer still. They weren't letting up.

Full of terror, she felt the malice in their actions. That whoever it was behind her was trying to deliberately run her off the road.

And all she could think of was Jacob, sleeping soundly in the back. How they were putting him in danger, gambling with his life. She pressed the handsfree button on the steering wheel.

'Call Carl!'

'Missing me already...' Carl began, only Alessia spoke over him.

'Carl!'

'Alessia?'

Alessia could barely speak. Her gaze flitted from the rear-view mirror to the road in front of her as she clung to the steering wheel.

She almost didn't see the car ahead of her as it attempted to pull out onto the road in front, from where it had been sitting on a driveway. But she was going too fast. She couldn't stop now. Aware the entire time how close the car was still behind her, she swerved. There was an angry screech of tyres as the car that had just tried to join the road was forced to make an emergency stop, sounding their horn loudly at her.

'Alessia? Are you okay? What is going on?' Carl's voice shouted out through the car's speakers.

'There's a car behind me. I think it's trying to run me off the road.'

'Pull over...' Carl started to say.

But his words were drowned out by another screech of brakes, louder this time, and the sound of metal loudly crunching against metal as something hit her from behind.

The jolt startled Jacob awake and he started to cry.

'Alessia? Alessia? Are you there?' Carl shouted down the phone, his voice frantic.

'It's okay, baby! The car is just playing up and scared Mummy,' Alessia said in an attempt to soothe her son, now that they had come to a stop.

'Alessia? Are you okay?'

'They hit me,' she said, in shock at what had just happened, before she realised that Carl was still there at the end of the line. Listening to her. That he heard everything. It made her feel less alone.

'Idiot!' Alessia said, furious now as she removed her belt and got out of the car, ready to give a piece of her mind to the other driver over their diabolical driving.

It was only then that Alessia realised that the other car hadn't stopped. It had kept going, speeding up and racing past her, as if they didn't want to be seen.

Alessia made her way around the back of the vehicle to inspect the damage. There was a concave dent in the bumper, and a deep gouge of paint scraped out all down the side of the car.

The side where Alessia and Jacob had been sitting.

She got back into the driver's seat.

'They're driving off.'

'Did you get the number plate?'

'I can't see... they're going too fast,' she said as she glared after the car and strained to read the number plate as it quickly drove off into the distance. She managed to recite the first few letters and digits to Carl before the car finally turned the corner at the end of the street and disappeared.

'Are you okay?' Carl asked as Alessia went back to comforting the scared and crying Jacob.

'Mummy! I want Daddy!'

'It's okay, baby. We're fine, thank God! We just got a scare, that's all. We're fine now, aren't we, Jacob?' Alessia said as she smiled at her son and his tears gradually subsided, unsure who she was trying to convince with her words more. Her blood was boiling at the thought of how serious it could have been. How Jacob could have been hurt.

'I'm coming home,' Carl said as Alessia started up the engine again.

'No. Don't do that. It's done now. They're gone,' she said, now that Jacob had stopped crying and begun to settle again. She got back into her seat and placed her hands in her lap, trying desperately to control their trembling.

'No. I'm not doing that again. This time, I'm reporting them. I'll get an Uber. I'll see you at home,' Carl said, tight-lipped, before hanging up the phone.

Alessia bit her lip as she pulled away. The familiar unsettled feeling of the last few days bubbled away again in the pit of her stomach. Carl was right. It wasn't okay. None of this was okay. First, a brick had been thrown through the window. And now this. They couldn't just be coincidences, could they? Separate, random attacks. Alessia was frightened. Because it felt as if the threat had been directed at her. That it was personal. It was Sarah. She was doing this to her, Alessia was certain of it.

11

NOW

'I don't understand why you won't let me report it. You could have been seriously hurt. Jacob could have been hurt. They were driving like a bloody nutcase.'

'It's not that I won't let you. I'm just saying, is it worth it?' Alessia said, matching Carl's curt tone. 'Because we weren't hurt. It was just some idiot who was too impatient to sit behind me or wait for me to move out of their way. You know how people drive around here. Like absolute idiots. It was just a scrape, Carl. A small dink in the bumper. It's not even worth the insurance claim. And besides, they'll be long gone now. There was no one else around. No one saw it, so what's the point in reporting it? It's done. You'll just be wasting the police's time.' Alessia sat Jacob down on the bottom step in the hallway and took off his jacket and trainers as he wiped his eyes, not happy about being woken up by all the drama and carried out of the car. The rare sound of his mother and father arguing was making his bottom lip quiver.

But Carl was too wound up to notice. Having immediately left the office in an Uber, he'd arrived home just minutes after Alessia. And despite Alessia's protests, he wanted to call the police. Right now. To report the arsehole that just rammed her off the road, intentionally or not.

'What, like you not reporting the brick that got thrown through the window to save wasting police time? Come on, Alessia! You heard what Harriet said: these are real crimes. We need to report them. I mean, Jesus, what if they are linked?' Carl said, as if it had only just occurred to him that there had been two separated incidents this week, both aimed at his wife or his home. Because this was a huge coincidence.

'Linked?' Alessia said incredulously, unable to control the shake in her voice as she raised her voice, determined to play down Carl's suspicions. To defuse the situation so that it didn't get completely out of hand. She didn't want the police involved. 'Don't be ridiculous. I already told you, the brick was probably just kids.'

'Probably. But we won't ever know that, will we?' Carl pressed, picking up the phone, 'because you didn't report it...'

'I didn't report it because it was nothing. Just like this. And to be fair, today was probably half my fault. Jacob was asleep and I was daydreaming. I was driving really slowly and probably riled up whoever it was,' Alessia said, the reasoning more for her own benefit than for Carl's. Because she wanted to believe that version of events. The other version terrified her. That it had been a planned attack. That Sarah would go that far.

'This isn't just nothing, Alessia. And it's actually an offence if you don't report it. You could be the one who ends up getting fined. You heard what Harriet said about the brick, anything like this is not a waste of police time. We should report it. I mean, what if they do it again to someone else? What if next time, someone gets hurt, or Heaven forbid, killed?'

Alessia wavered then, knowing that Carl was right and she didn't have a leg to stand on. Carl wasn't going to back down.

'Fine, call Harriet then, run it by her, see what she says.' But she was unable to squash the sickly feeling deep down in her stomach that their friend would have no choice but to start looking into the allegations, and that she might find something out that Alessia didn't want her to know. But what other choice did she have?

She saw the concern on Carl's face, the genuine worry in his eyes and the relief there, too, that she was going to report it this time. And she knew that she was being too defensive and too hard on him when he was just trying to make sure they were all safe. She softened.

'I'm sorry. You're right. Of course, you are!' she said finally, taking a deep breath and calming down. There was no point in saying anything else to dissuade him: Carl would call Harriet, regardless.

'I just don't want to cause a huge fuss over nothing, that's all. But you are right. Call Harriet. I'll go and settle Jacob into bed,' Alessia said as she watched Carl pick up the phone.

The chances were that it was just a random driver.

And that she was just being paranoid again. And Harriet wouldn't find anything, anyway.

12

NOW

Stepping off the tube, Alessia made her way out onto the high street, walking beneath the refuge of the tightly knit buildings that towered above her in a bid to keep out of the rain.

She cursed herself for not bringing an umbrella, but she hadn't anticipated the grey looming clouds that had opened up as soon as she'd left her house this morning. Her mind had been on other things.

She pulled up her hood in a futile attempt to stay dry. The rain was coming down heavy now, cascading down her face, big droplets dripping from her hair. Her clothes were already sticking to her skin.

She crossed the road, being careful not to tread in any of the deep pothole-filled puddles that lined Islington High Street, and stared ahead towards the tall, grey building that she'd googled earlier. This was the place. This was where she worked now. Immediately Alessia could feel a knot of anxiety twist in her stomach.

Part of her wondered if she was stupid to come here as she huddled against a wall for shelter for a few minutes while she worked out what to do next. Because she hadn't thought this far ahead.

Harriet was so lovely for insisting on helping her out and giving her a day off, telling her that an afternoon shopping and having a relaxed coffee would be just what she needed. And maybe it really was. Maybe she shouldn't have come, she thought. Maybe she should have done what Harriet had suggested instead of standing out here, in the cold and the rain. Because in truth, she was probably just wasting her time. What happened back then felt like a lifetime ago now; what if she didn't even remember her? And even if she did remember, she was taking a risk in coming here and dragging it all back up.

A risk that this might open up Pandora's box on the life that she'd buried all those years ago.

But still she waited, unable to drag herself away, in the vain hope that she might catch a glimpse of the woman she once knew. Because curiosity had got the better of her now, and she wanted to see her. She needed to see her.

She watched as hordes of people frantically rushed past her in a bid to get out of the heavy downpour. Heads down, unseeing. The few stares that did reach her showed her no acknowledgement. People simply stepped around her as if she was invisible. Like she wasn't even there. Which was one of the things Alessia had actually grown to love so much about London.

The anonymity of the city. How you could be a somebody or nobody, everything or nothing and no one really cared. No one took any notice of you because they were all too preoccupied with themselves. Still, she waited.

The day darkened and the streetlights flickered on, casting their bold yellow hues into the reflection of puddles that lined the ground, as the rain continued to fall.

And she saw herself then, finally, as others might, had they bothered to glance in her direction and take any notice of what she was doing. Standing out here for hours in the pouring rain, with her arms wrapped around herself as she shivered, in a bid to keep warm, while she stalked the ghosts of her past.

'What are you doing?!' she muttered quietly to herself. 'The is the definition of madness, isn't it?'

She laughed as she realised that if she was going crazy, then at least she was definitely in the right place for it. She dragged her gaze away from the Children's Services building she'd spent all her time focusing on since she'd arrived and rested her gaze on the building next door instead. A psychiatrist's office.

What am I doing here?

It was stupid. Coming here. She gave up and decided that she wanted to leave. She'd catch the tube, go home and relieve Harriet from her childcare duties and cook Carl something nice for dinner. And she'd try and forget this crazy notion of why she'd come here today. To see her. And part of her felt almost relieved. Because she had felt so nervous about dragging everything up again, unsure if it would do any good. And even if she did see her, what would she say or do?

About to leave, her eyes went to the building's entrance one more time. Like a challenge as she willed a final call to action. As she gave herself one last chance to see her. *If it's meant to be, it will be.*

'What the...?' An involuntary gasp crawled up her throat and burst out of her mouth without thought as she narrowed her eyes and held on to the wall behind her in a bid to stay upright.

It was her. She was there. She was really there. What were the chances? Or was she seeing things that weren't really there? Were her eyes deceiving her? Because Alessia had only caught a fleeting glimpse of the woman's face before she flung her bag over her shoulder, tossing back her long dark hair, and disappeared underneath an umbrella. But it looked like her. Though she was standing at a distance. And heavy sheets of rain hammered down between them.

But still, every part of Alessia's body reacted to the sight of her. Every cell. Every breath. Every heartbeat.

She needed to be sure. She needed to be certain. Without

thinking straight – without thinking at all – Alessia walked, her feet moved one in front of the other robotically, her limbs took over. Like an out-of-body experience that she had no control of, she followed the woman from her past.

13

THEN

She's lucky.

That's what her social worker, Amanda, had told her after their last meeting together, before she brought her here to this strange, unfamiliar home. She thinks about that as she stares up at the bedroom ceiling, her eyes tracing the pretty pattern that the lampshade casts across the room. She's given up trying to count the thousands of tiny squares that float like a puzzle above her.

Instead, she is listening to the family downstairs. The TV is blaring loudly and she can hear cups clanking together in the kitchen. The sound of water running and the kettle boiling. It sounds normal, mundane, homely. If she closes her eyes she could be back at home. Not here in this house full of well-meaning strangers.

The foster care is only temporary, until the trial, Amanda had said. And that's all that Emma-Jayne can think about as she lies on this unfamiliar bed in the sparse room of the picture perfect two-up, two-down house on the outskirts of the West Sussex countryside. She eyes the window. Outside, the tops of the trees tap at her window. Beyond that, they stand to attention like soldiers in neat rows as they line the sprawling fields.

The hustle and chaos of London seems worlds away right now.

The concrete greys replaced with vivid pockets of green, all stitched together like a patchwork quilt that spreads across the landscape for what looks like miles. But that's the point of all of this, she figures. Of them moving her here. As far away from possible from her old home and her old life.

She blinks the tears away as she thinks back to the police station. To that night. Recalling her mother's ashen face, her expression of pure disbelief. How she'd doubled over. Folded in on herself when they'd told her what they'd done. And Emma-Jayne had tried to tell her the truth. She'd tried to tell her what had really happened, but her mother hadn't listened to her. She hadn't wanted to listen to her. She'd just wanted to scream and lash out, and her words had echoed all over the station, bouncing off every wall. Ringing in Emma-Jayne's ears.

You're a liar!

Later, Amanda had muttered quietly to Emma-Jayne that her mother hadn't meant what she'd said. That she was in shock too. But Emma-Jayne knows she meant it. She'd meant every word of it. That her mother blamed her solely for everything. That she probably wished it was her that was dead.

And Emma-Jayne thinks about that a lot too. Her body stone cold, lying in a pit, deep down in the ground. The soil piled up on top of her. Unloved and unclaimed. Dead. Because she deserves that, doesn't she? If what they say she did is true. A life for a life.

She's still sure she didn't kill anyone, but her mind won't allow her to go back there. It keeps blocking the memory out. And every time she tries to think about it her chest tightens and she feels the shortness of her breath, as if there's not enough air inside her lungs.

And that's when she starts to worry that she really is guilty after all. The room starts to wildly spin and she feels dizzy, and she is forced to do that thing that Amanda has taught her. Like she does now. *Breathe!*

She sits up, swinging her legs over the edge of the bed. Wincing at the sight of the jagged splay of cuts and scars that zigzag all down her legs, she plants her bare feet firmly on the floor, spreading her toes out and burying them in the thick pile carpet, wriggling them back and forth as she breathes deep gulps of air back into her lungs.

Grounding herself as she repeats Amanda's instructions like a mantra.

Slow and steady. In through the nose, back out through the mouth.

The panic attacks are coming more frequently than ever now, the closer they get to the trial. Sometimes she catches them in time and manages to stop them before they engulf her entirely. Other times, they catch her first. Today she wins and the rapidly growing panic subsides inside of her. She thinks about the trial then, and she doesn't think that she can face it. She doesn't think she can face *them*. Her mother. The jury. Her demons. All of them. And she's scared of what her fate will be, even though Amanda says that they might go easy on her. That they'll see she's still a child. Just twelve.

But Amanda has told her that she needs to speak up. To be in with any chance of being offered any sort of leniency, she needs to tell the truth. Only Emma-Jayne can't find the words. Her brain can't make sense of any of it. And she thinks about what she overheard the police officer saying to Amanda at the station, when they stood outside the cell and thought she wasn't listening.

The hushed voices that had talked about children being on trial for murder in England from the age of ten. How the police officer had told Amanda that if the judge found her guilty, she'd likely go to a youth detention centre, and when she turned eighteen, she could be moved to an adult prison.

How Amanda had said that it wasn't as simple as that. That Emma-Jayne's case was complex. That there was more to it.

Was there more to it? Emma-Jayne still doesn't know what she had meant by that. All she really knows is that the thought of prison terrifies her. But she's not sure telling the truth will help her. Because it hasn't so far. Each time she tries to tell them that it hadn't been her, that it had been Sarah who had done it, it falls on deaf ears. And she knows why. Because Sarah must be telling them lies. She must be blaming this all on her.

And they believe her.

That's why they don't want to hear it. That's why they are not listening. They don't believe her version of events. They want her to say something else, something that isn't true.

Her head throbs as she tries to envisage it now. That night. What happened.

And she tries really hard. Only, even now, her mind won't allow her to go there again. Why can't she remember?

And the doctor that had looked over her had told her that it was the brain's way of protecting herself. He had said that the mind is wider and more vast than the entire sky. It was complicated. That it has its own special way of blocking trauma out. He'd told her that even though she's trying really hard to remember, a part of her might not want to. The same part of her that can't bear to relive what she's done, to admit that she was the one responsible. That she caused all of this. Because deep down she knows that it must be true. And that's why she takes the pills, reaching into the bedside cabinet for the little pot that she'd purposely stashed away, wanting to do it properly this time. She swallows them down and then lies back on the bed and waits for the darkness that she craves to come. For this to all finally be over.

She closes her eyes and feels herself finally slip in and out of consciousness. Unsure of what is real and what isn't. She sees him there. Standing quietly. Watching through the gap in the doorway. Watching her. And then he's gone.

But there's noise suddenly and she's aware that she is no longer alone. The room is full of people. Shouting. The phone is being dialled. An ambulance is coming. It seems God won't even allow her to die. Maybe it's too easy an escape? She thinks as she feels the warmth of hands and arms around her as they hold on to her tightly, pulling her back.

14

NOW

The rain was relentless. It lashed down violently and hit the concrete and sprayed up from the puddles that had pooled at her feet. Alessia pulled her coat tightly around herself and clasped the zip with a closed fist as she pulled it down, to ensure that her hood stayed up – as she shielded herself from being seen as much as from the downpour. She sped up. Her heels clicked against the wet pavement, in time now with the woman ahead of her.

She watched as her quarry stopped suddenly. Standing at the kerbside as she scanned the gridlocked traffic. The lights were still red. Alessia had time to get there. Time to catch up. Only the woman didn't wait – she made a run for it, weaving expertly through the stationary traffic just before it started to move again, and Alessia wasn't quick enough to do the same. The traffic was moving fast by the time she approached. A red bus pulled up beside her and blocked her view.

Alessia panicked; stranded on the opposite side of the busy road, she ran the length of the vehicle, her eyes scanning the busy high street in search of a glimpse of the woman. But she was gone.

And she ran then too. Spotting a small gap in the traffic seconds later, she plunged into it, ignoring the angry beep of an oncoming car and squeezing her eyes tightly shut for a second as she braced for it to hit her. She somehow made it to the other side in one piece, breathless, as she finally caught sight of the woman again, making her way up Seven Sisters Road.

She breathed a sigh of relief before she continued to follow, her gaze fixed on the woman. She daren't let it stray, not even for a few seconds. Closer now, Alessia observed the woman's ill-fitting suit. How the trousers were too long, the ends wet from where they'd trailed through the puddles behind her. Closer still, so close that she could smell the woman's overpowering cheap perfume.

The same perfume from back then? A memory floated into her head of how the pungent floral perfume had once lingered, stuck at the back of her throat. Distracted now, not concentrating on her step, their bodies collided as Alessia slammed into the back of the woman.

'I'm so sorry!' she muttered as the woman twisted unsteadily on her feet. 'I wasn't looking where I was going.' She nodded up to the oversized hood on her coat that had slipped down, conveniently covering the top of her face.

'No worries,' the woman said, graciously accepting the apology without question.

Before their eyes met.

Alessia noted how the woman had aged. How her eyes crinkled at the sides as she searched them for a flicker of familiarity or recognition. And for a second, she thought she saw it. As the woman's stare lingered just those few seconds longer than was comfortable. A look crossing her face as if she was searching Alessia's features, trying to place her. But the inquisitiveness was short-lived as the rain continued to pour down around them.

'Doesn't look like it's going to stop anytime soon,' the woman said with a curt nod, as if to break up the awkwardness and her blatant staring. Then, muttering something about catching a cold, she was gone, hastily continuing her journey. Eager to get out of the wet. And Alessia couldn't help but feel a wave of disappointment wash over her that this woman who played such a pivotal part in her life had no recollection of her. Or had she?

Because Alessia was almost sure that she she'd felt it. That gut feeling of mutual familiarity as their eyes had locked together in those few seconds. She should turn back, go back to the tube, back home to Jacob. But she didn't. She continued to follow.

Onwards, up Upper Street. Hanging back as she watched the woman turn into St Mary's Church Gardens. Along the pathway that ran through the middle of the old cemetery. Passed the empty, rain-sodden benches, taking a short-cut to the small block of flats the other side. Alessia hovered patiently behind a small white van, watching as the woman fumbled for her keys, before she dropped them, her hands shaking as she twisted the key in the lock before finally disappearing inside.

She waited, though she had no idea what she was waiting for. What the point was of coming here, other than at least now she knew where she lived. She wanted to ask for help, to speak to someone who would understand – though maybe she won't understand. Maybe she wouldn't get it at all. If anything, it might be the opposite. She'd think she was mad, turning up here like this, out of the blue. Following her home. Still doing and saying all these crazy things again. After all this time. She should go.

About to leave, she saw a light flicker on, downstairs, beneath the wrought-iron railings, illuminating the flat's basement. Alessia pressed herself against the brick wall, watching as the woman walked across the room. The kitchen. The walls around her were painted a garish bright blue. Her coat was still on as she reached into the fridge and pulled out a bottle of wine, pouring herself a large glass before she opened her laptop.

Alessia watched as she downed the wine in one before immediately pouring herself another glass. The MacBook fired up and she tapped away at the keyboard. Alessia peered in, her eyes strained to see. But even from here, she recognised the image that flashed on to the screen.

The young girl's face staring back at her. And the headline across the top of the article that read 'Twelve-year-old Arrested for Murder'.

Alessia jumped at an eruption of noise behind her, startled –
loud laughter from a group of workmen as they passed her in the
street. One of them made a comment, aimed it at her, causing the
other men to all laugh in unison. Though she didn't hear what they
said, and she didn't care.

She'd already zoned out.

Because she knew now that Amanda had recognised her after
all. Even after all this time. And it had hit Alessia like a punch to
the stomach then. The blow severe as she realised that she'd put on
an act and pretended that she didn't recognise her. Amanda had.
Yet still she'd turned her back on her and simply walked away.

15

NOW

'Did you have a nice day?' Harriet said as she jumped off the sofa at the sound of the front door closing. 'You've just missed Jacob. He was hungry so I fed him and I gave him a bath and put him to bed. I hope that's okay? Only, I didn't know how long you were going to be.'

Alessia nodded her head absently as Harriet's gaze swept her body.

And she could read Harriet's thoughts, the concerned look on her friend's face, as she stood there soaking wet, trembling from the cold, her clothes stuck to her skin. A large white box was in her hands, which Harriet eyed curiously. 'Ooh, what's that? Did you buy yourself something nice?'

'Oh, this?' Alessia said, looking down at the box and shaking her head as if she'd only just realised she was holding it. 'No. It's a delivery. It was out on the doorstep.'

She could barely remember her journey back here. She'd been so lost in her thoughts inside her head, that she'd somehow found her way home in a complete daze.

'Oh, sorry, I didn't hear the door go,' Harriet said. 'Here, let me take it. You know what you need? A nice hot cup of tea!' She took the box from Alessia before she led her through to the kitchen and set it down on the kitchen counter. 'Do you want to get out of those clothes while I make us both one?'

Alessia barely heard her words let alone registered them.

'I take it that your shopping trip wasn't very successful then?' Harriet continued as she switched the kettle on.

'Sorry?' Alessia said, wondering how Harriet knew she'd lied and hadn't gone to the shops today.

Harriet had some kind of a sixth sense about things. She'd always put it down to strong intuition, which had always come in handy in her line of work. But Alessia had occasionally mentioned how it freaked her out sometimes, how observant and accurate Harriet could be.

'You haven't got any bags!' Harriet grinned. 'And I know you well enough to know that you'd clear out most of the shops given half the chance.'

'Oh, yeah, right! Sorry. No. I didn't really see anything I liked,' Alessia said, unconvincingly, realising that not having any shopping bags was a giveaway and that she'd have to rethink her story about where she'd been all afternoon.

'That's always the way. Every time I have money burning a hole in my pocket, I can never find a single thing, and yet when I'm skint, I want to buy the whole damn shop!' Harriet smiled.

Alessia did too. But it was a few seconds too late.

'Oh, and you were right about the dinosaurs from outer space game!' Still Harriet persevered, and Alessia could sense that her friend was trying to distract her and keep things light between them, even though she could obviously tell that there was something going on. And Alessia happily played along. She didn't feel willing or able to confide in her friend about what it was that was really bothering her.

'Yeah, Jacob really is nuts over those dinosaurs!'

'Isn't he! Such a vivid imagination. And his energy! He's like one of them Duracell Bunnies. On and on and on.' Harriet grinned and playfully rolled her eyes, feigning exhaustion.

Alessia was miles away again. Staring into space, aware that Harriet was talking, but her mind elsewhere.

'Are you sure that you're okay, Alessia? I hate to pry, really I do, but you seem... a little off. Has something happened? Are you and Carl okay?' Harriet said, pouring them both a tea before staring at Alessia and trying to read her expression. 'You look as if you've been crying.'

'Crying? Oh God, no! It's probably just the rain, no mascara could withstand that heavy downfall,' Alessia said, catching the concerned look on Harriet's face.

'And Carl told me about Sunday. With the car. He said that someone had hit the back of you.'

And Alessia knew how much Harriet would have been waiting for her to say something to her about it. How she would be thinking it was strange that Alessia hadn't even mentioned it until Harriet had to practically prise it out of her.

'The car thing was an accident. Carl is just overthinking things now, what with the window being broken the other day. Look, I didn't tell him because I was embarrassed to admit it, but I was distracted when it happened. I had turned to check on Jacob. It had only been literally a few seconds. I must have slowed right down and that's what caused the car behind me to lose their patience with me,' Alessia lied.

She realised that she needed to snap out of her wistful mood. That Harriet would only worry about her more if she didn't. And Alessia could do without her raising her concerns with Carl too.

And that she needed to get her story straight.

'I didn't want Carl to think that I was acting irresponsibly while Jacob was in the car with me. I felt that it was partly my fault.' She tried to read Harriet's expression and suss out whether or not her friend believed her. The last thing she needed was Harriet and Carl both conspiring against her. At least if she could convince Harriet that the car incident had been nothing, then Carl would believe her too.

'And me and Carl are fine. We're great. Everything's fine,'

Alessia continued, her voice sounding too forced even to her own ears, but she hoped it would be enough to throw Harriet off the scent. And also because she didn't want to seem ungrateful. Harriet had been kind enough to offer to look after Jacob for the day, and Alessia didn't want to throw that back in her face. 'I'm so sorry that I was out for so long. I really did just lose track of time. And you're right, I wasn't in the mood for shopping in the end. But I did manage to find a nice café and ended up reading a whole pile of trashy mags while getting wired on way too much coffee and a very large slab of chocolate cake. It was pure bliss! Or at least it was bliss, until I stupidly decided not to bother with the last tube and walked back. In the rain! Look at the state of me!' Alessia laughed. Relieved that she sounded so normal. That she'd managed to pull the façade off. 'Thank you so much for minding Jacob for me. You know what, though, I think I'll give the tea a miss. You're right. I do need to change out of these things. I might grab a shower and an early night, seeing as Jacob's already down.'

'Are you sure? I don't have any plans tonight. I can hang around. I could order some food in if you're hungry?'

'No honestly, you've done more than enough for me today as it is. And knowing Jacob he'll be out for the count now until the morning,' Alessia said, but she knew Harriet wasn't stupid. She would be aware that she was being dismissed and, no doubt, she would have already convinced herself that Alessia was keeping something from her. But still Alessia persevered. 'I should make the most of it.'

Harriet eyed her friend.

'Alessia. If there was something, you would tell me, wouldn't you?' she said carefully.

Her voice was soft and Alessia could sense the effort she made to try and coax her in to telling her what was really going on. Harriet wanted Alessia to know that she wasn't fooled by her act. Only, typically, Harriet wouldn't spell that out to her, because she knew when not to overstep the line.

'Thanks. But there's nothing to tell. I'm fine. Everything's fine,'

Alessia said without skipping a beat. Shutting the conversation down.

Harriet nodded then, seeming to take the hint.

'Well, look, I was thinking, we can always make this a regular thing, you know? I could come over once a week and you could get a few hours' rest, or maybe have another go at shopping again?' She paused. 'I just want you to know that you're not alone. I mean, I know you have Carl too, but if you need me, please call me, okay?' She grabbed her bag from the stool before she slipped her coat on and made her way to the front door. 'Oh and just so you know, Jacob didn't eat all his dinner. He made a beeline for the biscuits though, and well, I couldn't refuse that cute blooming face of his. Sorry, I'm still babbling on, aren't I? When all you want to do is get out of those wet things and crawl in to bed. Okay, I'm off. Go on, off to bed with you! Get some rest and I'll call you tomorrow.'

Alessia laughed too, and kissed her friend, before she closed the door behind her and leant back against the thick PVC panel for a few moments. She closed her eyes while she caught her breath as she enjoyed the sound of the house being in complete silence.

She could finally think straight at last. She could work out all the pieces that were hurtling around inside her head. Today had really taken it out of her. Harriet was right about one thing. Getting out of these clothes and getting some rest was just what she needed.

Making her way into the kitchen, she poured herself a glass of water and drank it back in one before her eyes went to the white box that she'd left on the side. It was probably for her. Carl rarely got parcels sent here for him, whereas Alessia was forever buying Jacob the latest toys and outfits she'd spotted online. But she saw there was no address label on it. Had it been delivered by hand?

Curious, she cut through the packaging and peeled back the cardboard.

It was a display of flowers. Dark green foliage entwined with a cluster of lilies and white roses. She smiled. Carl always bought her flowers. It was one of the many things she adored about him.

How he would buy them for her 'just because'. Never only after one of their rare arguments or on days where it was expected, like Valentine's. Just on days that he had been thinking of her. Except, he normally delivered them himself, bringing them home with him from the local florist around the corner. Having them delivered and left on the doorstep wasn't his style.

Frowning, she reached inside the box and picked the display up in search of a card. The overpowering smell hit her first. Putrid and rancid, like rot. And she realised that the flowers were all dead: withered and flaccid, they hung from the wreath. And it was only then that she saw it. Splayed out at the bottom of the box. A mass of brown fur. Alessia let out a scream. Her hands gripped the wreath so tightly that the sharp jagged thorns from the dead roses embedded themselves into her flesh. She dropped the arrangement as if it was on fire. A thick drop of blood trailed down her finger and landed on the message card that had floated down to the floor, red on white, blurring the line of striking bold letters.

MURDERER!

No! No! She cried silently to herself as she thought of Jacob, lying so innocently in his cot upstairs. Sleeping soundly, so blissfully unaware of any of the horrors of this. Her heart hammered forcefully inside her chest, her lungs constricted and the room started spinning, violently. *Breathe*, she told herself as wild panic rose up inside of her.

From the very second that the brick came flying through her window the other day, she knew in her gut that her past had finally caught up with her. Because she'd made a promise to Sarah that they'd always be friends, hadn't she? But Alessia had broken her promise when she'd been forced to leave Sarah behind in the end. It was the only way that she'd been able to move on. The only way she'd been able to have any kind of life of her own. By blocking Sarah out. By blocking it all out. But now Sarah had found her again, and she was going to make Alessia pay for casting her aside, for forgetting all about her.

And when Carl found out the truth about her, she would lose him too. He would take Jacob from her and she'd lose them both. Her family. The one thing she treasured more than anything else in her entire life. Staring at the box as tears ran down her cheeks, this only confirmed it for her.

Her darkest days had returned. Sarah had somehow found her again. And maybe part of her had always known that she would. Part of her had been expecting her.

16

THEN

They are back here again. In the doll's house. Only today the mood feels sombre, and Emma-Jayne isn't sure why. But the doll's house feels like a horrible place. Cold and dirty, and almost infectious in how it makes her feel cold and dirty too. She wrinkles her nose up at the pungent smell of the place – the stench of wet socks and rotten wood, musty and earthy – and she shivers.

The damp always seems to have a way of crawling under her skin and deep down into her bones. Lingering there for hours afterwards, even once she gets home, it's in her hair, her clothes, her skin. And she's sure it's getting worse each time she comes here, like the place is decaying before their very eyes. This sanctuary of a den that they both made is crumbling into squalor around them. It doesn't feel like a nice place to be any more. It doesn't feel safe.

'What is that?' Emma-Jayne says, getting up from the damp floor and smoothing down her school skirt as she scans the floor.

'Can you see it?' Sarah says. Her eyes flash with excitement as the creature scampers across the room, a blur of brown fur against grey concrete. Then, seeing the angst on Emma-Jayne's face she laughs.

'Chill out! It's just a little rabbit.'

'It was smaller than a rabbit, though!' Emma-Jayne says, dancing from foot to foot.

'It could be a baby rabbit?' Sarah shrugs.

'It was faster than a rabbit though. And why would a rabbit come in here? Inside? With us. It would be too scared,' Emma-Jayne says, not listening to her friend. Not buying it. 'Rats come inside though.'

'It's not a rat. I saw its fluffy tail. And it hopped,' Sarah says as the two girls stare at the pile of rubble by the back bare wall, listening to the scuffling sound coming from behind where the creature is now hidden. 'And I bet you're right. The poor little bunny is more scared of us than we are of him!'

Emma-Jayne isn't sure about that. She has a bad feeling. Her palms are sticky now, and she feels hot and sick. Untrusting in Sarah, because Sarah always makes up silly stories and pretends that they are true.

'Half-truths,' Sarah had said defensively when Emma-Jayne had called her out on a few. But if they are only half true, that means they are half lies also. Though Emma-Jayne doesn't ever say that out loud. She just thinks it, quietly, to herself.

'Let's go look!' Sarah says finally, knowing it's the only way to shut Emma-Jayne up. To prove to her she didn't have anything to be scared of. That this time she isn't lying.

Emma-Jayne shakes her head, and Sarah shrugs again.

'Okay then, watch!'

She tiptoes towards the rubble as quietly as she can while Emma-Jayne watches with trepidation. Then she pounces, screeching loudly as the furry creature tries to escape from the predator hunting it. It runs back the way it came, towards Emma-Jayne. And Emma-Jayne is screeching now too as the thing comes bounding her way. Beady eyes. That long snake-like tail. Sharp rodent teeth. And she needs to move. To run. To get away. Only her legs betray her, and she can't move. She's glued to the spot. And she feels it clutch on to her shoe. Its sharp claws scamper up her leg. She screams louder. Piercing, echoing. And the rat quickly realises its error and scampers back down her leg again, running across the floor and out the doorway. Leaving the two girls in silence again.

'It was a rat! I told you!' Emma-Jayne is crying. And Sarah is beside her as they both look down at the small puddle that has formed at Emma-Jayne's feet where she wet herself.

'It's okay, I won't tell anyone,' Sarah says, tucking her hand into hers.

17

NOW

'Jesus, Carl! I didn't hear you come in!' Alessia shrieked as she continued to shove what looked like the remnants of a dead bouquet of flowers into the bin.

'I'm sorry, I didn't mean to scare you!' Carl laughed as he held his hands up to show that he came in peace, surprised that his sudden presence in the kitchen had made Alessia jump out of her skin.

'Here let me,' Carl said, watching as Alessia tied the bin bag in a double knot and noted the flustered look on her face and how her cheeks were burning red. 'Why don't you grab a bottle of red and go and sit down? I'll take the bin out and then we can both chill and have a drink,' Carl insisted with a smile, sensing that his wife had had a bad day and reaching to take the bag from her.

'Now that sounds like a plan.' Alessia nodded, grateful, before she took a deep breath and stepped away from the bag. She grabbed a couple of glasses and the bottle of red from the rack on the dresser and made her way into the lounge.

'And don't start without me! I know what you're like!' Carl joked, still making light of the other night when he and Andrew had drunk far too much of the stuff.

Though tonight if anybody was going to neck back a bottle of red, it would be Alessia going by the strained look on her face. He'd been working too hard lately. The hours had been longer than usual and they were both starting to feel the strain. An evening together would be just the remedy for them both, he hoped, as he dragged the bag from the bin and carried it outside and down the pathway that ran along the side of the house towards the wheelie bin. But as he lifted the lid, he recoiled as the sudden stench of something rotten hit him with its full force. 'Jesus Christ, Jacob!' Carl chuckled to himself. He held his breath to try and block out the rancid smell of his son's dirty nappies. It never ceased to amaze him how such a small boy could make such a gigantic stink.

About to toss the bag inside, he narrowed his eyes at the sight of the large white box at the bottom, the lid flung open just enough so that he could see that there was something inside.

He peered in, doing a double take as he realised it was a small creature of some kind.

'What the hell...?' Carl grimaced, shaking his head as he realised he was looking at a dead rat. Instantly, Carl was set on edge. Because it hadn't got in there by itself, surely, so had someone put it there? Alarm bells rang inside his head. Alessia? Had she put it in the bin? Though he knew there was no way that she would have been able to bring herself to go anywhere near a rat, alive or dead.

He'd joked about it at first, when they'd first got together. When he hadn't understood that Alessia didn't just not like the idea of rats, she actually suffered from musophobia, a genuine fear of the creatures. Alessia had told him that her phobia had stemmed from her childhood, that she'd been bitten by one in the garden as a child. And now just the thought of them completely terrified her. So much so, that she could suffer a panic attack just at the thought of them.

But how else would the rat have got there? And if she did put it in the bin, why hadn't she mentioned it? He wondered then if that was why she had seemed flustered in the kitchen just now. Distracted almost. So much so that she hadn't even heard him come in. Because she had seemed jumpy, hadn't she? More than normal. That wasn't just his imagination, was it? Staring back into the bin, Carl turned his nose up at the putrid sight once more, unable to comprehend how she hadn't mentioned it. She'd been just about to come back out here too. He recalled the flowers he'd seen her shove into the bin before she tied the bag up. Twice. In a firm double knot. Her expression had been flustered. As if he'd just walked in and caught her doing something that she didn't want him to see. He hadn't bought flowers for ages and now that he thought about it, he couldn't recall seeing any displayed anywhere in the house for a while now.

Curious, Carl untied the bag and saw the splay of dead, wilted flowers. Where had Alessia got them from? Pulling the bunch up in search of a card, he frowned as he realised that the display was set on a circular plastic frame. It wasn't a bouquet. It was a wreath. Why would they have a wreath of flowers in the house? There was only one way to find out. Tying the bag back up, Carl threw it inside the wheelie bin before making his way back inside the house.

'Alessia, do you know that there's a rat in the bin?' he called out to the lounge as he washed his hands under the kitchen tap.

Alessia didn't answer.

'Alessia?' Carl said, drying his hands on a towel as he walked into the lounge.

'Huh?' Alessia said as she moved quickly away where from where she'd been peering out of the lounge window. Watching him? Apparently so distracted that she hadn't heard Carl's question. Or perhaps, Carl thought before he repeated himself, she was just buying herself time.

'There's a dead rat. Outside, in the bin.' He saw her falter as if she was trying to recall her well-rehearsed answer.

'Oh... yes. I found it in the garden. A cat must have got to it or something. And I didn't want Jacob to see it and get scared.'

Carl nodded. Her answer was plausible. To anyone who didn't know her. Because Carl had seen her reaction to rats in the past.

How her phobia made her act completely irrationally. How it locked her into a trancelike state, so much so that she couldn't even breathe properly, let alone think straight. Would the thought of Jacob even factor in during a panic attack?

'So... *you* boxed it up and threw it in the bin?' Carl stared at his wife suspiciously. Yet somehow, she was managing to hold her own. To stay calm and not react. She was acting.

'It wasn't exactly going to hurt me.' Alessia shrugged, her tone defensive. 'It was already dead. So, yeah. I got rid of it.'

And Carl saw it. The way that Alessia deflected her eyes from his when she answered and briefly glanced down at the floor. That moment her lie rolled so easily from her tongue, because Alessia had always been the worst liar. She didn't lie to him often. But whenever she did slip up with a little white lie, he always knew. She knew it too.

But why would she lie to him about a dead rat?

They sat there in silence after that, the TV on, but neither of them really watching it. Alessia was constantly making some excuse or another to leave the room, to look for her phone, or needing her jumper, but Carl had seen her on Jacob's baby monitor, how each time she'd gone upstairs she'd poked her head into Jacob's bedroom to check on him. As if the baby monitor alone wasn't enough and she had to see him for herself.

And Carl sat there festering. Thinking about the fact that picking up a dead rodent just wasn't Alessia's style. That was the kind of thing that would freak her out so much that she'd at least have called him at work, demanding that as soon as he was home he was to get rid of it for her. And then he'd tease her playfully but tell her that he'd do it. Knowing how much it affected her. Knowing how much she'd want it gone. And what about the wreath? Where had it come from? He was just about to ask her when Alessia spoke.

'Did you hear that? Do you think he's awake?'

Getting up from her chair again, ready to leave the room, Alessia sounded as if she was almost willing it to be true. For

Jacob to wake and join them, so he'd ease the tension in the room.

'You'd hear him on the monitor. We both would.' Carl narrowed his eyes, nodding to where the monitor sat in the middle of the coffee table. Next to it were the two glasses of wine. Alessia's remained completely untouched.

He wondered then if perhaps he was being too hard on Alessia. Maybe her behaviour tonight wasn't about her trying to cover something up; maybe this was all part of the after-effect. Maybe the dead rat had pushed her over the edge. And instead of a panic attack, she was deflecting. Aiming all her irrational fears towards Jacob.

He watched as Alessia sat back down, her eyes still on the baby monitor as she chewed at the skin around her nails.

'Jacob's okay, isn't he?' Carl asked as he wondered if perhaps he was unwell or that he'd had a bad day and maybe Alessia just hadn't told him yet. Maybe that was why she'd been acting so strangely and out of character. Maybe she was just worried about their son.

'Yes. Jacob is fine.'

'And you're okay, Alessia? Only you're acting very weird tonight,' Carl said finally. He knew that if he didn't just come out and say it, he'd never get an answer.

He was convinced now that something was up, because as much as they both completely, besottedly adored Jacob, they adored their evenings alone together equally as much. And Alessia had barely even looked in his direction this evening, let alone made any kind of real conversation with him. And she definitely seemed distracted. As if she was a million miles away.

'Yeah, I'm fine. Oh, Carl, I'm sorry! I'm sorry!' Alessia said as she sank back on the couch and wrapped her arms around him in a sudden admission of guilt. 'No, I'm not. I just can't settle tonight.'

'You're not sick, are you?' Carl asked as he kissed Alessia on the forehead and saw the genuine strain on his wife's face. How pale and tired she looked.

'I think I'm just a bit run-down or something.'

'You do look a bit peaky,' he said gently, treading carefully so as not to offend her.

'Do I? Yeah, I feel it. I might go to bed and get an early night,' Alessia said. 'Maybe I should take the spare room just in case I am going down with something. It's probably nothing but I wouldn't want to pass anything on... You don't mind, do you?'

'Not at all. Go, sweetheart. Leave the monitor, I can check on Jacob if he wakes tonight. You get some rest,' Carl said.

Alessia blew him a kiss before she took the stairs.

He sat back in the chair and eyed the monitor. As he waited for her face to appear again at Jacob's bedroom door, which it did just seconds later, he smiled to himself before he shook his head. Alessia just couldn't help herself. Jacob was always her number one priority. Which was one of the things he loved about her the most.

Drinking back the last of his wine, he finished Alessia's glass too. Unsettled then. Unable to shake the images of the dead rat or the wreath from his mind. And the fact that Alessia had lied to him. That she was holding something back. The question was, what?

THEN

Emma-Jayne hears the front door slam. Footsteps marching up the stairs. Pulling the duvet tightly up around her, she holds her breath and listens intently, praying that whoever is home has just forgotten something. That they'll come and go quickly. That they won't come into her bedroom and find her here. But her hope is short-lived as she hears the steps directly outside her bedroom door, before the door handle creaks and her mother's voice fills the room.

'What the hell are you playing at, Emma-Jayne?' Her mother storms in and throws open the curtains. The room is suddenly flooded with bright light.

'Urgh!' Emma-Jayne complains loudly, hoping that her mother will go easy on her if she pretends that she's disorientated, having just been dragged from a deep sleep. 'I'm not well. I feel sick so I went back to bed.'

'You had this planned all along, didn't you? When you sat at the breakfast table eating your cereal this morning, you knew then that you had no attention of going in to school, didn't you?' Brenda shouts, still furious that she'd received a phone call at work from the school telling her that Emma-Jayne hadn't turned up *again*.

'Again?' Brenda had mouthed down the line to the teacher who had called her, unable to hide the shock in her voice that this was the first she'd heard of Emma-Jayne truanting. She must have sounded like a bumbling idiot.

And at first she'd thought maybe she'd misheard the teacher. That she had got it wrong and there had been some kind of a mistake. Because Emma-Jayne was never sick and she rarely ever took time off from school. It turns out she was wrong there.

'Her attendance has declined rapidly the past few weeks,' the teacher had informed her. 'We've sent letters home asking you to make an appointment to come in and see us. To discuss Emma-Jayne's disruptive behaviour. But we hadn't heard anything back from you. So I thought I'd call.'

'Letters?' Brenda had said, guessing rightly that Emma-Jayne would have kept them from her. That she wouldn't have wanted her mother to know she'd been truanting from school, nor that they were unhappy with her disruptive behaviour whilst she was there. So she'd driven home, purposely wanting to catch Emma-Jayne out, red-handed.

'I told you I felt ill this morning,' Emma-Jayne mumbles from where she lies, the covers still pulled up over her head to block out the light. To block her mother's voice out.

And it wasn't a lie, she thinks. She slept so deeply last night, as if she'd been knocked out. But when she'd woken this morning, she'd still felt so tired and groggy that she could barely keep her eyes open. And when she stood up, she felt it, how her whole body ached. Tender and bruised. A sicky feeling inside of her. That feeling that something really bad had happened to her, only she can't really remember what. Her head still feels fuzzy even now. But despite all of that, she'd still got dressed and sat at the breakfast table. Not wanting to cause a fuss. Not wanting to say anything. Not while he was there.

'Look E-Jay,' Bobby had said, throwing his sister a goofy grin. 'Look! A Lellow car,' he said, pointing at the yellow one. 'And this one is geen.'

'Yellow and green, you stupid idiot!' Emma-Jayne had huffed, her eyes down, without bothering to look up from her bowl of cereal. Because she'd known that Robert would be glaring at her, his expression burning with rage. He was so precious about Bobby. His first and only biological child.

Which was partly why Emma-Jayne did it, why she was always so mean to her brother. So that she would get a rise from him.

'I see you're being your usual sulky, miserable self,' her mother had said, making light of Emma-Jayne's comment and doing what she usually did, trying so hard to sweep the sudden tension in the room neatly under the carpet. Extinguishing the fire before it had properly started.

'I'm not sulky. I don't feel well.'

'Well, you're well enough to get dressed for school and eat cereal, so you're well enough to go to school. And don't speak to your brother like that!' Robert had chastised her. 'Apologise.'

It was the only time Robert spoke to her. When he was angry with her. When he was telling her what to do.

'Sorry,' Emma-Jayne said with a shrug. Knowing that she wouldn't win. That it was quicker and easier for them all if she just did as she was told. Because otherwise he'd make her pay later.

'No. That's not good enough. Apologise to your brother properly,' Robert said again, glaring at Emma-Jayne. And Emma-Jayne could see it in his eyes. The enjoyment he was getting from her humiliation.

And if she could see it so clearly, surely so could her mum? Only her mum acted oblivious to it all. Just as she always did, with everything. Moving quickly between the cooker and the kitchen table, serving Robert his perfectly cooked eggs just as he expected. Sunny side up and just so. His toast served with a crunch and just a smear of butter.

'I'm sorry, Bobby!' Emma-Jayne said through gritted teeth. Her expression deadpan as she saw the hurt look on his face, and the way he'd gone so quiet.

Too angry to focus on her guilt at being so mean to her brother, she'd forced it down. Waiting until they'd all left the house so she could crawl back into bed.

'I tried to tell you this morning, but you don't listen. You never listen,' Emma-Jayne says now, her voice still muffled underneath the duvet.

'Listen to what? The way you speak to us all? All the silly lies you make up?' Brenda asks, gritting her teeth. 'If any of us should be in bed, it should be me. I'm exhausted, Emma-Jayne. You think it's easy for me working two jobs? Spending my days at the college and my evenings cleaning a bloody office block for a bunch of stuck-up solicitors? And I have to do pretty much everything here. The cooking. The cleaning. All the washing. And all I ask, Emma-Jayne, is for you to give me a break. Give him a break,' she says, her voice almost pleading.

Because they both know what this is really about. The mutual hate that Emma-Jayne and Robert have for one another. The bad feeling that always hangs in the air between them. And the older Emma-Jayne grows, the more distance she seems to place between them. The more time she spends up here alone, in her room. It isn't healthy.

'Get up. You're going back to school,' her mother says, glaring at the mound on the bed, getting angrier the more she speaks, and the more Emma-Jayne ignores her.

'I said get up!'

She's lost her temper. Emma-Jayne can hear her crossing the room towards her.

'Stop!' she shouts as her mother wrenches the blanket from her.

'You're going to school. Right now, get up!'

And Emma-Jayne sees it. The horrified look on her mum's face as her eyes slowly make their way down her body. Stopping at her legs, which she normally makes sure she keeps well covered, that are etched in what looks like a road map of long winding cuts and scratches that snake up both of her calves and shins.

'Oh my god! How did this happen? How did this happen to

you?' she asks, her jaw dropping, her expression horrified. Thinking the worst. That someone has harmed her child.

There are so many cuts though. Some still bright red, jagged and fierce. Others have scabbed over. Some of the lines are just fine white raised scars. And she knows by the way that Emma-Jayne simply shrugs, without offering any explanation, that Emma-Jayne has done this to herself.

'You did this?'

Emma-Jayne's eyes go to the floor. To the carpet. To anywhere other than her mother's face.

And Brenda sees her daughter's cheeks burn red hot. She's never felt so completely shocked. So utterly astounded.

'But why? Why would you hurt yourself like this? Why would you do this to yourself?' Brenda asks, trying to work out why she would harm herself intentionally. So brutally. What would she gain from it?

And Emma-Jayne doesn't know what to tell her. Because there's so much bad stuff inside her head, and if her mother can't even deal with this – cuts and scars – there's no way she'll be able to cope with anything else.

But she knows she must start somewhere. And part of her is relieved.

'I found a chunk of glass at the doll's house. I took it. Me and Sarah...' Emma-Jayne starts, only she can see that her words instantly strike the wrong chord.

How the wavering look of sympathy on her mum's face is quickly lost, replaced with anger.

'Stop!' she says, shaking her head. 'Enough about that bloody girl. We've spoken about this before. What is wrong with you? What the hell is wrong with you?'

And she's pulling her then, forcefully, by the crook of her arm, wrenching her upright from the bed. Done with her stories and done with her lies. Not willing to hear any more stories about Sarah.

'We need to take you to see someone. This isn't right. None of this is right,' her mother says. She makes her way over to the wardrobe and grabs the hanger with Emma-Jayne's school uniform, her eyes going back to the cuts on Emma-Jayne's legs.

'If this is what you are doing to your own body, self-harming. I saw a programme about it. How teenagers would hurt themselves by slicing in to their own skin. A cry for help, they'd called it. Attention seekers, Robert said. And I think maybe he has a point.' She shakes her head, faltering. Because Emma-Jayne isn't like those other kids that cut themselves. She has a family and a happy stable life.

'Why do you do it?' she asks, as if Emma-Jayne's actions have been aimed at her. Like a personal attack. Another thing she did to punish her for marrying Robert. For going on to have Bobby. For trying to make them a new life. A good life. Only Emma-Jayne seems determined to destroy it. 'What if Bobby saw this? What if he copied you? What would you say then?'

And Emma-Jayne shakes her head and starts to cry. Because her mum won't listen. She never listens. And her mother doesn't pull her in close or hold her tight. She doesn't fill her with words of reassurance. Instead she just stares at her with an angry expression fixed to her face. A look that tells her she doesn't understand. She could never understand.

'You silly girl!' Her voice is full of disappointment now. 'Put your uniform on. I'll drive you to school. We'll talk about this later.'

And Emma-Jayne nods, knowing that they won't talk about this again.

Because this is what her mother does. She pretends not to see things. Not to hear things. She floats around in her own little world, not wanting to admit that their lives are far from perfect. And maybe doing all of this to herself is a cry for help. Maybe she is crying out, begging her mother to see the pain she is in. The secrets locked away inside of her. Only it doesn't seem to matter how loud she cries, her mother is completely deaf to it. The only person who listens to her, the only person who understands, is Sarah.

19

NOW

'I'm sorry to call so late. Alessia has just gone up to bed, and she'd lose her rag if she finds out that I'm calling you and talking to you about her behind her back. But I'm worried about her, Harriet,' Carl said, feeling a twang of guilt that he was going behind Alessia's back. Because he knew how much Alessia valued her privacy. About their relationship, about what went on between them. And Carl respected that. He found it refreshing, even – that talking and gossiping about their marriage hadn't ever been Alessia's style.

'I just wondered if you had anything back about the car that hit Alessia?'

'No, sorry, I've put the feelers out. But finding this car would be like looking for a needle in a haystack. Oh, the glorious chaos of London's roads, eh! But without the full number plate, I'm limited,' Harriet said, unable to keep the concern from her tone.

'Is everything all right, Carl? Are you and Alessia okay?'

'Yeah, I am fine. We're fine.' Carl rubbed his head and drank back the last dregs of the bottle of red wine before he spoke again. 'At least I hope we are fine. I don't know, I know how this is going to sound, and it's nothing I can really point my finger at. Nothing major anyway, at least I don't think. But Alessia doesn't seem herself right now. Ever since the brick came through the window. I mean, she says she's fine, but she seems... I don't know. Distracted? And I just wanted to see what you thought. How did she seem today, when she came back from her shopping trip? Did you notice anything strange?' Carl said, realising then that Alessia hadn't mentioned anything about her day off shopping, and half hoping that Harriet would tell him that the day was fine, that he was worrying about nothing.

Only he wasn't expecting the pause at the other end of the phone. Harriet's silence made him suddenly even more anxious.

'Harriet? Is there something you want to say?' Carl said, sitting forward on the sofa and bracing himself for whatever it was that his friend was clearly hesitant to tell him. He'd only asked because he trusted Harriet. He and Alessia both did. And he knew that she was always straight with them.

'Look, I wasn't going to say anything, I guess because I didn't think it was such a big deal, but yeah, I noticed it, too, how distracted she seems. When I asked her she shut me down. Tried to make it all seem so less trivial than it actually was,' Harriet admitted.

And Carl knew that Harriet was struggling with telling him because she didn't want to appear disloyal to Alessia. The two women were friends too. Harriet only had his wife's best intentions at heart.

'I just don't understand why she's playing these things down. Because if you ask me, she seemed pretty shaken up about the whole window incident. But why is she so defensive? And the car hitting her, she knows she can always talk to me. Only she isn't doing that either,' Harriet said, clearly still hurt that Alessia hadn't confided in her about the whole thing.

'You know Alessia, she just doesn't like the drama. Anything for an easy life,' Carl said, defending his wife and trying to make Harriet feel better.

'I know. I know,' Harriet said. 'I do think it's shaken her up a lot more than she's letting on. I spoke to her out in the kitchen the other night, while you and Andrew were sinking back all that wine. I wanted to know if she was really okay. And she said that she was. She said that she just felt a little overwhelmed lately. And today when she got back from the shops, she just didn't seem herself.'

'Overwhelmed by what though?'

'Well, I mean, do not take offence when I tell you this. This is strictly between us, but she did hint that you've been working longer hours and she mentioned that she's been on her own with Jacob a lot. And I do mean hint, Carl. Most of it was me reading between the lines. And she said that she's not been sleeping so well. That she's tired...' Harriet said, treading lightly.

The phone was silent for a few seconds while neither of them spoke.

'And before you think the worst, let me just add that Alessia did not once speak badly of you. In fact, she was so vague and unforthcoming that I had to practically drag the little she did say out of her.'

'I've dropped the ball. Haven't I?' Carl said, feeling guilty that he hadn't been more present at home, with Alessia and Jacob. Of course she was feeling overwhelmed. She'd been doing it all on her own lately, and Carl had barely been here. 'I've been so wrapped up in work and this deal. I didn't even realise.'

'Hey, don't be so hard on yourself. It happens. Trust me, I'm guilty of it too. Poor Andrew is always left to fend for himself while I'm working overtime or covering for someone else's shift at the last minute. It happens. That's life,' Harriet said lightly. 'Look, I know that there may be some truth in what she said, about being tired. Jacob can be a wild one. I mean he made me play dinosaurs from out of space about three billion times with him today. That's enough to tire anyone out.' She laughed affectionately. 'But I kind of got the feeling that she's keeping something from me, still. I just got the feeling that she was holding back on me about something, you know?'

'Oh, I know!' Carl nodded in agreement. Feeling exactly that.

'And when she came back today, she really didn't seem herself at all. Firstly, she hadn't bought a single thing when she was in town – that alone should send out alarm bells.'

Carl smiled at Harriet's attempt at lightening the situation. Before she continued to tell him about how Alessia had come home soaked through. As if she hadn't even been to the shops today at all.

'She said she wanted to get an early night and I got the impression she didn't want me to stay.'

'Well, she didn't go to bed. She was still up when I came home from work. I found her in the kitchen. Shoving some flowers into the bin. I got the feeling she was hiding something from me.'

'Woah! Shoving flowers into the bin? Yeah, that does sound a bit shady now you mention it. And you didn't think to report that to the police, Carl?' Harriet teased, knowing that there must be more to this, because Carl had never called her out of the blue before about Alessia.

'I know it sounds mad, bear with me. They weren't just any old bunch of flowers. It looked like a funeral wreath. The flowers were all dead. And when I put the bag out in the bin, I found a box at the bottom of the dustbin with a rat inside.'

Carl paused then, knowing how crazy he must sound.

'A dead rat. Alessia claimed that she put it there. She said she found it in the garden, a fox or cat must have got to it, and she didn't want to scare Jacob.'

'Well, that's understandable...' Harriet said. 'I mean, I know how terrified she is of things like that, so maybe she doesn't want Jacob to pick up on her phobia.'

'I'm overthinking all of this, aren't I?' Carl said, realising that he was stupid to doubt Alessia and think she was keeping things from him. That maybe there was a perfectly reasonable explanation behind her behaviour tonight. Rats were one of her biggest phobias, and maybe it had affected her more than she wanted to let on. Which is why she had just gone to bed. That and because she was genuinely tired and run-down.

Only Harriet didn't answer and, picking up on the awkward silence, Carl prompted her to speak.

'Harriet?'

'Look, it may be nothing, but...' Harriet paused again as if gathering her thoughts. 'The box you saw in the bin, it wasn't a large white one, was it?'

'Yeah. How did you know?' Carl asked, suspicious. Wondering for a split second if he'd got this all wrong, and it had been Harriet who had disposed of the rat for his poor, helpless wife.

They would have told him by now, though, if that had been the case. Harriet certainly wouldn't have let it string out this long. Especially seeing as he was calling her so late in the evening and sounded so genuinely worried about Alessia.

'Because there had been a delivery while Alessia was out today. Only I didn't hear the door. She'd found the box on the doorstep when she got back. And I mean, I know some of the delivery drivers happily drop-kick parcels from the side door of the van, especially if the item's marked as fragile,' Harriet joked. 'But thinking about it now, I don't recall seeing anything on the packaging. No name or address, or anything like that, when I carried it into the kitchen. It just looked like a plain white box. So, it must have been hand-delivered, right? You don't think that...'

'That what? Someone sent a wreath and a dead rat on purpose?' Carl said, realising that Harriet had just hit the nail on the head. Of course that was what happened. That was exactly why Alessia seemed so shaken up tonight.

'You think someone's starting some kind of hate campaign against either myself or Alessia?' Carl said, shocked at the realisation. He rubbed his head, part of him convinced that that couldn't be a viable possibility. 'That someone is doing all these things on purpose. First the brick, then the car. Now this. Sending us things to our house. Dead things? And wreaths?' But another part of him realised that was the only real explanation. 'Shit! But why and who? Who would be so sick and twisted as to send stuff like that? And to almost run Alessia off the road while she had Jacob in the car with her. They could have been seriously hurt. I can't think of a single person that either of us could have pissed off that would bring themselves to do something as messed up as that.' Carl pursed his mouth, his brow furrowing. None of this added up.

'People can be strange, Carl. And let me tell you from experience, even that's a huge understatement,' Harriet said. 'If it is personal – and I do mean "if" because we have nothing concrete to go on right now – personal doesn't always mean there's a motive. It could be someone acting out on impulse, out of spite or jealousy. It could be part of a malicious game, maybe from someone you know. Or a weird fixation from someone you don't. All of this could be down to a complete stranger.'

'But you think that it's all intentional, all of these things that have been happening lately,' Carl said. Seeing Alessia's shocked face when he'd walked in the kitchen. How she'd been trying to shield him from what she'd discovered. How she'd stood at the window anxiously all night and kept checking on Jacob every five minutes. She thought it too. And then it dawned on him. The thing that deep down was bothering him the most.

'Only if someone is doing this on purpose. If they are doing this to us. Why is Alessia keeping it to herself? What isn't she telling me, Harriet? And who is she trying to protect?'

'I was just asking myself exactly the same thing!'

20

THEN

'Blooming hell, Sar!' Jumping as the sudden movement catches the corner of her eye and she sees the dark figure that lingers in the kitchen doorway, Emma-Jayne drops the butter knife down on the plate, next to her half-made crisp sandwich. 'You scared the life out of me!' Her expression of fright quickly turns to a frown as she recognises her friend standing there.

She should be used to Sarah sneaking up on her because she does it all the time. Sneaking into the house as soon as her parents are gone and Emma-Jayne is home alone. Which makes her wonder now, just how much time Sarah must spend watching her house. Only she isn't alone this time. She's looking after Bobby.

'You can't be here. If they come back, they won't be happy,' she warns her friend. Which is the truth, though only half of it.

Emma-Jayne's parents don't like Sarah. So much so, that her mother has forbidden her from saying her name. She'd said that they didn't like the influence Sarah had over her. Or the way that she behaved when she was around her. Or the way that Sarah had changed her. They acted like Sarah was a troublemaker. The instigator. She was the reason that Emma-Jayne was so distracted and difficult. Nothing Emma-Jayne could say to defend Sarah would change her mind. Her mother wouldn't listen. And Emma-Jayne couldn't bring herself to tell Sarah the extent of her mother's dislike. So, she played it down, trying to spare her friend's feelings. Keeping Sarah a secret as much as she could. But if Bobby saw her, Bobby would tell.

'I can't go out. I've got to look after Bobby,' Emma-Jayne says, nodding towards the lounge where her younger brother sits, transfixed, as he stares at the TV screen. Part of her is glad that she is supposed to be looking after her young brother. Because she knows why Sarah is here. She wants to go back to the cottage again, and Emma-Jayne doesn't want to go there any more. She doesn't like it there. Last time had been too much, and she'd been unable to shake the terror that she'd felt creep through her veins ever since. The horror of that place. The sinister things she felt once went on between those old, decaying walls. And even if it meant falling out with Sarah, then Emma-Jayne was prepared to do it.

Because sometimes she wondered if it was worth it, all these lies and secrets and the sneaking around. Sarah wasn't always very nice to her. She would shout and swear and call Emma-Jayne names. Telling her that she had to do things. Things that she didn't really want to do. Things she couldn't do. In school they had a talk once about bullying. The teachers had said that bullies would intimidate you into doing things that you didn't feel comfortable doing. Was that what Sarah was? A bully? She wasn't sure. Anyway, Emma-Jayne always forgave Sarah everything because deep down she knew that it wasn't Sarah's fault that she was like that. That she acted that way. She was damaged. And what was the saying she'd heard on the TV just a few days ago? Hurt people, hurt people. Especially the ones closest to them. And Sarah was hurt.

So more often than not Emma-Jayne just gave in. She didn't bother to fight back or stand up for herself, because the truth was, she just didn't have it in her. Not when it came to Sarah – she felt too sorry for her. And sometimes she wondered if that was what made their friendship work. How they were both polar opposites of one another. Like chalk and cheese. Sarah with her hard jagged edges, and Emma-Jayne soft and submissive.

Today, though, she is going to stand her ground. She isn't going to let Sarah persuade her otherwise.

'Sorry!' She shrugs, her tone clearly anything but as she stares at Sarah defiantly. Ready for her friend to beg and plead with her and then when that didn't work, the manipulation. The name calling. Until she got her own way.

Except, Sarah doesn't do any of those things. Instead she looks sad, and diverts her eyes down at the floor, tracing a line on the tiles with the pointed toe of her trainer. Her head down, avoiding eye contact with her friend. And it is only then that Emma-Jayne sees the tears falling from her face.

'Are you crying?' Emma-Jayne says, not meaning to sound so shocked as she speaks, but she's never seen Sarah cry. Not once. In fact, Sarah rarely shows any kind of emotion at all. Except for anger. She is always angry at something or someone. Always lashing out.

'What's the matter?' Emma-Jayne falters, her frosty exterior slipping away as she realises whatever upset her friend must be bad if it's made her cry.

'Something really bad has happened,' Sarah says finally. Her voice barely a whisper as she tilts her head and looks Emma-Jayne dead in the eye. 'Really bad.'

And Emma-Jayne sees it then, the extent of the bruising that spans across her friend's face. The bright purple and blue bulge of her eye where she's been hit by something. Or someone.

'Who did that to you?' Emma-Jayne asks, recoiling at the sight of the horrific injuries. But she already knows who. She's seen the bruising on her friend's body before. Finger marks embedded in her skin that she tried so hard to conceal. And she'd seen the way that Sarah walked sometimes. Slow and awkward, with trepidation, as she winced in pain at the injuries he'd inflicted upon her.

'You need to come.'

And Emma-Jayne nods without question. The decision is no longer hers to make.

21

NOW

Turning the bedroom lamp on, Alessia slipped out of her clothes and into her dressing gown. Sitting on the edge of the bed, she eyed the bedroom door as she listened intently while Carl moved around downstairs. A glass clanking, a door clinking shut. And she imagined him pouring himself a second glass of wine and lying back on the sofa with his feet up, watching something trashy on the TV that she would never have approved of.

She was glad to be in the spare room tonight. Because she needed to be alone with her thoughts. She needed to make sense of all the things that were floating inside of her mind. Her head felt as if it was spinning, her thoughts sporadic and out of control, and she'd felt that way since she'd come home today and found that package waiting for her.

The image of the dead rat was still engrained in her mind, and she knew that she wouldn't sleep tonight, and even if she did, her head would be plagued with bad dreams. She clasped her hands tightly together, closed her eyes and silently prayed that she wouldn't slip back into that dark place again. Because she could feel herself slowly slipping back there. She'd tried so hard to put her past behind her and start a new life. A better life. But she could feel the pull of *her*. Dragging her slowly back there. To her past. To her childhood.

Sarah was back. She could feel it.

And she was angry. Angry still? Even after all these years? Of course she would be. Because they'd betrayed each other, hadn't they? They'd been forced to turn against each other. And in the end, they had both been punished, she guessed. Though she had never seen or heard from Sarah since. Alessia had done that deliberately. She'd purposely cut her out. And now this was her punishment.

Though the truth was that she'd thought of Sarah often over the years. More often than she'd ever care to admit to a single living soul. Her complicated best friend. That ripe, blistering anger that she stowed away deep down inside herself. The way she forced you to take notice of her.

Was that what she was doing now?

Forcing Alessia to take notice of her.

Alessia had wondered often over the years if Sarah's life had mirrored hers. If she too had been sent to a foster family. If she too had felt her legs tremble beneath her at the thought of taking the stand at the trial. If she too had retreated inside herself, too scared to interact with anyone for months when she was sent to the secure mental health unit.

Had her life been ruined just like hers? The early years at least. Because Alessia had worked hard to build her life back up again since then. She'd done everything in her power to put herself back together. To overcome the dark secrets of the past.

She had started again. From scratch. Giving herself a new name. A new identity. She'd put herself through further education at a local collage. Administration and secretarial procedures, while working part-time doing a mundane job as a receptionist at a doctor's surgery. Enough to keep her busy and out of trouble. And the meagre wage she'd earned had been just enough for her to get by. She'd paid her bills and managed to keep the kitchen cupboards of her tiny bedsit full of food.

And for a while it had been enough. That simple, honest life. Living in such a routine and structured way that she'd become used to it. The normality of it all had been everything that she'd craved and it had made her feel safe. Going home each night, with only her cat, Kirby, for company. It had been enough, more than enough, until one day it wasn't. That was the day that Carl had walked into the surgery. The day she realised everything that she'd been missing in her life.

Carl had taken an instant liking to her, even though she'd been so acutely shy at first. Unable to hold his eye contact or come back with anything interesting to say when he spoke to her. She had probably seemed cold and distant. Aloof. Which wasn't how she'd wanted to seem. It had just been her way back then. That was how she had been for years – keeping herself to herself, her head down and simply doing her job.

But Carl had seen something in her that no one else had, and he'd persisted. The more awkward and disinterested she seemed the more Carl must have seen her as a challenge. And later, when she'd finally put him out of his misery and accepted his invitation to dinner, he'd told her as much. Confiding to her the lengths he'd gone to win her over.

How he'd exaggerated symptoms so that he could make appointments at the surgery just to see her. For little things really, like a suspected allergy he'd learned long ago just to live with or that mild, niggling neck pain that sometimes irked him but he'd never done anything about. Any excuse he could find just so that he could come into the surgery and see her.

And she'd confided in him that she had thought he was a hypochondriac. He'd laughed at that. Really laughed until tears had run down his cheek. And Alessia hadn't let on how flattered she was. That he'd made so much effort to get close to her. To get her to notice him. And it had been her turn to laugh louder still when he'd asked her if she thought he was a weirdo. For knowing the second that he set eyes on her that she was the one. Because Alessia had never really had that in her life. That kind of a connection. Within weeks they had become inseparable, and Alessia finally allowed herself to believe that maybe, now, she could have more. Maybe she deserved more.

And then they had both been blessed with Jacob. Becoming a mother had changed Alessia, entirely. Her darling boy had given her a purpose, a real purpose. Filling her with a kind of indescribable love that she'd never known before or probably would ever again. And because of Jacob, and Carl, Alessia strived to be her best and do her very best in everything. To give her son the very best start in life.

What if Sarah didn't have any of that? What if that was why she seemed so determined to destroy it all for her?

What if this was Sarah's way of reminding Alessia that she couldn't just block her out and leave her back there, in her past? That she couldn't just move on with her life and pretend that she didn't exist. And it terrified Alessia because she had so much to lose now, if everything got dragged up again. All her secrets.

She eyed the wardrobe in the corner of the bedroom and took a deep breath, feeling its unwavering pull. It had been calling to her all day. For a few days actually. Ever since the brick had been thrown through the window.

Alessia crossed the room to the wardrobe, and pulled the doors open before she bent down and searched through the mountain of small boxes that she'd stored away inside, tucked away at the very back. Old things. From her old life. Before she had met Carl.

She picked up the first box. She peered inside the lid, smiling as she saw the photo frame on top. A picture of Kirby as a kitten. She'd found him lurking one day in the back garden of the bedsit she was renting. And he'd been the one to claim her, really. He'd wrapped his scrawny little body around her ankle and purred up at her. At first she'd tried to shoo him away but hadn't been able to resist that lost look in his big blue eyes. The same lost look that was mirrored in her own. And as she put a saucer of milk out for him, and a small dish of tuna, she had promised herself that she wouldn't make a habit of it. That it would just be this once. But the kitten kept coming back, and it had of course become a daily ritual. Alessia would set down the dishes and the cat would purr around her feet gratefully. And before she knew it, Kirby was at her window for her every day. Sitting there, waiting patiently for her to come home, his face against the glass. Until eventually he just never left. And Alessia hadn't wanted him to.

Because Kirby was the closest thing she'd had to love since she was twelve years old. He was a friend of sorts. Her only one in the world. And that cat had meant more to her than anything or anyone. She still found it painful, even now, to see photos of him, remembering how one day she'd woken up to find his saucer of milk untouched, and no sign of him outside the flat. How she'd waited anxiously for days, pacifying herself with the notion that he'd just moved on to someone else. That he'd found someone more needy of his love than her. But she knew deep in her heart that he wasn't coming back. That something bad had happened to him. Because he would never have just stayed away.

Placing the lid back down, Alessia picked up the next box. An old handbag and some clothes that she had no intention of ever wearing again, yet somehow, she couldn't bring herself to throw them away. About to put the lid back on, something shiny caught her eye. She fingered the shimmering gold necklace. The pendant shaped like a key and embellished with the number 18. Amanda, her social worker, had given it to her to mark her eighteenth birthday. And to mark the start of her new life. Before she'd left the secure unit. Away from there finally. To start a life of her own in a pokey little bedsit. Free at last.

She stared at the final box, knowing full well what was inside. Because this was what she had been thinking about all day. She'd made a point of hiding this box away properly, tucked at the back of the wardrobe, at the bottom of the pile, In the hope it would never be found by anyone other than her. Lifting the lid, she eyed the small bundle inside, still wrapped in a thick navy scarf adorned with purple butterflies. Taking it out, she laid it down carefully on

the bed, and unwrapped the scarf slowly as if the contents inside
were delicate and might break.

The doll. She stared down at the ragged, worn dress. She
hadn't been allowed to keep in touch with Sarah, but she had kept
the doll. She'd clung on to it, for all this time, as if her life
depended on it. Though part of her could never explain her attachment to it. Why it felt so important. Why she couldn't bear to part
with it. Reaching out, she touched it with trembling hands.
Running her fingers down the frayed fabric of the doll's dress.
Twisting the dry, matted hair between her fingertips.

And she realised she was crying. Huge tears were rolling down
her cheeks, a strangled sob threatened to escape her mouth. She
picked the doll up and wrapped her arms around it as she hugged it
tightly to her, before she rocked back and forth. She recalled the
day they'd found it tucked away in the chimney of the cottage.
How she'd told Sarah to put it back. How she'd begged her.
Pleaded with her. And she was glad that Sarah hadn't listened to
her in the end. That she hadn't put it back. Because even though
everything had changed after they had found it – everything had
turned bad after that – the doll was all Alessia had left of her.

22

THEN

'He's dead,' Sarah says simply, having dragged Emma-Jayne to the doll's house. The two girls stand silently in the middle of the room. Taking in the vision of the twisted, buckled corpse that lies in a tangled heap, sprawled out at their feet.

'He's dead? He's really dead!' Emma-Jayne's voice comes out strained. She clamps her hand over her mouth. Her eyes are wide with horror as she repeats her friend's words like a mantra, trying to make sense of the scene before them.

And he is dead, she thinks as she stares down at him. Noting the way his head lolls to one side. How his glassy eyes are wide with an expression that could only be surprise. His skull is caved in on one side of his head, a missing chunk of flesh. She looks down at the dark red blood-soaked ground for the missing piece of the puzzle. What had he landed on that had killed him? She looks for a rock, or a ledge, wondering if his skull had broken his fall as he'd landed.

'Still clutching his can for dear life, though,' Sarah says, twisting her mouth in disgust. Her tone laced with sarcasm as they both look at his hand, wrapped tightly around the can of cider that had spilled out its contents on the floor beside him. Cider mixed with the pool of blood. His limbs are splayed out on the step next to him, leaving him crooked and awkward. 'Always did love a drink!'

'Have you called for an ambulance?' Emma-Jayne asks, feeling her chest tighten at the onslaught of hyperventilating. This can't be real, can it? This can't be really happening? Why is he even here, at the doll's house?

She's never seen a dead body before. She'd always imagined it would look like you were just sleeping, not like this brutal and horrific sight. A blood-soaked, empty shell of a man at their feet.

'They won't believe me that it was an accident. They won't believe us. And it's not like they can bring him back to life again, is it?' Sarah says with a nonchalant shrug, squatting down and reaching out her hand, before prodding his forehead with her finger. 'Ew, his skin feels so weird. Hard and cold like ice. Wanna feel?' she says with a shudder, though her eyes stay fixed on him, filled with fascination as she takes in the sight. And something else burns brightly there, behind her pupils. Triumph.

'No!' Emma-Jayne looks down at her friend with horror, fighting back her tears at the madness of the situation. How surreal it feels. And all the while Sarah is acting weirdly. Like any minute now she's going to burst out laughing. And Emma-Jayne wonders if perhaps she's in shock. Maybe they both are.

Is that why she's in no hurry to call for help? Maybe this is what happens to people when they can't cope with a trauma. They behave strangely like this. But there's something about the way that Sarah is acting so genuinely disconnected from the fact that there's a dead man sprawled out at their feet, his head caved in. And there's something about the blood that's pooling out around him, the fact that there is so much of it, that makes Emma-Jayne feel uneasy. And she knows. Deep down in her gut, she knows. This wasn't just an accident. He didn't just fall down and bang his head. He's been murdered.

23

NOW

Alessia couldn't sleep. She'd been lying in bed, wide awake, for hours. Staring up at the ceiling, restlessly tossing and turning beneath the covers while her mind spun into overdrive, as she dragged up the past and everything that happened back then.

Unable to lay there in the darkness, alone, for another minute thinking about it all, she got up. Because going over it again and again in her head wouldn't help her. It would only make her feel more confused. And she already felt as if she was teetering there, on the edge. She thought of Jacob before she tiptoed quietly across the landing and snuck into the nursery as quietly as possible so as not to wake him. And instantly she felt that pull of love. That grounding that she so badly craved at the sight of him, lying there, sleeping so soundly. His tiny little body splayed out in his cot-bed. His eyes closed; his head full of only beautiful dreams.

This is clarity, she thought to herself as she stared down at her beautiful baby boy. This is her reminder, right here, of how far she'd come. Of how hard she'd fought for this life. And it was the reminder she needed that she could never go back there, to that girl she once was. A reminder that this was why she had had no choice but to leave Sarah behind. And they'd all been right in the end, hadn't they? The people around her who had told her that letting go of Sarah would help her. In some ways it had saved her. Blocking her out, leaving her back there, in the past. And this life had been her prize.

Only the guilt had been eating her up inside lately. Taunting her, because it was always there, lingering in the dark recesses of her mind. And lately it had been worse, almost too much to bear. And she had tried to convince herself that these days she was better. That her life was better. If only she kept believing. If only she forced herself not to think about it too much.

But she felt herself slipping. Back there again, to that space in her head that they'd told not to trust. To that girl she used to be. And it was a terrifying feeling. Like free-falling from a great height and knowing that any minute now her whole world was all going to come crashing down around her.

She thought about all the times she had tried to hurt herself. Just to feel the release. To feel something that was real. And then there were the times that she'd attempted to take her own life. Though she hadn't really wanted to kill herself, had she? They had been cries for help. Cries loud enough to make them all listen to her. But still they hadn't. And in the end, she'd had to help herself the only way that she could.

She wiped the tears that streamed down her cheeks as she stared at Jacob. Knowing how much she needed this reminder. How much she needed to stay focused. Sarah might have found her again but that didn't mean that Alessia had to let her back in. If she tried hard enough, she could still keep her out.

Taking a seat in the corner of the room, she wrapped herself in the blanket that was draped over the back. Her hand traced the little silver train-shaped money box on the side, before running across Jacob's first teddy bear that sat so prominently on his dresser.

Having spotted his nursery book bag on the floor beside her, where Carl must have left it earlier, she picked it up. Wide awake now, she thought she might as well check over his reading log book and see how he was doing. The teacher's comments always brought her so much comfort. And pride.

Jacob is a happy, confident little boy. Jacob enjoys Storytime and often tries to join in. She smiled as she thumbed the pages, then faltered as a loose page fell out and landed on the floor.

She bent down and picked it up, just managing to stifle the scream that threatened, as she registered the headline that ran across the top of the paper. A wild panic spread through her as she stared in horror at what had been planted inside Jacob's book bag.

Her hands trembled as she held the paper, the image of the goofy looking twelve-year-old staring back at her. Her hair tied in two neat plaits; her nose speckled with freckles. The photo of her.

Hammer Horror

The headline screams out of the page.

And suddenly she drops it. As if the paper she is holding is toxic and she has no choice. It's as if the ink could burn through her skin. The words could burn through her eyes.

She watched as it floated down to the floor.

Terrified that this was the extent that Sarah was willing to go to get to her. Because this was all just a game to her, wasn't it? Showing her how close she could get to her. And closer still. How she could make everything come crashing down again, around her. How she could rip her whole world from under her. She was trying to scare her. And it was working.

24

NOW

The sound of glass smashing from somewhere off in the distance woke her. Disorientated, she opened her eyes and wrenched herself from her dream. She must have been out cold. Exhausted from the heavy week at work and the bottle of wine she drank before falling into bed. She stared at the clock. It was only 3 a.m.

Had something woken her? The flat sat in silence now and she wondered if she had imagined the noise, if perhaps she'd dreamt it. She turned over to go back to sleep, but then she heard it again. Louder this time.

It was coming from the kitchen. And before she had time to think straight, she registered the sound of footsteps, treading lightly at first before getting louder as they reach the hallway outside the room.

Her heart hammered inside her chest as the door handle slowly moved and the bedroom door creaked open.

She heard the sound of someone shuffling quietly as they made their way around the bed. Rigid with fear now, she felt the presence of someone standing beside her. Their slow, laboured breathing as they stood there, under the blanket of darkness next to the bed. Another sound then as they moved away towards the end of the bed. She heard the creak of her dressing table chair.

Were they sitting there? Watching her, waiting? And for a few seconds the only sound she heard was the banging of her heart as it pounded dramatically inside her chest.

Too terrified to move, she lay there, weakly, putting on an act that she was still asleep. That she had no idea she was no longer alone as she tried to work out what to do.

Her phone.

She forced herself to turn over and let out an exaggerated yawn as she fumbled for it and checked for the time. And with one swift movement she grabbed it and slid it back under the duvet with her.

Knowing that the bold move would need a distraction in order for her to carry it off, she immediately hit the touch lamp that sat next to her bed. She sat up, just as the room flooded with light. Despite being terrified of who she might see there, she had no choice now but to face her intruder head on.

The entire time, her fingers fumbled underneath the covers for the numbers 999. Only she faltered the second she saw her intruder sitting there. Watching her. Waiting. The last person she'd expected to see.

'Emma-Jayne?'

NOW

'I wasn't sure if you'd remember me, Amanda!' Alessia said, her voice tinged with relief that Amanda hadn't forgotten her after all this time. That she still remembered who she was. That Alessia hadn't been completely irrelevant after all.

'Though it's not Emma-Jayne any more. I haven't been Emma-Jayne for a long time. I'm Alessia now.' She shrugged. Not bothering to add why she'd decided to change it. They both knew why. 'I heard it somewhere, on TV, I think. I can't remember now. But it stuck, and I like it.'

'It's lovely.' Amanda nodded, her mouth dry, the panic inside her only growing more heightened as she tried to work out why Alessia was here. How after years of Alessia having seemingly disappeared into thin air, Amanda had seen her twice in one week. And she wondered now if Alessia was capable of harming her.

'And, of course, I remember you,' Amanda said as she gave Alessia a nod and a warm smile, making a point to keep her expression friendly looking instead of startled. Trying to appear calm. When she was anything but. Alessia's face looked puffy, as if she'd been crying, and she was dressed in her pyjamas with a coat thrown over the top as if she'd just rolled out of bed. 'I've thought about you so much over the years. Hoping that you're okay. Are you... okay?'

Amanda played the game that she'd become an expert at over the years. Reading people's body language and observing. And in Alessia she sensed the anguish that festered there. The rawness of the obvious pain behind her eyes. After all this time, it hadn't left her. And she tried to work out the best way to connect with Alessia and defuse the situation. To stop things from escalating. From anyone getting hurt.

Act normal, she told herself. Act like waking up in the middle of the night to find a child who had once been under your care years ago, had broken into your home and sat at the end of the bed while you slept, was completely normal. A child that you had failed.

'I'm better now.' Alessia paused.

And Amanda tried to hide her sceptical look as Alessia looked down at herself. As if she was suddenly seeing herself for the first time. Seeing herself the way that Amanda was too. The way she noted the pyjamas she still wore underneath her coat. The way she recognised how this must seem, the fact that she'd broken in to Amanda's flat, in the middle of the night.

'I was better!' she corrected herself as she pressed her teeth into her lip and bit down, staring around the room as she took in her surroundings now that the light was on. Her eyes moved fleetingly to the sound of a cat meowing out in the kitchen, disturbed by the unexpected visitor.

'I like cats. I used to have one,' Alessia said politely.

And Amanda could see the sadness in her eyes at the admission. How the loss of her own beloved cat seemed to overwhelm her.

How she was trying so hard to appear normal. As if this was a completely rational conversation to be having. Comparing pets.

Alessia continued to eye the bedroom's shabby wallpaper, the mismatched bedding, and Amanda could see her world, her life through Alessia's eyes, and caught the vague judgement there.

Disappointment. That this was all that had become of Amanda. The woman she'd once pinned all her hopes on. Lived here, in this dingy flat. Alone. Her kitchen full of empty wine bottles and nothing more than a pet cat to keep her company.

'It's not much, but it's home,' Amanda said defensively. Knowing that she was the typical cliched social worker. She'd dedicated her life to helping others sort their messy, neglected lives, only to let her own fall down around her.

'I have a son now. Jacob,' Alessia continued, clearly not fussed.

And Amanda could tell how much Alessia wanted to share that news with her. How much she wanted her to know how different her life was now. That she meant it. That she really was better now. Despite how she might appear.

'He's almost three. You should see him. He's so smart and so funny. He knows his numbers up to ten. Can you believe that?' Alessia shook her head in wonderment. 'It's not just me that thinks it. Everyone says how advanced he is!'

And Amanda nods. Aware how hard she was trying to not sound like every other mother out there who believed their own child to be extraordinary.

'I'm happy for you, Alessia. You deserve to be happy.' Amanda smiled warmly at Alessia, seeing the look of complete adoration in her face when she spoke about her child.

And she meant it. Emma-Jayne's – Alessia's – case haunted her, her entire career. When the story made it to the national newspapers, the press had turned the tragedy she'd lived through into a witch hunt against her, publishing stories about her by other family members and discrediting her name. There had been no sympathy for what she'd been through. She'd been made out to be manipulative and evil. All those people in the system, her colleagues, who should have helped her, who should have offered her support, had instead placed Emma-Jayne underneath a microscope and let the world judge her for the crime she'd committed. They had failed her. Amanda had failed her.

Amanda had lost faith in the entire system after that. She'd lost faith in her vocation too. These days, it was just a job to her. A means to an end as a way to barely pay her bills.

Though she didn't say any of that to Alessia. Because whatever she had suffered since, she knew that Alessia suffered far more. That she lost everything and everyone around her. Including herself for a while.

'I looked for you,' Amanda said. 'They said that you'd moved into a bedsit. That you were in Ealing. Only I couldn't find you, and they said that they lost touch.'

It made sense now, how Amanda had never been able to find her. Because Amanda had been searching for Emma-Jayne. And Emma-Jayne no longer existed.

'That was the point. I wanted to start again. I wouldn't have been able to do it otherwise.'

Amanda nodded understandingly. And it was only then that she saw the doll on Alessia's lap. The sight of it made her flinch, as if she'd been hit by a surge of electricity.

She remembered the day she'd walked into the police station and first set eyes on Alessia. Sitting in the cold, clinical police cell, wrapped in a blanket, clutching the doll tightly to her as if her life depended on it. And Amanda had tried to hide her disgust at the young girl's seemingly treasured possession. The tatty worn fabric of the dress, that matted, brown synthetic hair. Alessia followed Amanda's gaze.

'It's been in a box at the back of my wardrobe this whole time,' she said, staring at the doll, too, as if she was only seeing it for the first time, as if she'd only just realised she had picked it up and brought it with her. 'It's stupid, isn't it? Keeping stuff like this. Little reminders of the past, but I couldn't bring myself to part with it.' She shrugged before she laughed at the irony. The sound was so small and strangled, and she quickly composed herself.

And Amanda understood. The past that she wanted to escape in some ways, but in others, she still clung on to so tightly.

'It's all I had. I guess I'm sentimental like that.'

And Amanda nodded again. Remembering how Emma-Jayne

had clung to the doll that first day at her foster home too. Like a comfort blanket, she hadn't let it out of her sight, not for a single second.

'You followed me yesterday, didn't you?' Amanda said as the silence lingered between them. 'You were outside my office. And then as I cut through St Mary's Garden, I stood at my flat just opposite the park's entrance, and I thought I caught a glimpse of you, but I wasn't sure.' Amanda spoke as clearly as she could, forcing a calmness to her voice that she didn't really feel, as adrenaline surged around her body. And she fought the tremor in her limbs, wondering if she was right to feel this scared. She wasn't sure. She kept clutching her mobile phone in her hand under the covers.

'I didn't think you recognised me. When I bumped into you,' Alessia said, cautiously.

'I wasn't sure at first,' Amanda admitted. 'It was so long ago, and, well, look at you now. You've grown into such a beautiful young woman. But it was your eyes that gave you away. That look...' Amanda smiled but it was only to try and conceal the sadness she felt at the recognition of emptiness she'd seen there behind Alessia's grey eyes. How she'd been able to see past them, recognising the angst and the pain.

'I thought that you were following me afterwards, but I convinced myself that I was just being paranoid.' Amanda laughed at the realisation that Alessia clearly had.

'And then, I couldn't get you out of my head. Because I think about you often, Alessia,' Amanda said again, another genuine admission. 'And I searched for you. Many times over the years. I was worried about you. But I don't blame you for wanting to start again. We all deserve a second chance. You of all people deserve a second chance.'

'A second chance?' Alessia couldn't help but laugh at that. 'I didn't even get a first chance. Tell the truth you said. And I did tell the truth. But they didn't believe me anyway.'

'We needed more time. I couldn't get you to open up to me.

And that was understandable, you'd been through so much. But I only had what you gave me, Emma-Jayne. Alessia, sorry! I could only tell them the very little that you told me, and it wasn't enough.'

They were both silent. Thinking about how deeply trauma-tised and terrified Alessia had been back then. How things could have been so different if they'd had more time. If Alessia had trusted her.

'Why are you here?' Amanda said, treading cautiously still but feeling braver now that Alessia seemed willing to listen. 'It's three o'clock in the morning. You have broken into my home.' She needed Alessia to realise that this wasn't okay. This wasn't how they were going to solve her problems.

'Will you help me?'

'Of course I will. What can I do?' Amanda said, blindsided by the neediness in Alessia's voice. The last thing she ever expected was Alessia to ask for her help. From her. After everything.

'I need to find Sarah. I need to make her stop. She's taunting me. Doing all these things to me. And she won't stop.'

Amanda nodded to show Alessia that she understood. She needed to tread carefully, not wanting to place any judgement in her tone.

'You stayed in touch with Sarah? All this time?'

Alessia shook her head.

'No. I haven't seen her. Not since the... the day that the police came.'

The day of the murder, Amanda thought. Still Alessia wouldn't say it. Still, after all this time, she was blocking it out.

She thought back again to that first day they'd met at the police station. How Alessia had searched Sarah out amongst the sea of curious faces that she'd passed in the corridor as she'd led her out of the station. How despite seeming so scared and intimidated by her surroundings, she'd forced herself to meet the eye of everyone she passed in search of her friend.

And how her gaze had rested on the eyes of her mother.

Amanda had seen the iciness of her glare as she'd stared back at Alessia. How the woman's expression had been stone cold and empty, as if Alessia no longer existed to her. And it had broken Amanda's heart to see the girl so wounded by her mother's dismissal. She'd felt Alessia physically wither beside her, shrinking into herself. Amanda had wrapped her arm around the young girl as she'd led her out to the car before taking her to her first foster placement.

'She found me,' Alessia continued, searching Amanda's face for a reaction as she spoke. 'She threw a brick through my window. And at first I wanted to believe that it was kids, you know, messing around and playing a joke. That they'd run off afterwards so that they wouldn't get in trouble. But I knew as soon as I saw it, all that broken glass. The note. It was that day. That same day. The anniversary.' She was almost whispering. She added, 'I'd been back there. To the house I'd grown up in. For the first time since the police took me away. Only, it looked so different. The house. The street. The people. None of it was how I remembered.'

Alessia shook her head and stood, forgetting about the doll that had been sitting on her lap as it dropped to the floor. She began to pace the room, her words pouring out of her, as she told Amanda everything that had happened, clearly relieved at finally being able to open up and talk about it all. To someone who knew. To someone who was there back then.

And Amanda could see the confusion there. How Alessia still seemed as if she was trying to make sense of it all herself. How she was raising her voice, trying to ensure that Amanda understood the gravity of the situation.

But it was almost as if she was trying to understand what all of this even meant too.

'She sent me things. A wreath. And a dead rat. A dead fucking rat!' Moving her hand up to her mouth. Her body full of nervous energy, she shivered at the thought of the dead rodent. The menace behind it. 'She rammed our car off the road, and she didn't give a shit that Jacob had been in the car with me. That she could have really hurt us.'

'You saw her?' Amanda asked, trying to hide the disbelief in her eyes. Because she knew that would only anger Alessia. She'd come here for help not judgement. She'd had enough of that to last her a lifetime.

'No, she drove off. But I know it was her. It had to be her. And tonight, I couldn't sleep and when I went to check on Jacob, he was sleeping so peacefully. I sat there in his room, going through his things, reminiscing, and when I looked inside his nursery book bag, I found this.'

Alessia held up the crumpled newspaper cutting, straightening it out, so that Amanda could read it more clearly.

Hammer Horror

She flinched at the very thought of Carl being the one who found it, instead of her.

'So, you think Sarah has been in your house?'

'No. I don't know. I think maybe she got close to Jacob at the nursery. That she planted the article in his book bag for me to find. Don't you see? She is trying to scare me. She's trying to show me how close she can get to me!' Alessia shivered. 'How close she can get to Jacob. It's a threat.'

That was why Alessia had come here tonight. Because she'd had no other choice. She needed someone who had been there with her, someone who understood. Only, despite seeing the article for herself, Amanda was still bewildered.

'But why would she do all this, Alessia? And why now?' Amanda said, trying to reason with Alessia. To stay rational as she tried to talk Alessia back down from her panicked state, because she wasn't making any sense.

'Because she's enjoying this, playing games with me, messing with my head!'

Amanda nodded understandingly, but she could see how

fragile Alessia was. How much she truly believed what she was saying. How volatile she still seemed. And she wasn't sure if it was too late, if she would even be able to reach her now. If she'd even be able to help.

'But why?' Amanda asked, still not convinced.

'You know why! She's angry. Because I told the police that it was her. That she did it. She felt betrayed. Betrayed by me. And then I cut her out. And now she wants me to pay. She wants to ruin my life. Ruin everything. Because that's what will happen if Carl finds out what I've kept from him. He won't want me then. And what about Jacob? What kind of life will he have, having a mother like me?'

Alessia cried. Openly sobbed.

'She won't stop until someone gets hurt. Somebody close to me. I need to see her. To speak to her. To make her understand. Will you help me?'

'I'm so sorry but I can't, Alessia...' Amanda started as she shook her head. Her tone was full of sympathy because she knew how this conversation was going to end. The impact that it would have on Alessia. And Alessia could sense her stalling. She could sense the trepidation in saying anything more.

'Please, Amanda. Please! You owe me that, at least. You know where she is, don't you? Please, you have to tell me.'

'No,' Amanda said, trying to sound more final. Letting Alessia know that this wasn't something that she could persuade out of her.

'But surely you can make enquiries? You can find out? There would be information about her somewhere. The foster family she'd been placed with would be on file. Or maybe she's still in touch with them too, and they'd know where she is now?'

Amanda opened her mouth to say something else, only her words were drowned out by the noise of sirens blaring loudly. Both women stared towards the window, hearing the cars screeching to a halt outside the flat. The flash of blue lights that pulsated across the ceiling and walls.

'You called the police?' Alessia said, incredulously, up on her feet, already making her way towards the back door as panic set in.

'But you said. You said you'd help me?'

'Alessia. You broke in to my flat. You seem... irrational,' Amanda said, still treading gently, her mobile phone still gripped in her hand underneath the covers. Immediately she doubted her actions as she witnessed the terror spread across Alessia's face at the thought of being arrested. At the thought of the police taking her away again. Fearful that all her deepest secrets would come out. Part of her wished then that she hadn't been so weak. That she hadn't acted so hasty in making the call. But she'd been scared too. And unsure of Alessia's motives for breaking in here, she'd had to put her own safety first. And it was too late to take it back now.

'I was scared. Alessia, you must understand that. I haven't seen you for years, and then you just turn up like this. Breaking in to my flat. In the middle of the night. I thought you might...' Amanda tried to explain.

'You thought I might what?' Alessia said, her eyes wide with indignation at the unspoken accusation as the penny dropped. 'You thought that I might hurt you? That I might kill you?' Alessia laughed but her words were full of sadness, and the humour didn't meet her eyes.

'Alessia, you're not well. You're sick...' Amanda tried to explain gently, seeing the genuine hurt in Alessia's eyes. The way that she looked as if she'd had her heart broken all over again.

'No!' Alessia said, shaking her head. 'You're not doing that. You are not doing that to me again. No! You promised me that you'd help me once, and I thought you meant it. I thought that I could trust you.'

'You can, Alessia...'

'No!'

The door banged. Alessia heard shouting.

'*Police. Open up.*'

She ran. Towards the back of the flat and out through the back door. And with that Alessia was gone.

THEN

'Did you do it?' Emma-Jayne asks, gulping down the hot bile that threatens at the back of her throat. A pool of anxiety forms deep down in the pit of her stomach as she waits anxiously for the answer, her eyes not leaving the crooked body splayed out in the middle of the room. The doll's house feels cold and empty as their small voices echo around the room.

'What? No! He fell, didn't he?' Sarah's answer is deadpan, followed by another shrug.

Emma-Jayne notes the glistening of her eyes as she speaks, her gaze unwavering from the sight of him. The way that her mouth is twisted into a suppressed smirk.

'Where were you? When "it" happened?' Emma-Jayne asks. Her question is loaded. It's an accusation and they both know it. For a few seconds neither of them speak. The allegation lingers in the air between them until Sarah finally answers.

'I was asleep.' She shrugs sounding bored now. 'I heard the thud! It woke me.'

Thud. Emma-Jayne shivers at the emptiness behind the word that comes from Sarah's lips. So final. A thud. His skull caving in. Blood seeping out from the open gash in his head. She doesn't believe her.

But she doesn't let on, she simply nods her head, unable to tear her eyes away from Sarah, studying her reaction. Or lack of one.

And Sarah looks at her, finally. Acknowledging the doubt she sees in Emma-Jayne's eyes.

'What? You think I did it? You think I killed him?' Sarah says, her voice challenging Emma-Jayne.

'Well, did you?' Emma-Jayne says, her chest pounding. The walls feel as if they are slowly closing in. Was the doll's house always this small? Always so claustrophobic?

'Because you said before... a while back... That you would do it. That you would kill him,' Emma-Jayne says, unable to hide the tremor in her voice as she continues. Because the truth is, she honestly doesn't know what to believe. All she knows is that Sarah is capable of it.

She hated him. Sarah would vent and call him names and say how much she hated him sometimes, but other than that, the conversation always felt forbidden to go beyond that.

But they should have spoken about it, shouldn't they? That was what friends did, wasn't it? They turned to each other when they were in need.

And Sarah had been in need. Because he had done things to her. Bad things.

'You said if he did it again, you'd do it. You'd kill him.'

'Well, I guess I don't have to now. He fell. He's dead,' Sarah says, turning to her friend then and flashing her a fleeting look of warning.

She was stepping too close to the line. They didn't talk about this stuff. They couldn't talk about this stuff. It was too much. And Emma-Jayne knew not to push Sarah on it. Because she'd seen it sometimes. The rage brewing there behind Sarah's eyes. The way that she fought so hard to suppress her anger. But sometimes the anger got the better of her, and Emma-Jayne knows that she is more than capable of murder.

Thud.

'We need to tell someone. We can't just leave him here like

this,' Emma-Jayne says. Knowing that it won't make a difference now. What is done, is done. He is gone, there's nothing that anyone could do now that would save him. That could bring him back.

But calling for help was the right thing to do, wasn't it? They need to tell someone.

'We can't!' Sarah says, shaking her head forcefully as the two girls stand and eye the blood that pools out from his body. Slowly getting bigger before their eyes. 'They won't believe us. They'll think we did it.'

'No, they won't. Not if we tell them the truth. That he fell,' Emma-Jayne says, her eyes sweeping the bruising on Sarah's face. Her eye bulbous and closed up.

They'd see her bruising. They'd know about the other stuff.

'No,' Sarah shouts. Snapping out of her own daze and taking control of the situation. 'We can't tell anyone, because no one will understand. No one will help us. Who will believe us? We're just little girls. He told us, remember, they won't believe us! No one will.'

And Emma-Jayne nods her head dutifully as she recalls how they'd both heard those words before. How he had said it.

No one will believe you.

'We should leave him here, all alone. It's what he deserves, isn't it...? To rot,' Sarah says. Her voice is hard. Final almost, as if she's worked it all out. What they should do with him.

'We can't. We have to tell someone. That he fell. They'll believe us then. If we both say the same thing,' Emma-Jayne says, eventually. After a few minutes of silence. 'He fell and he banged his head.' She speaks clearly, letting each syllable roll carefully from her tongue, as if testing how the words sound as they leave her mouth.

Like she's practising. And she is practising. Because she knows she'll have to say something. When they eventually find him here. Dead. And she wonders if she can get home without being seen by anyone. If she can put her bloodstained clothes in the bin and wash her blood-soaked skin. And isn't it a good thing really? That he is dead. It feels like it's a good thing, only she's scared. Really scared. And instead of feeling relieved, she starts to cry. She cries so hard, so much, that the big, wracking sobs shake her entire body and she fears that she may never stop.

'He can't hurt us any more,' Sarah says. Her voice is softer now, as she stands close to Emma-Jayne and places her hand inside hers. Warm and comforting, their fingers locked together. And Emma-Jayne looks at her dead in the eye as something passes between them both. An unspoken promise to each other that only they would ever understand. Sarah did it for her. She made it stop, for her.

Emma-Jayne squeezes Sarah's hand tightly, knowing in this moment that everything has changed. Nothing will ever be the same.

NOW

'How was my day off? Ooh, where do I start? First I hit the West End for a slap-up meal, then we ended up in a fancy new cocktail bar in Soho. Ended up getting off my face on a goldfish bowl of sangria, and before I knew it, I was singing karaoke and dancing on the bar!'

'So another typical night doing sweet FA then!' Rufus, one of the younger PCs, said. He raised his eyebrows and shot Harriet a knowing grin as they all stood in the locker room at the station, getting changed at the changeover of shifts.

'Damn it, how did you know?!' Harriet laughed. It was a long-standing joke between them all, that half the time they were so overworked here on the job, that by the time they were due a day off they were too exhausted to actually do anything. 'Okay, what did I do really? I looked after my friend's son, Jacob, for a few hours. He's almost three and trust me, his energy levels make this job seem like a walk in the park. And then I went home and sat on my bum, watching absolute trash on TV all evening. And I'm talking obscenely, mind-numbing telly viewing. While feasting on the world's biggest pizza delivery you could ever imagine.'

'Oh, I bet Andrew loved that. Some quality time with Waynetta Slob, sprawled out on the sofa.'

'Andrew was working nights actually! So I had the whole lot for myself. And I even managed to drag the hoover around while I was waiting for it to be delivered, so when he wakes up this morning, he'll think I spent the whole evening being the perfect little housewife! He'll have no idea about the level of slobbery I can descend to.' Harriet chuckled, tapping her nose playfully, knowing full well that Andrew wouldn't care one bit if she slobbed around on her evening off. He always said that she worked hard and had earned her rest. She hadn't dragged the hoover around for brownie points. She'd done it because she'd felt guilty for always being at work and never being home to get anything done.

And the pizza and movie had been her reward.

'So, did I miss out on any drama last night?'

'Not really, actually it sounds like your night was probably more eventful than ours,' Rufus said, throwing his jacket on and rolling his eyes. 'We had a few arrests in the high street after the pubs kicked out. Brought a drunk driver in. He was four times over the limit!' Rufus shook his head in disgust. 'The bloke couldn't even walk straight, how he even managed to get his keys in the ignition, I'll never know. We pulled him just as he left a friend's house. So thankfully he'd only just made it off the driveway. Oh, and there was some weird "domestic" over in a flat by St Mary's Church, in Islington. Potentially a break-in.'

'Potentially? And what's a weird domestic when it's at home?'

'Yeah! Potentially, because when we got there the woman who made the call suddenly acted all cagey and tried to retract the fact that she'd alerted us to her flat being broken into.'

'So it wasn't a break-in, then?'

'Oh it definitely was. The kitchen window had been smashed where they'd tried to gain entry. Only, for whatever reason, the woman no longer wanted to pursue her complaint and kept trying to convince us that she'd made a mistake and that no one had tried to break in. We've got the whole of her 999 call on tape and, trust me, going by the two women's voices on the tape there was definitely a break-in. But I'm going to put my money on it being a lovers' tiff. I don't know what was going on between them, but it sounded messed up.'

'Messed up? How so?' Harriet asked, intrigued. They often came across some strange people and situations in their line of work but she never tired of hearing the stories.

'I don't know, at one point they were talking about someone sending a dead rat or something. None of it really made sense,' Rufus said, shaking his head as he laughed at the craziness of some people.

'A dead rat?' Harriet narrowed her eyes as she thought back to the conversation she'd had with Carl the night before. How he'd told her that he'd found a dead rat in his dustbin. Her first thought was Alessia. But that would be complete madness, wouldn't it? Linking her to last night's incident. It couldn't have had anything to do with her friend, obviously. Still, Harriet couldn't help but feel spooked out by the coincidence.

'Is that a thing now then? Sending dead rats to people? You had any more reports of that happening recently?'

'Not that I know of. Maybe it's just for the Real Housewives of Islington, their version of sending someone a horse's head.' Rufus grinned. 'Anyway, the woman didn't want to press charges, and we didn't bother cautioning her for wasting our time. Figured it wasn't worth the whole tree worth of paperwork that went with it.'

'But we got it all on tape?'

'Yeah, why? You want to have a listen?'

'Oh only if I get bored on shift today. You know, if I end up twiddling my thumbs with nothing else to do!' Harriet said, rolling her eyes and playing down the fact that that was exactly what she wanted to do.

'Yeah well, good luck with that,' Rufus said, grabbing his bag and flinging it over his shoulder. The station was always manic. There was always something happening, something to do, and some days they rarely had time to go to the toilet, let alone follow up every single situation they came across that appeared to be more than it seemed. 'Catch you later. Hey, I might even treat myself to pizza for breakfast now you've put that in my head.'

'Do, you've earned it!' Harriet smiled, watching as Rufus walked out of the changing rooms. Then following him just a few minutes afterwards, deciding to make the call handlers' office her first call of the day before her shift officially started.

It was pure curiosity, nothing else. At least that was what she told herself as she made her way to the call handlers' office. Because she didn't want to admit that she had a nagging feeling of doubt forming in the pit of her stomach that she also wanted to rule her friend out of the equation too.

THEN

The doll's house is even worse now than before. The walls rickety and crumbling. Closing in, it feels so much smaller than usual. Claustrophobic. Thick mould sweeps across the walls and ceiling. The smell, musty and stagnant, so much worse than either of the two girls can remember. Lingering, forcing them both to hold their breath. His body is dead weight, heavy like lead. And they are exhausted from dragging him across the cold concrete floor. They drop him now – *thud* – before both slumping down on to the cold floor next to him. Emma-Jayne looks down in horror at the smears of mud and bloodstains on her clothes. Long thin streaks and splashes. The two colours merging, almost undistinguishable from the other. And there is so much blood. How is there so much?

'Now what?' she asks as she stares around the bare shell of the cottage. She closes her eyes tightly and opens them again as if adjusting her gaze. As if suddenly seeing these four walls and the thin roof for the very first time. Has it always been so small here? Just the two tiny rooms?

She eyes the hole in the wall where the window used to be. Past the curtain of cobwebs that drape down from the ceiling and swing gently against the draught of the breeze. Outside, the brambles climb and twist their way up the brickwork, blocking out the light in place of where the glass used to be. And beyond that, the woodland. Thick and dense and overgrown. Sinister looking now, as the light of the day fades to evening. Emma-Jayne shivers as the feeling of something eerie, sinister hangs in the air around her.

Death.

'Why was he here? At the doll's house. How did he find us?' she says, shaking her head, still trying to make sense of what happened. To piece it all together. Because her head feels groggy again and she can't keep her focus.

'You know how!' Sarah says bluntly. And she stares at him. Her gaze unwavering, as if she's wary to drag it away from him, as if she's wary that he's not really gone.

But he is dead. Emma-Jayne knows it. And part of her isn't sure why they are both still sitting here, just staring at him, watching silently as the pool of blood seeps further out on the floor around him. Why haven't they called for help? Because they should tell someone, shouldn't they? The police, her mum. Someone. He's dead. They should tell somebody.

'He found the doll,' Sarah says, taking the doll out from where she's hidden it, carefully buried between the folds of her oversized cardigan.

Clutching the doll to her side, as if it is her most treasured possession.

Emma-Jayne instantly recoils, her blood running cold at the sight of the thing. It is bad, isn't it? The doll.

'But you put it back. I told you to. I saw you do it,' she says, shaking her head, as if she's seeing things. Because the doll couldn't be here. It was back inside the fireplace.

And she is unable to explain the terror she feels. How the doll sets something off inside of her. How she knows that there's so much rage and anger and sadness attached to it. How much trouble it could get them in.

That's why she had insisted that Sarah put it back in the first place. And she'd watched her do it. She'd seen her get down on her hands and knees and crawl back into the claustrophobic chimney space and put the doll back where they'd found it.

Only Sarah shakes her head. 'I told you I didn't want to leave it here. I told you that I wanted to keep it. He found it though, didn't he? Oh, he wasn't happy one bit. He thought you took it,' Sarah says matter-of-factly. '"You shouldn't have taken it, Emma-Jayne. You shouldn't be touching things that aren't yours. Why can't you just do as you're told? You are always causing problems around here. Always causing trouble."' Sarah puts on a deep voice. Mimicking his words. Laughing now, believing she's being funny. That Emma-Jayne will laugh too.

Only Emma-Jayne doesn't laugh. Her face doesn't even crack a small smile.

'Stop it. You're acting like a stupid baby!' Emma-Jayne says, annoyed at how childish Sarah can be sometimes. How she shows her age, two years younger.

Sarah shrugs and Emma-Jayne senses that she has no regrets.

'Well, I'm glad we took her. I didn't want to leave her here, in the cold, on her own. How would you like it?'

Emma-Jayne shivers. Because she knows the question is loaded. That she is terrified of being here, alone. In the doll's house.

Sarah knows it too.

'We should have left it where it was,' Emma-Jayne says. 'We should have left it there. We should never have moved it. Because now look what's happened. We should hide it. We should put it back up there,' she says, panic in her voice as she speaks. She snatches the doll from Sarah's grasp. Wanting her to know how angry she is with her. How she's blaming her for all of this.

This stupid doll is the only thing that Sarah really cares about. And all the while, her eyes still on him. Dead on the floor in front of them. Blood pooling out around his head.

'No, we can't. Don't put her back, Emma-Jayne. Please, don't put her back. Let's just keep her. Please?'

'Fine, whatever!' Emma-Jayne shrugs and gives in.

What does it matter now? She feels her tears threatening again as her body begins to tremble. Vibrating wildly, the fear and terror she feels all rolls into one. Her hand clasped tightly to the doll as she stares down at the body at their feet. The blood still pouring out onto the floor. Sarah's not taking any of this seriously. She doesn't care. And all she keeps going on about is the stupid bloody doll.

And they are going to be in trouble now. Big trouble.

NOW

'The main switchboard put the call through,' the call handler said as she pulled up the recording from the night before onto her system and nodded to Harriet to take a seat before pressing play.

'Emma-Jayne?' a woman's voice says.

'That's the caller's voice you can hear. A Miss Amanda Langshot. A social worker, apparently.'

'I wasn't sure if you'd remember me, Amanda!' Another woman's voice now.

And though it sounds vaguely familiar – the same London hue –the woman has identified herself as Emma-Jayne. Harriet relaxes. Full of relief that her initial gut reaction was wrong. And that this incident last night had nothing to do with her friend.

Of course it didn't. She was right to be suspicious, though, and rule out the connection. Because she'd been in the job long enough to know that things were not always as they seemed. Assume nothing, believe nobody and confirm everything. She lived by that. Thankfully, this time her gut reaction had been wrong.

About to tell the call handler to switch the tape off so that she could go and start her shift, she faltered. Figuring that the woman might deem it strange that she only listened to the first sentence of

the conversation, after she'd taken the trouble to stop what she was
doing and go through it all with her, Harriet politely waited it out.

'Can you hear that?' the call handler said as Harriet strained to
listen to the rhythmic noise on the recording.

'Tapping! The caller tapped constantly the entire time they
were on the call. So that we wouldn't be suspicious that the caller
wasn't talking to us or think it had been made by accident or as a
hoax. It's why I stayed on the line and listened. Whoever it was,
knew how to alert us that they needed help. She was smart enough
to give us her location too, without giving herself away... Here, have
a listen for yourself.'

*'It's not Emma-Jayne any more. I haven't been Emma-Jayne for
a long time. It's Alessia now.'*

Harriet felt her senses heighten as she recognised Alessia's
voice. Her name. Wishing it to be different, wishing suddenly that
she'd ended the recording a few minutes earlier. Now her mouth
went dry. She could feel her heart as it hammered inside her chest
at the realisation that this was Alessia she was listening to. Alessia
had broken into this woman's flat in the middle of the night.

She tried to listen to the words, to stay focused, only there was
a whooshing sound in her ears, and her head was spinning. The
call handler was still talking, giving her own running commentary
as the tape continued to play in the background. *Focus.* She heard
a few random words about Jacob. About a cat. She heard Alessia
say that she's better now.

Had Alessia been sick? Had she been unwell? Harriet tried to
concentrate, homing in on the words that were being spoken. But
the call handler kept interrupting.

'This is the bit where I knew where to send the cars. She gives
me her location without letting on to the intruder.'

'You followed me yesterday, didn't you?'

Harriet's brain whirled then. *Yesterday.* Harriet had offered to
look after Jacob, and Alessia had been gone all afternoon. Coming
home soaking wet and looking like she'd been crying. Pretending
she'd been sitting in a coffee shop all afternoon, and that she'd got

caught in the downpour on the way home. When in reality, she'd been following this woman instead. Planning to break in to her flat? And then she'd come home to Harriet and lied straight to her face.

The recording went silent, and Harriet waited for the woman to speak once more.

'From my office, up along Upper Street. I wasn't certain but when I cut through St Mary's Garden I had a feeling that you had followed me. And as I stood at my flat, just opposite the park's entrance, I turned and thought I caught a glimpse of you...'

'See, smart woman! She's speaking clearly, probably for our benefit. She must have known that I couldn't dispatch a unit on the call trace alone. It wouldn't have been specific enough. I needed an address, and she gave me one. That's when I dispatched a unit to the address. They didn't know which property to go to, but they checked out all of the flats opposite the park's entrance and saw a broken kitchen window, which is how they suspect the intruder got in. Though as you already know, the suspect was already gone, and the caller insisted she didn't want to press charges or take things any further.'

Harriet nodded, still in shock that Alessia had anything to do with any of this. She knew that she should speak up. That she should tell the call handler that she knew the identity of the intruder. That she recognised Alessia's name, her voice. That she knew her. But for some reason she didn't. She stayed quiet.

And she wasn't sure why. But something deep inside her stopped her from reacting at all. Instead, she sat there silently. Holding her tongue. Forcing herself to swallow down the words that were lodged in the back of her throat. Because there had to be more than this that met the eye, surely? This wasn't the Alessia that she knew and loved. This wasn't Alessia at all.

Harriet waited for the women to continue, to see if she could piece any more of the puzzle together. Alessia started talking about someone called Sarah. Blaming her for throwing the brick through the window and sending the dead rat. Claiming she had run their car off the road just a few days ago. Alessia had known all along who it was, yet she hadn't told Carl? Why?

'Police! Open up!'

The last words on the recording played out, and the call handler ended the tape.

'That's it. That's our lot!' the call handler confirmed. 'Rufus gave me an update, he said that the caller didn't want to press charges. It's a complete waste of our time and our resources. Personally, I would have cautioned the caller for wasting police time, but, again, what can you do?'

'Yeah, it's certainly a strange one, all right,' Harriet said, though part of her was relieved that whoever this Amanda was, she hadn't given the police any more details about Alessia.

And Harriet wondered if that was intentional. And if so, why? Was she trying to protect Alessia too? And if so, from what?

'Well, I guess at least no one was hurt.' Harriet shrugged before flashing the call handler a grateful smile. 'Right, thanks for that. I best get on. I'll catch you later.'

Leaving the room, Harriet's head was spinning as she went to chase up the details about the car that had run Alessia off the road. She'd thought it would come to nothing. That it was just another careless driver on the London roads. Only now she knew that the chances were, it was more sinister than that. That the incidents could well be linked.

For the first time in her entire career, Harriet had just gone against the oath she'd made to protect and serve and guarantee impartiality. She'd just put her loyalty to her friendship before her career. And that didn't sit well with her at all. Because now she felt like the guilty one, that she was the one covering up. She had no idea what she was covering up for, for Alessia. She was going to have to pull a sicky from her shift today. She'd tell her colleagues that she wasn't feeling well. She needed to speak to the woman on the recording, today, and find out what the hell was going on. And, more importantly, who Sarah was.

30

NOW

'Come on through. You'll have to excuse the mess. I've only just got out of the shower. I was just having breakfast,' Amanda Langshot said, having opened the front door to find Harriet standing on her doorstep so early in the morning. 'Though, like I said last night, I'm not sure that there is much more I can tell you that I haven't already told your colleagues. It was all a misunderstanding, you see.'

Amanda showed Harriet through to the lounge and offered her a seat before taking one opposite her.

'Well, Ms Langshot, we actually have a telephone recording that suggests it was more than that,' Harriet said, sensing Amanda's annoyance, though in fairness the woman tried to keep her tone light. Harriet had figured that Amanda would be wondering why she was here. Why the police hadn't let go what happened last night, despite their assurances that they would. But before she got a chance to explain why she'd come, Amanda was already on the defensive.

'Look, I am sorry that I made the call, it was a mistake. Your colleague last night said that you wouldn't be taking it any further.'

Then seeing the anxious look on the woman's face, Harriet immediately softened, reminding herself that if she wanted this woman to open up to her and be honest, she needed to make sure that she didn't alienate her.

'You're not in trouble, Amanda.' She paused and glanced around the room. 'It's a nice place you have here.' She searched for something amongst the mess and chaos to compliment the woman on. But she couldn't really see anything worth praising. The flat's décor was cold and tired, dressed with sparse, worn furniture. A stale smell of sweat and alcohol lingered in the air.

'The rooms are nice and big!' she said finally before clearing her throat and smiling. Wanting to show Amanda that she was friendly. That she was here on good terms.

'I'm sorry to call in so early, I just wanted to catch you before you left for work. My colleague informs me that you're a social worker?'

'Yes! For my sins,' Amanda said with a smile, visibly relaxing now that Harriet had told her that she wasn't in trouble.

Though Harriet could tell that the smile was for her benefit. To emphasise that she was joking about her job. But she could also tell that part of her meant it too. She guessed that being a social worker hadn't been the easiest vocation for the woman. Nor the best paid. And she wondered if Amanda had sensed her judgement of her as she'd looked around her tatty front room.

'I've been doing it for over twenty years. It's been full-on! I don't really get time for much else.'

Harriet nodded. She understood that only too well herself. How the job so often took over. It was an age-old excuse but a genuine one. As to the amount of tidying or decorating, it could eventually mount up. Tasks that you meant to do but just never had the time to get around to.

'Look, I'm not sure what I can help you with today. I'm really sorry that I made that call. I really didn't mean to cause such a fuss. The other officer said you wouldn't press charges against me for wasting police time. So, I'm not sure why you are here? It genuinely was all a huge misunderstanding.'

'It's okay, Amanda, like I said, you're not in any trouble. I just wanted to ask you a few questions if that's okay?' Harriet said before taking a deep breath.

She knew full well that if Amanda worked in Children Services, she'd be more than used to wearing a poker face. Unreadable, not giving anything away. So if Harriet wanted her to open up to her, she was going to have to lay all her cards on the table and come clean about why she was really here. It was a huge risk, but Harriet was willing to take it.

'Look, Amanda. Can I be completely honest with you?' Harriet said, pausing for a few seconds. Because she was jeopardising everything by coming here. One phone call back to her sergeant at the station and Harriet's career could be over.

'I came here alone today. None of my colleagues know that I'm here. And this conversation is completely off the record. So, if anyone could get in trouble today, then it would be me. I'm laying a lot on the line to come here and speak with you.'

'Why? Why would you do that?' Amanda asked, giving Harriet her full attention.

'Alessia is a friend of mine. She is married to one of my best friends, Carl.' Harriet paused, trying to gauge Amanda's reaction to this information. Praying that her instinct was right. That Amanda hadn't told the police anything in order to protect Alessia, and that that must mean they must both be on the same page. That they only had Alessia's best interests at heart.

'I listened to the recording. I know it was her who came here last night. I know she broke in,' Harriet said. 'I haven't shared this information with my colleagues. Not yet. Not if I don't have to. So, I need to know why! It's so out of character for Alessia to do something like that. I don't understand what her motive was. Why was she here?'

'She is scared,' Amanda said simply. 'Fear makes even the best of us act irrationally.'

And Harriet saw Amanda physically relax.

A sign that she believed her, and that she no longer felt as if she was the one placed under scrutiny.

'Scared of what though exactly? I mean, I know she is going through some stuff right now. But she won't tell me what. And I'm really worried about her. She hasn't seemed herself lately. So, if there's anything you can tell me, anything at all, that might help, I give you my word that this conversation won't leave these four walls. It's just you and me.'

Harriet watched as Amanda nodded understandingly, before twisting her hands together nervously in her lap. But the other woman seemed reluctant to start. 'You clearly know each other?' Harriet pressed. 'I heard you talk about the past?'

'Yes. No. Sorry. Yes,' Amanda said, full of anxiety now that she was faced with a barrage of questions. 'I don't know Alessia. I knew her before. As Emma-Jayne. But I haven't seen her in a very long time.'

'Can I ask how you knew her?'

'She had been in my care, as a child. I had been assigned as her social worker,' Amanda said, clearly finding it difficult to open up about their connection. Harriet could hear the emotion in her voice. She could see that Alessia had never been just a case to Amanda. Amanda had really cared about her.

'It didn't sound like last night was a joyful reunion.' Harriet had sensed the tension in the conversation she'd listened to. The way the two women had danced around each other, almost in riddles.

'Well, how would you have felt?' Amanda laughed, her tone almost mocking. 'Waking up in the middle of the night to find someone sitting at the end of your bed that you hadn't seen for almost twenty years! A shock is putting it mildly.'

'Yes, of course!' Harriet nodded, feeling foolish then. Still unable to separate the Alessia she knew from this crazy person who had broken into someone's flat in the middle of the night. Still unable to get her head around it. That wasn't normal behaviour. Of course Amanda would have felt shocked and scared.

'So, you felt scared of Alessia? Did you think she was capable of causing you physical harm?'

Amanda sighed before shaking her head. 'No. It was more shock than fear. Deep down, I don't think she would have hurt me. She just wanted my help.' Amanda got up and walked to the dresser. Opening the door, she took out a bottle of vodka, holding it up.

'Want one?' she offered.

Harriet shook her head. Which didn't deter Amanda from pouring herself a large measure and drinking it back.

'This is what happens when you spend a lifetime working our type of job!' Amanda said, sounding almost defensive that Harriet might be silently judging her for drinking so early in the day. 'Social workers, police. We're all the same really. Treated like vermin by the very people we do the job for. It gets to you eventually, doesn't it? Wears you down.' She justified as she immediately poured herself another one, unapologetically. Figuring that if they were both going to lay it all out there, she may as well just be herself.

'I'm sorry, I must sound so hard-faced. I wasn't always like this. The system is so unbelievably flawed. And sometimes people slip through the net. Kids slip through the net.'

'And Alessia, or Emma-Jayne, was she one of the kids that slipped through the net?' Harriet asked, wondering why Amanda was going off in that direction. Almost as if purposely making a point.

Amanda nodded again before she continued. 'Has Alessia ever told you anything about her family? Or about her past? Has she ever spoken about anything that happened back then?'

'No nothing.' Harriet shook her head. And now that she thought about it, she realised she didn't know anything about Alessia's family or her childhood. Alessia had always shrugged the subject off and talked about something else. And Harriet had guessed that there were tensions there, things that Alessia hadn't wanted to talk about. Families could be complicated like that, so Harriet had never tried to push it.

But it was odd, wasn't it? How she knew so little about her friend's past. Seeing as they were all such good friends.

'Well, where do I start?' Amanda sighed. 'When I first set eyes on Emma-Jayne, sorry, Alessia, she was just twelve years old. She was sat in a police cell. Wrapped in a blanket, trembling with terror. I don't think I've ever seen a child look more terrified and more alone than Alessia did then.' Smiling sadly as she recalled the memory. So vivid and sharp it was as if it had happened only yesterday.

'Why was Alessia in a police cell? What had happened to her?'

'What happened to her? Oh, no...' Amanda shook her head. 'Alessia had been arrested for murder. The murder of her stepfather, Robert.'

'Alessia murdered her stepfather?' Harriet repeated the words robotically, unable to absorb what Amanda was telling her. She wondered if perhaps she'd heard her wrong. Because Alessia wouldn't hurt a fly. She was always so thoughtful and considerate. So normal.

'She'd been clinging to this doll for dear life,' Amanda said, picking the doll up that Alessia had left behind last night in her haste to get away from the police, and holding it up to show Harriet. 'It's hard to believe that this grotesque-looking doll could be such a beloved treasure to a child, but Alessia wouldn't let it out of her sight. I guess it brought her some kind of comfort, and God knows she needed it.' Amanda placed the doll down on the table in front of Harriet. 'I didn't mention it to your colleague last night. I didn't want them to take it. Because I know she'll want it back. Could you take it for her?'

Still rendered silent from the shocking revelation about her friend, Harriet simply nodded. To show that she would. And that she was listening. Because still she couldn't speak, still she couldn't find any words to fill the silence. Instead, she just sat there, dumbfounded, as a million questions swirled around inside her head. Of all the things she'd imagined that might get said here today, Alessia murdering someone hadn't been one of them.

'The night I met her, Alessia had been in a really bad way. She was in shock, understandably. Hallucinating and talking in riddles. She didn't make an awful lot of sense, but from the very little she did say, I believe that she had been sexually and physically abused by her stepfather.' Amanda's voice was raw with emotion.

'Oh my god!' Harriet said, feeling the blood drain from her face at hearing this, and part of her not wanting to hear any more. But she knew that she must. That she needed an explanation. She'd let Alessia into her life. She deserved to know the truth about her.

'It's a lot to take in. I know,' Amanda said, pausing and giving Harriet a few minutes to absorb the harrowing news of what had happened to her friend. 'I was there, yet I still find it hard to get my head around it all.' Amanda shook her head bitterly at the memory and took a moment to compose herself before continuing.

'She refused to let a doctor examine her. And when I tried to speak to her mother to gain permission and to explain to her the little that Alessia had confided in me, her mother point-blank refused to believe Alessia's claims about the abuse. I thought that maybe her mother was in shock or perhaps denial. I mean, a mother hearing that had been going on, that her husband had been doing something so despicable like that to her child... Well, it would be hard for anyone to believe, wouldn't it? But it wasn't either of those things. Alessia's mother was adamant that Alessia was making up the claims. She had screamed at her. Called her a liar, an attention seeker. She even went as far as to make a formal statement against Alessia, claiming that her daughter couldn't be trusted. It was absolutely heartbreaking to witness. I tried talking to her too, but she was adamant that Alessia had made the allegations up.'

'But why on earth would Alessia make up something so horrifying? Why wouldn't her mother believe her? Her own child! Abuse isn't something you just make up?' Harriet said, sickened at what she was hearing. Dumbstruck that any mother could turn their back on a child when they most needed them.

'A number of reasons, I guess. Denial being the most obvious one. She simply couldn't cope with hearing the truth. It would have been too much of a burden to bear if she admitted that it had happened, then there would have been a huge element of self-blame and guilt on her. I guess she would have felt partly responsible. And if she wasn't partly responsible, then the onus would be on her being the one to stop it. Only she did neither. Maybe it was easier for her to believe it was all a lie.' Amanda shrugged. 'Alessia's mother told the police and the courts that Alessia was a troubled child and that the relationship between Alessia and her stepfather had been a difficult and strained one, and that it had mostly been Alessia's doing. That she hadn't been happy about her mother's relationship with Robert. Or about the pair having another child. Her brother Bobby. Her mother said that she was jealous and purposely disruptive. And that she'd set out to destroy their family any way that she could. It was pretty brutal and damning, her own mother saying all of that. But unfortunately, the school backed up the claims that Alessia was troubled. Confirming that Alessia often truanted from school, and when she did attend, she would purposely distract other students. That she craved attention. It had become a pattern.' Amanda's brows furrowed angrily even now at their reasoning.

'But I couldn't help but wonder if that was the point. That Emma-Jayne, sorry, Alessia, had been reaching out for help. That acting up and being troubled and disruptive had been part of that, because let's face it, in my experience, those are not signs of a happy, well-adjusted child. Unfortunately, she wouldn't talk to anyone after that. So her disruptive behaviour ended up being used against her, instead of going in her favour. Her mother publicly disowned her and the media had a field day with the story. Alessia simply shut down after that. She wouldn't speak at all, to anyone. Not to me, the police or the child psychiatrist. She just completely clammed up,' Amanda said sadly. 'But I guess you would, wouldn't you? After going through all of that and even your own mother accuses you of lying about it.'

'Yet you believed her? About the abuse?'

'One hundred per cent. If a child tells me they have been abused, my job is to support them in any way I can. But Alessia didn't make it easy for herself or for me. She wouldn't talk about what had happened to her. And she wouldn't talk about the murder either. Which made things worse for her ultimately, because her silence only added fuel to the fire of her mother's claims. And the way she just completely shut down came across as heartless. It looked to people on the outside that she had no remorse for what she had done. That she didn't have any feelings at all. But despite all of this, the only thing she was adamant about was that she didn't kill her stepfather. She claimed from the very start that she hadn't committed the murder at all. That her friend Sarah had been the one to kill him.' Amanda shook her head sadly. 'That's when things really took a turn. Alessia being so adamant that Sarah had done it. She sounded really convincing. So much so, that even I started to doubt that Alessia had done it. But the police only found one set of fingerprints on the murder weapon. Alessia's. She also had fragments of brain matter and blood all over her dress and in her hair. It was conclusive.'

'Yet, she blamed it on Sarah? The same Sarah that she's convinced is terrorising her now?'

'Apparently so!'

'Apparently? You don't think that it's the same Sarah doing all these things now. Because Alessia seems convinced.'

'Has Alessia ever spoken to you about Sarah?'

'No. The first time I heard her name was on the telephone recording, here, last night. But clearly, Alessia thinks that Sarah is the one that has been doing all the things to her? Tormenting her. Throwing a brick through her window. Running her off the road...'

'That's why she broke into my flat last night. She said that she found an old article about the murder in Jacob's nursery book bag. She was terrified at how close Sarah was able to get to her. To Jacob. How far she was willing to go to scare her. She wanted me to help her find her. To help her put a stop to it all.'

'And you wouldn't? Only you said on the recording that you

couldn't help her,' Harriet asked. Understanding then why Alessia might have acted so desperately. If she was genuinely terrified for her or Jacob's life. If someone had got that close to Jacob to make their point. They might go even further next time. And Alessia was just trying to protect him. To protect herself. That was why she'd been driven to do something so out of character, so crazy, like breaking into someone's home in the middle of the night. She had everything to lose.

'It wasn't a case of I wouldn't help her.' Amanda shook her head. 'It's more that I can't. Sarah isn't behind any of the things that Alessia is claiming to have happened.'

Harriet narrowed her eyes under the scrutiny of Amanda's gaze. Confused at the way Amanda could speak with such certainty over something she'd only just learned the previous night.

'She's not claiming that they've happened to her. They have happened,' Harriet said defensively. 'She's not making it up. Someone is tormenting her. They are stalking her. And I'm worried that she might be in real danger. I might not know everything about Alessia's past, but I do know her now. If she thinks it's this Sarah doing all of this to her, then she's clearly got good reason to believe it.'

'It's not Sarah,' Amanda said with finality.

'But how can you be so sure?'

'The same way I'm certain that Sarah wasn't behind Robert's murder. Because Sarah isn't real. She doesn't exist.'

31

THEN

The dreams keep coming. Nightmares really. Mainly about the doll that they found. Emma-Jayne has been plagued with them ever since she'd last been to the doll's house. Unable to get the images of the ragged little dress and the child's small tooth from her mind.

Wake up, she tells herself. Because part of her knows that she's still asleep but it feels as if she's awake too? She feels as if she has the power to wake herself up. Properly.

Only there's a fogginess clouding over her brain, and her limbs feel too heavy for her to try and move. Is she awake? Is Sarah here in the room too? Because she can vividly see her face. Standing next to her and looking down at her as she rolls her eyes, her patience wearing thin.

Get up, Emma-Jayne. Come and play with me.

Emma-Jayne reaches out and grasps her hand. Holding her skin in hers, warm and soft. Their fingers locking. *Why is Sarah here in my bedroom in the middle of the night?* she thinks before the hand is snatched away from hers. And Sarah is gone again.

Was she just part of my dream? And it's only then that Emma-Jayne realises that it's not her bedroom that she's in at all. She's back at the doll's house. But it's so dark now. And she feels like she's here all alone. Only she can't be. Because she'd never go to the doll's house alone. Sarah must be here somewhere? But she can't see her or hear her any more. And she can't seem to move her limbs. They are weighted and heavy and she can only just tilt her head. And she sees it down on the floor, lying there as if it's been discarded. The doll.

And she can hear crying. The doll's voice. Or a child? Or Sarah? It sounds like Sarah. Like she is screaming for help, in pain.

The doll's house. The doll's house. The doll's house.

WAKE UP. WAKE UP.

Or is it the birds again? In the chimney of the doll's house. Chirping desperately for their mother and their next feed. She's not sure. And part of her is telling herself that none of this is real, that she's still asleep. Because everything is so vague at first, the sounds so blurry and faint. They are louder now though. Turning quickly into wild, piercing screams that fill her head, making her eardrums feel as if they might explode.

She places her hands tightly over her ears and tries her hardest to block it all out.

Trying to block Sarah out.

It's goes quiet then, as a deathly silence descends. And somewhere in the dark recess of her mind she knows that she is truly all alone now.

Sarah has really left her this time.

NOW

'Look Jakey, here's Mummy!' Carl said as he walked into the kitchen with Jacob clutched in his arms, all bathed and dressed. As Jacob screeched with excitement at the sight of Alessia sitting at the breakfast bar.

'Hello, baby!' Alessia smiled before she leaned in and kissed Jacob on his forehead, and breathed in that sweet, intoxicating scent of his skin, warm from his bath.

'Are you okay?' Carl asked as he placed Jacob into his high-chair beside her, and then narrowed his eyes as he realised that though she was still in her pyjamas, her coat was hanging over the back of her chair. Still damp from the early morning rain. As his eyes trailed downwards, he caught sight of the trainers that she was still wearing. The wet streaks on the floor beneath them. Self-conscious under the scrutiny of his stare, Alessia tried to tuck them out of sight under the breakfast bar, but she was a few seconds too late.

'Have you been out? I thought you were having a lay-in?' Carl asked, suspicious of what Alessia might be trying to hide. Where would she have gone at this time of the day?

'Yeah, I couldn't sleep. I got up early and went for a walk,' Alessia lied.

And the lies were coming more easily to her the deeper she was being pulled back there. She was becoming that person again. The person she'd fought so hard not to be. She tried to steady herself, pressing her palms against the breakfast bar to stop them from shaking.

'You want a coffee?' Carl said, trying to act normal. To not let on that Alessia's behaviour lately was starting to really worry him. That she didn't seem herself. She hadn't seemed herself for a while.

'Yes. Thanks!' Alessia said. Her body suddenly craving caffeine. And some warmth.

She stared up at the clock and realised that she'd lost track of time. It was almost nine thirty now.

She'd been sitting here in the kitchen for so long, trying to work out what to do, that her skin was tinged blue and her arms were prickled with goosebumps.

And still she hadn't worked out what she should say to Carl when the police finally came for her. Because they'd be looking for her right now, surely? Searching for her so that they could arrest her for breaking into Amanda's flat. Of course they would. Time was running out. What had she been thinking? What had she been hoping to achieve? Creeping around in the middle of the night like a criminal. Behaving like a crazy person.

And that's exactly what Amanda must think of her. That she was crazy. That was what Amanda always had thought of her. But the truth was she had felt desperate. As if she'd had no other choice. As if she had no one else she could turn to. No one who would understand. And she had thought that maybe Amanda, of all people, would. Despite it feeling like a lifetime ago now. She had offered her help once, hadn't she? She'd told her that she'd be there for her in any way that she could. And all Alessia had wanted was to put an end to what Sarah was doing to her. To ensure that she was safe, that more importantly Jacob was safe. She'd convinced herself that Amanda could make it all stop. That she'd tell her where Sarah was and help her to put an end to all this.

Only Amanda had said no. Because she still believed that Alessia was back there, didn't she? Still caught up with the crazy notions inside her head. And maybe she really is crazy. Because she can feel herself slipping slowly, sliding back into that dark, lonely place in the recess of her mind.

'Alessia?' Carl said softly as he placed a cup of coffee down on the counter in front of her. Interrupting her train of thought as she stared at Jacob.

'Alessia. Is everything okay? Whatever it is, you can tell me,' Carl said, and she saw the way that his eyes pleaded with her to confide in him. To tell him what was going on because he needed her to open up to him. To tell him what was troubling her.

She saw him study the distant expression on her face. The way he noted how her eyes were puffy, as if she'd been crying. How her cheeks were tearstained and flushed a bright red, the way that her face always gave her away in the rare few times that she'd been crying. And she knew deep down that he only wanted to help her. And he deserved to know the truth, didn't he?

'It's just, I was thinking about the rat. And that wreath. After you went to bed last night. Why didn't you tell me about them? It's almost like you tried to hide them from me,' Carl said, cautious. Not wanting to seem like he was attacking Alessia or accusing her of anything. He just wanted her to open up, to trust him. To tell him what was going on.

'And the brick coming through the window, and then that car that tried to run you off the road the other day. It's a lot.' Carl said, as if he really had put a lot of thought into it. As if he'd already tried and failed to piece everything together. 'I spoke to Harriet. And I'm sorry, because I know that you didn't want me to, but I was worried about you, Alessia. And I think I have every right to be. Because Harriet said that though she believes that the two incidents are probably not linked, but she also said that she wouldn't rule it out completely either. And I've been thinking that they might be. Linked. That someone is doing all of this to us or you on purpose. Are they? Is someone trying to threaten us? Or you? Are they trying to scare you? Do you know who's doing all of this?' Carl said, shaking his head.

And Alessia sees that it's almost as if he couldn't comprehend what he'd asked her but he knew that something wasn't right. That she was keeping something from him and he wanted to know what.

'No, of course I don't know who's doing these things,' Alessia said as she purposely cut him off, knowing that her protest sounded weak even to her own ears.

She turned her attention back to Jacob. Cooing and making silly faces as she used Jacob as a distraction, and Jacob rewarded her with a series of chuckles. Giggling away at her in hysterics. The comforting smell of coffee floating in the air. She squeezed her eyes shut just for a few seconds, tighter still to stop the tears from being able to escape. As she relished the sound, the noise, the smells. Wanting to savour these last few minutes of the life she created for herself.

Right here, in her home, in her kitchen with her family. Just the three of them. Safe. Before it was all ripped away from her again. Because the police would be here soon and then this would all be over. The truth would come out. Then Carl wouldn't love her any more. He wouldn't want to be with her. He wouldn't want her around Jacob any more. He'd take him away from her.

'I'm sorry! I'm so, so sorry...' she cried as the enormity of what she needed to do hit her.

She needed to tell him, because Carl deserved that. He deserved to hear the truth from her, not from the police, or from Harriet. He deserved to hear it from her. To know what he was dealing with here. For Jacob's sake if nothing else.

'Sorry for what? Alessia? You're scaring me!' Carl said, sensing her turmoil as she sat and cried so openly. Knowing whatever she was hiding from him was going to be bad. But still he needed to know. Still, he needed to hear it.

'Alessia, please tell me what is going on.'

Only she won't give him an answer. Instead she simply shook

her head. As her nose ran and her eyes filled with tears. All the while she looked at Jacob, drinking in the sight of him. So innocent. So perfect. And now she was about to ruin everything for them all.

And she was so angry at herself for fucking everything up. Because she brought it all on herself, hadn't she? She should have told the truth from the start. But instead, she'd chosen to keep her secret from everyone. Including Carl. And now she didn't even know where to start.

Where would she even begin? With her, she figured. Sarah.

Because it always came back to Sarah in the end.

'A long time ago, I had a friend...' she started. Deciding that he should hear it from her, his wife. Not the police. She should tell him that their entire marriage, her entire life, had been a lie.

She forced her mind back there, to the doll's house. The four cold, bare walls of that derelict room. Filled with the faint sound of crying. The doll? A child? No, it's Sarah voice that she hears. Alessia sees herself then. Lying there. Barely able to keep her eyes open for more than a few seconds. Her limbs weighted and heavy. Sarah is hurt and crying, small and crumpled, huddled in the corner of the room. And Alessia can't get to her. She can't reach her. And the sound of Sarah's voice comes and goes for a while. Filling Alessia with guilt and sadness. And she remembers how she just wished that Sarah would stop. Until she does stop. And the room is filled with a deathly silence. Which is worse. So much worse.

'Alessia? What is it, tell me?' Carl's voice again. Urgent, as he pulled her back from the vague snippet of memory of the dream she'd been having for most of her life.

It was just a dream, wasn't it? Or had it been a memory? She wasn't sure. There was something there, niggling. Teetering on the edge of her mind. And she tried to reach it, to hold on to the recollection. But it slipped quickly away from her. Like always. Yet some of it was still there, so engrained in her memory that it felt almost real. As if it actually had happened. Like it was important somehow? *Was it real?* No. They said it wasn't real. They told her, hadn't they? That it was just her mind playing tricks. *But it feels real.*

Sarah was real.

The room started to spin. She stood, her hands cupped over her already cramping stomach as the watery bile filled her mouth. *She was real?* Unable to make it to the bathroom in time, she lurched towards the kitchen sink, and emptied the contents of her stomach into it. Retched violently until there was nothing left inside of her. Until her stomach was empty, hollowed. Her mouth sour and burnt.

'Jesus Christ! Alessia? Are you okay?' Carl asked, horrified at the sudden deterioration he saw before him. The ferocity of Alessia being so sick. How her skin turned a sickly pale, ashen and prickled all over with beads of perspiration.

She nodded. But they both knew that she was not okay. She was not okay one bit. And Jacob must have sensed that too because he started to cry. Seeing his mum be so sick. And hearing the panic in his father's voice.

'It's okay, baby! Mummy's okay. She's just feeling a little poorly,' Alessia said as she stared into Jacob's big blue eyes and reassured her son.

Carl immediately went to him. Picking him up, he hugged him tightly. Soothing him as his cries gradually started to subside. And Alessia knew that she couldn't do this right now. She couldn't tell Carl about her past and destroy her perfect little family, not yet, not like this. She needed more time. She needed some kind of clarity. She needed to sort out her head and get her facts straight. But the room was still spinning and she felt so sick.

'I'm sorry. I think it's a bug. Do you mind if I go and lie down for a bit? We can talk afterwards. Once I've had some sleep.'

Carl nodded. And she felt his eyes on her as she crossed the room. And she sensed his relief too. Because even though he had no idea what was still to come, he couldn't possibly know, couldn't possibly even imagine what was to come, he had felt it. That once she said it, whatever it was that she'd been keeping from him. Once she said the words out loud, there would be no going back.

And Carl knew that it was something really bad. And he wasn't ready to hear it, and she wasn't ready for that either.

33

THEN

'Wake up, Emma-Jayne. Wake up?'

The voice wakes her. Sarah? She fights to open her eyes, only they feel so heavy, as if they are weighted down, just like her limbs. Her arms and legs pinning her down to the floor as she sinks into the cold concrete ground beneath her. She wonders how many pills he gave her this time. They always make her feel so sick and sleepy. And each time she wakes she feels strange. Aware that her body feels sore and broken. Aware of the things that he's done to her. But she can never remember the things. Not properly. And sometimes she feels glad about that. And she never knows how long she's been there. But it's dark outside now, so she guesses that it's late. And her head feels vague and fuzzy.

Only today, it's different. When she opens her eyes, the first thing she hears are the rats. They are everywhere. Climbing and scampering and scratching around under the blanket of darkness inside the doll's house. Writhing away around her feet. A high-pitch squeak. A swoosh of a tail.

She shudders and just about manages to pull her feet in tightly to her, scraping her bare legs against the cold floor. The feeling slowly coming back to her. Wanting to get up, but she's not strong enough yet. All she can do is look. But the rats scare her. So she turns her head and sees the doll. She's lying face down on the floor. Her tatty, threadbare dress submerged in a puddle of deep red. Blood.

Her eyes follow the trail that pools out all around the doll. The trickle that runs across the floor. To another pool of blood. From him. And she gasps at the sight of him lying there, on the concrete. The nearness of him. His mouth is wide open, his eyes glassy and staring vacantly up at the ceiling. His skin tinged grey. His head caved in. A strange, twisted look of surprise on his face.

'You did it for us!'

It's Sarah's voice again. Only she can't see her this time. She's not here. It's just her voice inside her head. So she shakes it, trying to drive the voice out.

'I didn't do this,' she says quietly.

And it's then that she sees the hammer. On the floor between them. Blood splattered all down the handle. And she's covered in blood too, she realises. It's all down her. Splattered up her arms, her legs. Her dress. It's in her hair.

'No, I didn't do this. Not this,' she repeats, over and over again as she slowly manages to sit up. Her voice is shaking. 'It wasn't me. I didn't do this.'

Sarah's voice comes again. The words coming out in that sing-song voice of hers.

'It's raining, it's pouring. The old man is snoring. He bumped his head when he fell out of bed and he couldn't get up in the morning.'

And it scares her. What she's saying. So much so that she starts to cry.

'I didn't do it!' she says again, but she knows that she did as the vivid image flashes in her mind. The hammer in her hand. *Thud.* How one hard swipe had been enough to bring him to his knees. She'd lost count of all the others, after that.

'Daddy?'

It's Bobby. And for a second, she thinks that she's imagined this too. But then she realises that his little voice, strained and scared sounding, is coming from where he stands in the doorway, his eyes fixed on the figure splayed out on the floor.

Wasn't I minding him? While Mum was out? Wasn't he watching the cartoons on TV? Had he followed her here? Why is he here? Watching me. And him. And the hammer and all the blood.

And Sarah's voice keeps ringing out inside her ears.

'*It's trembling, it's shaking. The old man's house is breaking.*'

'Shut up!' she shouts, wanting to silence the voice. To make her stop singing.

But she doesn't stop.

'*On the Earth's crack, he broke his back and he didn't wake up in the morning.*'

Only Bobby doesn't seem to hear her. Why can't he hear her? But she hears it. How Sarah's sing-song voice is drowned out. Replaced with Bobby's almighty scream.

34

NOW

Alessia sat on the edge of the bed in silence as she tried to calm her quickened pulse. To piece the story in her head together. But it was as if there were some missing pieces. Some parts of the puzzle that just didn't fit, they couldn't possibly fit. They had just been bad dreams, hadn't they? That's what the doctors had told her, back then, when she'd been unable to shake the dark memories of Sarah from her mind.

Sarah hadn't been real. And she'd tried to accept that. Even though she'd haunted her ever since. Even though she'd been unable to get that deathly silence that had come that fateful day, after the crying had stopped, out of her head. That nothingness. That void that could have only meant one thing.

Yet, she had tried so hard to do as they had told her. To accept that her memory of Sarah wasn't real. She'd spent years trying her hardest to block all thoughts of her out. To bury her image deep inside of herself. She'd had to. Otherwise, she would have spent a lifetime questioning her own sanity. Only now it seemed she was doing that anyway. Had they lied to her?

Because Sarah was doing all of this to her, she was sure of that. And the memory she'd just had in the kitchen, when she'd started to try and explain everything to Carl only confirmed that. The sight of Sarah, huddled on the floor in the corner of the doll's house. That familiar image so engrained in her brain. That had felt so real. And she knew for certain then that it hadn't been the snippet of a reoccurring nightmare that she'd endured over the years. That it wasn't something her mind had simply fabricated. She knew that the lines of her reality blurred a little, because of what she'd been through, she understood that, but today it had felt different. She'd sensed that connection. The emotion behind it all.

And she felt unsettled now. Wired and on edge, unable to stop her body as it trembled violently, as if she'd been shivering from the cold. Only she didn't feel the temperature. She didn't feel anything at all.

And the nausea had passed now. The exhaustion had set in, but she didn't want to sleep. Instead, she wanted answers. She needed answers. And part of her wished that she could crawl into the dark recesses of her mind and go back there. To that day. To when it happened. The places that her memory wouldn't allow her to reach. It was like she was trapped. Inside her head. Inside this house. And she needed to get out. She needed to break free of it all.

She paced the bedroom, unsure what to do with the pent-up energy that buzzed around inside of her. The doctors wouldn't have lied to her though, would they? They would have wanted to make her better. They would have wanted to help her. She needed to remember that. She needed to say focused on that.

'You can't be real,' she told herself quietly. Before she winced as she wondered if this too was madness. Talking to herself. Trying so hard to convince herself of what was real and what wasn't. Had she already slipped back there again? To that dark, messed-up place she'd once been in. The smashed window, the dead rat. Those things had happened. They had been real. Someone had done them to her, hadn't they? So she couldn't be slowly losing her mind?

'They said you weren't real,' Alessia said as she walked the length of the bed. Backwards and forwards, aimlessly. Her voice was louder now. Her body filled with bitter rage as she started scratching frantically at her arms, her nails raking thin delicate ribbons of skin in their wake. Just like she used to do. Back then. When she wasn't sure what had been a lie and what had been the truth. When she needed to feel something real. But now, as she clawed her nails through her flesh the buzz wasn't there. The pain was not nearly enough. She needed to stop.

She sat down. Pressed her palms down hard on the dressing table. Before she stared into the mirror. Instantly transfixed by the icy blue eyes that stared back at her. Sad looking. Those eyes. She shook her head. Unsure of who they belonged to. Were they hers? Were they Sarah's? Was she taunting her still? And right then, in that moment, she just wanted it all to stop. So she hit out. Her fist locked with the glass and when she looked again, the eyes had gone.

And it was her reflection she saw, staring back at her. Her distorted image staring out from the splintered mirror. A broken woman, shattered into a million pieces. She did it again. Slammed her fist into the jagged edges of broken glass. Craving that familiar release as the shards pierced her skin. Sharp and raw and real. And it was something, anything to keep her out of her head for a while, she thought to herself as the warm blood trickled down her wrist.

SLAM!

'Why are you doing all of this to me? Why are you doing all of this? You're not real. Sarah is not real.'

SLAM!

Her voice was so loud and hysterical that she didn't hear the bedroom door open behind her, nor did she register Carl as he ran into the room. Shouting her name. His voice full of concern, full of horror. As he dragged her back, away from the mirror and all the shattered pieces of broken glass. Away from the frenzied attack on herself.

She felt him wrap himself around her. Allowing herself to collapse against him then as they both sank down to the floor. Her legs grazed by the pieces of shattered glass.

'You're safe, Alessia. I'm here. It's going to be all right.'

She felt the pressure of his hold. The tightness of his grip. But she couldn't grasp his warmth. Because she was numb. To him. To the pain. To everything.

And she heard it, how Carl's voice was loaded with fear. And she knew that even as he said the words to her, even as he tried to reassure her, he didn't even believe them himself. He was afraid. Afraid of her. Of who she really was and what she was really capable of. And so he should be.

35

NOW

'Back when it all happened, Emma-Jayne became caught up in a media circus,' Amanda said, pausing for a few seconds, knowing how hard it would be for Harriet to get her head around any of this. It was a shock and Harriet had no idea about Alessia's background. Alessia had made sure that no one did.

'Her photo was plastered on the front page of every newspaper and every news channel on TV. Everyone was speculating about her. Judging her. Her mother was convinced that Alessia had fabricated the abuse to get people to feel sorry for her. So that she'd get away with the murder. She insisted that she'd made up her friend, Sarah, too. And of course, Alessia underwent a full mental health assessment. Which threw out some interesting theories about Alessia's state of mind at the time. One of the psychiatrists who assessed Emma-Jayne believed that she wasn't intentionally making up "lies" about a friend committing the murder. He suspected that the trauma Alessia had endured from the abuse she suffered, may have triggered a severe form of chronic dissociation. A multiple-personality disorder, if you like. But it was so hard to prove. A lot of practitioners and therapists back then questioned the diagnosis and the treatment of the disorder. Some even question the disorder's very existence. Some still do, even now.'

'I don't understand. So, Alessia was lying? Her mother had been right all along?' Harriet asked, sitting opposite Amanda and still trying to take in what she was telling her.

'Not exactly, no. The psychiatrist suspected that Alessia truly believed what she was saying. She wasn't lying. But her reality was somewhat distorted. He said that it was possible, in an attempt to cope with the severe trauma that she had endured, that Alessia may have "dissociated" herself as another child. She may have become this "Sarah". Her personality may have fractured, splitting into two parts, if you like. That Alessia created Sarah as a way to survive. So that, in her mind, she didn't suffer the abuse, because that way, it wasn't her who was present when it took place.'

'So this Sarah is really Alessia?'

'That was one theory, yes. In Alessia's mind, it was Sarah who had suffered the abuse, not her. Which is why Alessia may have been able to convince herself that she didn't kill her stepfather. She'd blamed that on Sarah. She couldn't seem to differentiate from the two. She believed Sarah was a separate entity. She really believed that. And trust me, Alessia was extremely convincing. Even I started to have my doubts about Sarah not being real. Alessia had been so adamant,' Amanda explained before getting up and pouring them both another shot of vodka. And this time she didn't bother to ask Harriet if she wanted one. She just poured it out for her and set it down in front of her, as if she knew that she probably could do with something to take the edge off. And she was right; this time Harriet didn't refuse it. Instead she took a much-needed gulp and listened as Amanda continued to explain.

'We had the trial coming up, and what we needed were definite answers not theories. We needed Alessia to talk to us. To tell us what really happened, and more importantly, why it happened so that we could get her the right help. Only, I just couldn't get through to her, no matter what I said or did. She just wouldn't open up to me. She wouldn't talk about the abuse she'd suffered, let alone the murder. In fact, the only thing she wanted to talk about was Sarah. It was as if she had been obsessed with her. Growing more and more frustrated when we told her she couldn't see her. And then, in the lead up to the trial she just completely withdrew from all of us. Her mother had disowned her by that point, and Alessia started self-harming and there were a few occasions she even attempted to take her own life.

'Which was when the judge had declared her unfit to stand trial. And Alessia was, instead, admitted to a secure psychiatric unit for treatment. She was there for almost six years, and in that time, she had been obsessed with talking about her weird, distorted dreams that she often had, about Sarah and this doll that they found together. It took a long time, but eventually, towards the end of her term at the institute, she finally stopped talking about Sarah completely. In fact, she acted like Sarah never even existed.

'The hallucinations stopped too, and the paranoia. As did the bad dreams. The healthcare team that had been treating her assumed that she'd finally moved past it all. They believed that she was "better". In her therapy sessions, she had started to open up about the abuse that she suffered too. She was beginning to accept what had happened to her. But she still wouldn't talk about the actual murder. She always claimed that she couldn't remember it. That she'd blacked out.' Amanda nodded down at the doll on the table between them both. 'The fact that she kept this, that she still has it, even now, proves my theory. She never really accepted that Sarah wasn't real. She had just pretended she did.'

'Pretended? What do you mean? Did she admit that Sarah wasn't real? That she'd made her up?'

'She admitted that Sarah may have been a fragment of her imagination, yes. Eventually. But I wasn't so sure. I could see it sometimes when I visited her, in her eyes, the loss that lingered there. Her grief for her had been real. And in all honesty, I just wasn't convinced that Alessia's confession was ever really sincere. I felt as if she was telling everyone around her what they wanted to hear. Because she wanted out of there. She wanted her life back.'

Amanda closed her eyes as if she could still feel the pain of what Emma-Jayne went through.

'And eventually she took it back. The last time I saw her, had been her eighteenth birthday. I'd visited her in the hospital, for what I hadn't known back then, would have been the very last time. I gave her a birthday card and a little necklace. A gold key with the number 18. I had written a little note inside the card, to say that the key was for her, to any door she wanted to open now she was old enough to build a life of her own. It was nothing much really – a token present really – but her eyes had filled with tears at the gesture and I could see that it meant something to her. I had hoped that she knew by then how much I really did care for her. That somehow I'd got through to her in some way. And I had hoped that we'd stay in touch. But weeks later, Alessia simply disappeared.'

Amanda shook her head bitterly.

'That last time I saw her, I pushed her too hard. I called her out on it. Quizzing her whether she was just admitting to making Sarah up, simply to get out of there. And she lied to my face. But I could see it in her eyes that it was the truth. Alessia knew that I knew too. She knew that I didn't believe the façade she was putting on. That I wasn't fooled like the others. I could tell she was acting. And sometimes I wondered about her detachment from her family. How she seemed so completely switched off from them all. How she'd learned so quickly just to cut them off. She never asked about any of them. Her mother, her brother Bobby. And of course, Robert.

'I never said it to her, in fact I never said it to a single living soul, but I wondered sometimes if there was more to some of her stories. If there was any truth to what her mother had claimed and if she had made some things up. Because Alessia was always so convincing. And she didn't seem to build real connections with anyone around her. In all that time, six years. Not even with me. And sometimes it felt as if she was just going through the motions. Like she was playing the part. Only, I never got a chance to dig any deeper because she disappeared completely after that. I lost all contact with her. And of course, now I know that she'd changed her name. That she started again, as someone new. And maybe she had to do that. Maybe she had to break free of all of it, break free of me too? The first time I saw her since then was last night.' Amanda shook her head, still gobsmacked that she'd somehow found her. That she'd turned up at her flat, in the middle of the night all these years later.

'And from the way she was talking about Sarah last night, I guess I was right all along. Alessia never accepted that Sarah wasn't real. She still believes that she's out there somewhere. Doing all these things to her.'

And Harriet sensed how part of Amanda was relieved that Alessia was okay. As okay as she could be, given the circumstances. But she was worried now about the state of her mind.

'But she's not lying about the things that have been happening to her. They are real. They have happened. The brick being thrown through her window. The dead rat. Her car being run off the road. They all happened. She's not lying about that.'

'I'm in no doubt that she believes they have happened, or at least they feel real like they've happened *to* her. *If* the psychotherapist that first assessed her was right about Alessia having a multiple-personality disorder, then it might be Alessia is doing all of these things to herself. Which is why she doesn't have any recollection of them happening to her; she only sees the aftermath. That's how MPD works. Our brain blocks memories out completely as a way of protecting ourselves. But something must have triggered it. Something must have happened to make Alessia suddenly start reacting in this way again.'

'So, you're saying that you think Alessia smashed her own window, and sent herself a dead rat?' Harriet said, unable to hide her utter disbelief at Amanda's far-fetched theory. 'No. No way! Seriously, Alessia has a huge phobia of rats. She doesn't even like seeing them on the TV. There's no way that she could do all of that, and still seem so frightened. So convincing. No way...' she said, unable to get her head around what Amanda was implying.

'I think it's a real possibility. It's something that I've looked into over the years. People with MPD can experience losing entire chunks of their memory. The brain is a very clever, complex organ. It works hard to keep both or all personalities separate. It's a survival mechanism. Alessia is convincing because it's her truth.'

'I think you're wrong. She couldn't have done those things. She was scared, really scared. I saw her...'

'Who was with her when the brick came through the window?'

'Jacob was there. Upstairs in bed. Alessia was home by herself that night because Carl was away at work. She said she'd been sleeping at the time.'

'What about the other times? Who was there when the dead rat was delivered?'

'I was,' Harriet said almost triumphantly, as if it proved that Amanda's theory had to be wrong. Because it was hard to think that her friend had been capable of doing all of this and having no recollection of any of it. That she could be so sick and Harriet hadn't had a clue the entire time.

'Well, I was babysitting Jacob, and the box was left on the doorstep...' She paused. Remembering how she hadn't heard the door knock or the bell ring. 'Alessia brought it in with her. She said that she'd found it there when she'd got home.'

Harriet saw the look on Amanda's face, the way she raised her eyes just slightly as she took in the information.

'Alessia found it there. She wouldn't lie about something like that... I know she wouldn't,' Harriet said. Doubting her friend suddenly. The enormity of what she was hearing today making her feel sick and light-headed.

And the truth was, from what Amanda had told her, Harriet didn't know Alessia at all. Alessia had purposely shut them all out, protecting her secrets. About to speak again, to ask Amanda what they should do in order to get Alessia help, because her friend clearly wasn't well, Harriet felt her phone vibrate in her pocket as a call came in. She reached for it and stared at the familiar name that flashed up on the screen.

'It's Carl. Alessia's husband,' Harriet said, apologising to

Amanda as she took it. But even before she pressed the button and accepted the call, she felt the familiar dread pool in the pit of her stomach. As she wondered why Carl was calling her. Whether he already knew that Alessia had broken into Amanda's flat last night. If he knew about any of this?

And part of her hoped that he did, because she had no idea how to break it to him if he didn't. How could she tell him that the woman he'd married, and had a child with, was a complete stranger to them all? And worse, a murderer.

Only she didn't get a chance to speak before Carl's voice rang out from the end of the phone.

'I'm so sorry to call, Harriet. But it's Alessia. She's hurt herself. I don't know what's going on but I think she's having some kind of a breakdown. I was going to see if you could come and sit with Jacob while I take her to the hospital?'

His words came out jumbled, fast and frenzied, and Harriet heard the panic there. The genuine concern. And she loved her friend even more for that. How he always put Alessia first. How happy they'd both always seemed. And she felt heart sorry for him. Because he had no idea how his life was about to unravel. And she wanted to help him. She wanted to make sure he was okay. Because as much as she'd grown close to Alessia over the years, Carl would always come first.

'You're still at home?' Harriet asked.

'Yes, but I need to get her to a hospital. She's hurt herself. Her arm is all cut up. It won't stop bleeding,' Carl confirmed.

'Okay, sit tight. I'll call Andrew and get him to come over and sit with Jacob. And then I'll make my way to the hospital. I'll meet you there!' Harriet said, not waiting for an answer before ringing off the call. 'It's Alessia. Carl thinks that she may be having some sort of a breakdown. She's hurt herself.'

Amanda nodded, unsurprised. As if she almost expected it. 'She used to do that a lot. Hurt herself,' she said sadly. Knowing how much pain Alessia must be in, to still be doing things like this to herself.

To still be so caught up in this nightmare. 'You want me to come too?' Amanda said, and Harriet nodded gratefully as she dialled Andrew's number.

Because even if Alessia didn't need her, Harriet probably would.

36

NOW

Carl was sitting in the chair in the corner of the cubicle of Chelsea and Westminster Hospital's Accident and Emergency Department, his eyes fixed on Alessia as she slumped back in the bed against the pillow. Still numb from what he'd just heard. Still unable to take it all in, the bombshell that she'd just delivered to him.

'That's going to leave some nasty scars!' he said finally. Dumbly, as if he needed to talk about something, anything else as he nodded to the long white bandage that snaked its way up Alessia's arm, from her hand to her elbow, now that the nurse had managed to extract all the tiny pieces of glass from where they'd been imbedded in the newly formed cuts.

Alessia had needed twenty-two stiches in total. Though Alessia was used to living with scars. He looked down at her legs, to her trousers. Noting how she always kept her legs so well hidden. How she'd always been so conscious of what other people would think of them.

'The other scars on your legs?' he asked, but as she closed her eyes, as if to apologise, he got his answer. He nodded. The accident she'd told him that she'd had as a child was yet another lie. She had fallen, she'd said. She'd been running too fast, and she had been careless. Not looking where she was going, and just before she realised, it had been too late. Her body had ploughed into a glass coffee table and she'd flipped and landed on top of it. Her feet had broken her fall, crashing through the pane of glass as it cut her legs to pieces.

Carl could almost have laughed at the craziness of the situation he'd found himself in. If it hadn't been so messed up. Married to what it appeared now was a complete stranger. All these lies that Alessia had told him from the first day they'd met. Half-truths she'd tried to justify to him as they'd sat here together in the cubicle, waiting for the nurse to return with Alessia's X-ray results to check there wasn't any breakage.

Alessia had murdered her stepfather. The words she'd just confessed to him still sounded strange and twisted inside his ears. He'd thought she was joking at first. And he'd stupidly sat there and waited for the punchline, for that goofy smile she shot him when she told him one of her awful jokes. Waited for her to hold her hands up and tell him that her sudden confession was all some sort of sick joke.

Only Alessia hadn't laughed. Instead, she'd kept her voice calm and steady. She'd kept her eyes on him the entire time as she'd told him everything. As if she was drinking in his reaction to the truth about her. As if she was assessing how he felt about it all. Now he knew the truth about her past. About how she'd been sent away to foster care and then a mental health facility. How she'd changed her name and started a new life. A new life with him.

And he had so many questions running round his head that he didn't know where to start. So he started with the most obvious one.

'Why? Why did you kill him?'

She had faltered. Not wanting to give him a reason but knowing that she had to. Carl deserved to know the truth about her. All of it. Everything.

'Because he hurt me. And he hurt Sarah.'

'Sarah?' Carl said, raising his eyebrows. Because she said the name as if it should be familiar somehow. As if he should know who she was talking about. As if he knew Sarah. And it was familiar. Sarah had been the name that Alessia had been calling out, shouting and screaming out, when he'd found her in the bedroom earlier that morning amongst the splintered shards of glass that covered the floor, trails of blood dripping down her arms.

You're not real. Sarah is not real.

'Sarah? I heard you say that she wasn't real.'

'She's not! That's what they told me. Sarah is my imaginary friend.' Alessia laughed then, her tone laced with sarcasm, and the sound was unnerving as it filled the space in the cubicle between them.

And Carl saw the sudden shift in mood in her. The way her face hardened. The way her eyes challenged him, as if she was daring him to say something. Daring herself to say something.

'Sarah isn't real. I see things. I see people that aren't really there!' She pointed her index finger to her temple and cocked her thumb to mimic that she was crazy. Because that was essentially what they had told her, wasn't it? That the things in her head hadn't been real. 'So, you see. I wanted to tell you. When we met, I wanted to be honest with you right from the start, but what would I have said? Oh, by the way, I murdered my stepdad and then spent six years in a mental institute because I blamed it on someone who wasn't real. My imaginary friend was the one that had bludgeoned him to death with a hammer...'

She stopped. Knowing by the look of horror on his face that she'd said too much. That she'd been too honest. Too open. And that had always felt like such a contradiction to her. She'd lost count of the times people had told her over the years that they wanted her to open up, and be honest with them, when the truth was, that they didn't really want to hear it. They said they did, they'd convinced her as much too, but they weren't really able to face the truth when she had finally given it to them. And she saw that now in Carl too.

That same look on his face. How he had begged and pleaded

with her to tell him what was going on. Why she'd hurt herself so badly. And in his defence, at least he had sat and listened. Patiently. Quietly, fighting to take it all in, his expression unreadable despite the fact that she knew that her revelation would have floored him.

And now he knew it all.

'He was bludgeoned to death with a hammer?' Carl said, his voice quiet, his skin pale and sickly looking as he gulped down a mouthful of burning bile in the back of his throat.

So it hadn't been an accident? Who was this woman? Who was this person that he'd married?

'I don't have any memory of doing it. I blocked it out,' Alessia said, her voice sounding small. Almost childlike, as if she was still dancing around the confession. As if she still, after all this time, couldn't accept it herself. And she wanted to explain. To tell him about the abuse she had suffered. To tell him of the horrors she'd been subjected to. But she couldn't even get to any of that now. It was buried too deep. And she wasn't sure that she'd be able to cope if she started to speak about it. Because she was already fragile. Weak. She was already slipping back there, wasn't she? She felt it. Which is why she was here now, at the hospital. Her wrists wrapped in bandages, to hide the new slices in her arms. She wasn't stable.

And she saw the way Carl looked at her. The same disappointment she'd seen a thousand times before from others, but she'd prayed she'd never see from him as he looked her up and down as if seeing her now for the very first time. This broken woman before him. Propped up in the bed. The medical trolley beside her still adorned with the towel that he'd wrapped around her arm before leaving the house. Soaked in her blood.

'I wish you'd told me sooner...' he started to say, but he stopped himself and looked down at the floor. More empty words. Because she knew he didn't mean them either. Not really. He couldn't possibly mean them. Because she'd told him now, and already she could see it. How it had changed everything.

If she'd told him then, they wouldn't even be here now. They wouldn't have even started. They'd have never made it this far. Because she knew how messed up it all sounded. The life she had lived had been fucked up. And she wondered for a second what it was that he'd been expecting her to confess to him when he'd asked her what was going on today. If perhaps he'd thought that she was going to tell him that she didn't love him any more. Or that she'd met someone else. That maybe she was having an affair. Normal tragedies that other normal marriages sometimes endured. Not this. Not this dark secret that Alessia had buried away.

Because there was no going back from here now, now that she'd said it out loud. Not now she'd seen that solemn look on Carl's face. She'd shattered the illusion of their perfect marriage and now they both sat here, trying to make sense of it all, amongst the ruins. Their life together had all just been make-believe. So lovely for a while. So perfect, the three of them. And there had been love. So much love but Carl could never have really loved her. Because how could you love someone that you really didn't know? And she felt heartbroken then, because that had been on her. For keeping so much of herself from him.

'When things started to happen. The brick through the window. The dead rat being delivered... I couldn't stop thinking about her. Sarah. I couldn't stop thinking that maybe it was her, doing all of those things to me. Because who else would it have been? It must be her; it must be her doing all of this,' Alessia said as she shook her head exaggeratedly. Because she was still trying to make sense of her thoughts. Still trying to piece everything together even now. 'But then I thought how can that be? How is it possible for her to have found me? How was it possible to do all of these things, if she's not real?' She narrowed her eyes and looked to Carl as if he'd somehow have the answers. Because he always did. Only this time, of course, he didn't. He just stared back at her blankly.

And she pursed her lips together tightly, as if she was contemplating trying to keep her next words firmly behind them.

Only she'd come this far now. And Carl loves her. Or loved her. She may as well be honest with him about everything now. Because she had nothing left to lose.

'So I clung to that. I told myself that it was impossible. That the doctors and social workers had told me that she had just been inside my head. A coping mechanism. But then I started to wonder about how I remembered her so clearly. So vividly. All the little things. Like, her icy blue eyes. Her crooked smile. All the games that we used to play together. All the silly songs that we used to sing. How we used to tell each other our secrets. And we'd pinky-promise to each other that we'd keep them, and never tell another soul. No matter what.' Alessia smiled sadly at the memory. 'And she had warm, sticky fingers. They used to snag on the knots when she combed them through my hair. Sometimes I'd wince with the pain, and Sarah would quickly smooth my hair back down again, to soothe me. And she'd twist the strands of my hair into two perfect plaits. My mum never did plaits for me... How do I remember all of that, if she's just a figment of my imagination?'

'I don't know, Alessia, I really don't know,' Carl said, still trying to get his head around it all. Before he glanced up at the clock on the wall, in the hope that Harriet would be here soon. Because he found Alessia's behaviour unnerving, how instead of showing any real emotion or remorse about what she'd done, she seemed numb and detached to it. She murdered one of her parents. She'd hinted that she had been abused as a child. And yet she was only focused on Sarah? Fixated on an imaginary friend, on something that wasn't even real.

Alessia seemed so fragile suddenly, and he was worried about saying the wrong thing. Worried that one wrong word would break her to pieces. So, instead he stayed quiet and let her keep talking.

'One minute Sarah was there, the next she was gone. And every time I tried to speak to them about her, I could see it. The disappointment on their faces. The looks of sympathy. Or pity? And I knew that they'd keep me in there forever if I didn't play along. They'd keep me there, locked away in that place. Forcing medication down my throat. Antianxiety tablets for the panic attacks. Antidepressants for my mood. Sleeping tablets to help with the insomnia. Antipsychotics to stop me seeing things that weren't really there. To stop me seeing her.' Alessia sighed before she leaned her head back against the pillow and closed her eyes. Exhausted now.

'And I did stop seeing her eventually. It was as if she'd vanished into thin air. A distant memory for a while and then it was as if she'd never even existed. And I thought that maybe they were right all along. I must have made her up. All that time, and she'd just been a figment of my imagination after all. Only I was so scared about how much I had believed that I'd seen her, how much I felt as if I really knew her. I felt as if I couldn't trust my own mind. And I became terrified of the power it had over me. And I just wanted to get out of there. Away from all of them. From that life. Away from me too. The old me. I wanted to start again. To feel normal. So the easiest thing to do was to go along with it and tell them that my mother had been right all along. That I'd made Sarah up.' Alessia looked genuinely sickened then.

'And they believed you?'

'Mostly. I guess.' Alessia nodded. 'Because they let me out. Eventually, when I was eighteen. But my mother had disowned me by then.'

Carl nodded. And he could recall the story that Alessia had told him about her mother dying of a heart attack. How she'd been a single mother, raising Alessia alone. And Carl had felt so desperately sorry for her, for not having any real family of her own. For not having that support system around her. And in the early days of their relationship, he could sense how much she craved a family of her own. People for her to love, and to love her back. And it was partly that, that had made him love her more. He'd wanted to give her that. That one thing that she'd never really had. But that had all just been lies too.

Alessia knew what he was thinking. She knew what would be running through his head.

'When I met you, I was Alessia. I wasn't Emma-Jayne any more.' Alessia saw him falter as he heard her real name for the first time. As if he believed that nothing else could shock him, nothing else could hurt him. But it had. He hadn't even known her real name.

Still, she continued as she clung on to the very last bit of hope that she had, that he would listen to her, that he would somehow understand. 'I wasn't that same girl, Carl. I'd moved on and started again. I made a new life for myself. Untainted by all of that and I wanted you to be part of that. The good me. Not the bad me. It wasn't all lies. We were real. We were the truth.'

She felt her tears come now. 'And when Jacob came along, there was no way I could ever tell you the truth then.' Her words came out fast, jumbled, in her haste, because she sensed that she'd lost him.

And he had every right to feel cautious. To question and doubt her. Every right to feel angry with her. Furious. She'd lied to him for their entire relationship. And she couldn't do it any more. No matter what it cost her.

'But something is wrong with me, Carl. Because I can't stop thinking about her. I can't get Sarah out of my head. And I have tried. Trust me, for all these years I have really tried to stop. But she's still there. In the back of mind. Creeping into my thoughts. And I'm scared because they'll say that I'm sick again, won't they? If I really believed that. That would mean that I'm slipping back into that bad place again. If I'm questioning it all?' Alessia said as she started to cry. Her whole body shook, overcome with huge wracking sobs. Because that was what she was really frightened of.

'I'm done with pretending, Carl. I'm done with all the lies. I need help.'

'And we'll get you help, Alessia. We'll fix this. You're not on your own this time,' Carl said as he took her in his arms and pulled her in tightly to him. And part of her felt relieved that he still felt that way. That he hadn't given up on her. At least, it didn't sound like he had. Not yet, anyway. 'Maybe it's just another slip up. Maybe with medication...'

She pulled back from him. Because she wasn't sure that he understood what she was trying to tell him.

'No, Carl!' she said as she shook her head. 'You're not listening. I don't need that kind of help. Don't you understand? I'm done with pretending that I didn't see her. That she wasn't there. I just went along with what they told me so that I could have my life back. The little that was left of it by then. And somewhere along the line, I started to believe my own lies. My own pretence. They made me put her in a box and leave her there. And I did that. I left her behind. But what if they were wrong all along, Carl?' Alessia said finally.

And Carl narrowed his eyes as doubt crept in.

Because what she'd just suggested was impossible, wasn't it? For Sarah to be out there somewhere this whole time. And for no one to have believed her. And if she was out there, that would mean that Alessia had spent her whole life doubting herself, accepting blindly what they'd told her. When deep down she'd always known the truth. And she'd built her whole life around that lie, just so that she could have a life of her own.

'What if I wasn't just imagining her? What if Sarah *was* real?' Alessia said. Because the more she thought about it, the more she'd convinced herself that it was true. 'Because she feels as if she was real. And someone has been doing all of these things to me. It must be her. And if it is Sarah, then she might do more. She might do worse.' She sounded genuinely terrified. As she thought of her son. Her precious boy.

'What if she hurts Jacob? Because she's not going to stop, Carl. Not until I face her. She's never going to stop.'

37

NOW

'Is she okay? Where is she?' Harriet asked as she made her way down the A&E corridor to where Carl stood by the coffee machine, a cup of steaming coffee cupped in his hands.

'Not really!' Carl said honestly. Still unsure what to make of everything. 'We're still waiting for the X-ray results. But the nurse thinks that she was lucky, that the stitches will be all she'll need. She doesn't suspect anything is broken. She's in a pretty bad way in her head though. She's not really making much sense,' Carl said gingerly, not capable of repeating what Alessia had told him in confidence less than an hour earlier. The revelation still felt so raw, so shattering. He couldn't get his head around it. And he needed to make sense of it before he said anything to Harriet.

Especially while they were in the presence of a stranger.

'I'm sorry to have dragged you both away from work...' Carl said, smiling almost apologetically at the woman who stood awkwardly at Harriet's side, assuming that she was one of Harriet's colleagues. Only Harriet quickly corrected him.

'Oh, no. Carl, this is Amanda. She used to be Alessia's social worker.'

Harriet paused when she noted that Carl didn't react to that. That he wasn't surprised to learn that Alessia once had a social worker. If Alessia hadn't been talking much sense, like Carl said, Harriet wondered exactly how much she'd told him. That much at least.

'Did Alessia tell you where she was last night?' Harriet continued. Treading lightly still.

Carl shook his head, recalling how he'd found Alessia early this morning, sitting in the kitchen. Her shoes still on, her coat damp and hanging on the back of her chair. She'd said that she'd gone out for a walk. Another lie, no doubt.

'She broke into Amanda's flat. Late last night. The police were called, but she'd fled by the time they had arrived.'

'She did what?' Carl said, unable to hide his shock as he rubbed at his temples in agitation. This was worse than he'd first thought.

Now he knew about Alessia's past. About the murder and the abuse. And now what, she was breaking into people's homes in the middle of the night? Smashing up their own house. Harming herself. When was this going to stop? What would she be capable of doing next?

'Shit, I'm so sorry,' Carl said to Amanda, embarrassed. Apologising profusely on his wife's behalf. 'That's not Alessia. She's not acting like herself right now...'

He stopped mid-sentence. Pausing, he took a breath as the painful realisation hit him that he wouldn't actually know how Alessia normally acted. Maybe this was her normal. Maybe this was the real her. Maybe she just wasn't acting any more. 'I think she may be having some kind of a breakdown.'

Amanda nodded in agreement. 'Please, do not apologise, Carl. I understand. And I think you might be right. I don't think Alessia is well. Not from what I heard last night,' she said, sadly. 'But I want you to know that she didn't break in to cause me any harm. She wasn't there with ill intention, not really. She is just scared.'

'Scared of what?' Carl said as he pieced together what Alessia had already told him and wondered what had happened last night to scare her into doing something so extreme. Because she had been at home. With him. She'd been safe. What would have scared her so much that she'd needed to leave the house in the middle of the night?

'She found a newspaper article in Jacob's book bag, about the murder of her stepfather,' Amanda said, treading gently. Noting Carl's lack of reaction to the revelation of a murder.

And Harriet saw it too. 'She told you? About the murder? You knew?'

'Yes. But only just now. I've only just found out. She told me all of it.'

'Did she tell you about Sarah too?'

'Yes. She said that she'd made Sarah up. That she wasn't real. But then she started backtracking. She started saying that she might be. She said that she'd just gone along with what the doctors had said because it had been easier that way. But that she thinks that Sarah is the one doing all of the things to her. The car being run off the road. The brick through the window,' Carl said as he looked at Harriet in search of some answers. In search of the tiniest bit of hope that Alessia wasn't losing her mind.

'The things that have happened,' Harriet agreed. 'Alessia might really *believe* that someone is *doing them to her.*'

'What do you mean?' Carl said as he read between the lines and sensed what Harriet was getting at. Before he rubbed his head again. To try and appease the dull thud of the headache that pounded aggressively inside his skull.

'There's a pattern, Carl. Alessia was alone when the brick came through the window. She was alone when she opened up the package and found the dead rat and the wreath. She was alone when someone ran her off the road, and when she found the news article in Jacob's book bag last night.'

'So what? You think that she's lying about all of that too? That she's making it all up?' Carl said, a look of disbelief on his face. 'But she can't be. I was on the phone with her the other day when she was in the car. I heard the whole thing. I heard the screech of brakes, the skid of the tyres. She sounded scared; I heard her screaming and Jacob, he was crying. It happened.'

'I'm not saying that she's lying. I'm saying that she truly believes that these things have really happened to her. But what if she's the one doing them?'

Carl stared at Harriet, confused at what she was implying.

'I know that it's a lot to take in, Carl. Really I do. But one of the psychiatrists who assessed Alessia before she was deemed unfit to stand trial, suggested that Alessia may be suffering from multiple-personality disorder. I've already explained it all to Harriet, but it was suggested that the abuse Alessia had endured back then had fragmented her personality. A survival mechanism if you like,' Amanda intervened.

Carl closed his eyes. Close to tears. Not wanting to believe any of this. But he'd seen her for himself. He'd seen how confused she seemed; how fragile she was. And now that she'd told him about everything else, the truth was he didn't know what to think any more.

'Christ, how did this happen? How did I not know any of this? How did I not know any of this about her?!'

'None of this is your fault, Carl. How could you have known? She only showed you what she wanted you to see,' Harriet said as she reached out a hand and squeezed Carl's arm affectionately. Letting him know that he wasn't alone in all of this.

'But why now? Why is she suddenly like this again now? If she's managed to hold it together for so long,' Carl said, still not entirely convinced at what Harriet and Amanda were telling him.

'No one knows why patients relapse. It could have been happening for a while and Alessia might have been hiding it. Or something could have happened recently that triggered it all. Recognising someone from the past. Recalling a vivid memory suddenly. A date...' Amanda trailed off. Narrowing her eyes as her own words died out. She reached in to her bag and pulled out her phone. Her fingers tapped at the calendar.

'What?' Harriet asked as she sensed that Amanda may have an idea about what had been the trigger.

'You said that this all started with a brick coming through the window? What day was that?'

'Er, Thursday, I think. Yeah, it was Thursday. I was away with work.'

'So, that would have been the fourth?' Amanda said as she screwed her mouth closed tightly, finally understanding. 'That's the anniversary of the murder. The fourth November 1998. Twenty years ago.'

'So, you think that what? Something about the date triggered her? And what? She's having some kind of a psychotic episode. Seeing Sarah again?' Carl said, knowing that whatever was going on with Alessia right now was bad. Really bad.

But before Amanda could say anything else, the nurse that he and Alessia saw earlier approached them.

'Carl. We got the X-ray results back.' She smiled to show him that they were the results they'd been hoping for. 'Just as we suspected, there's no breakage. But like I said, there was no harm in being extra thorough and checking Alessia over. Your wife was lucky she only needed stiches,' the nurse said, having seen how badly the woman had cut her arm.

'Thank you so much. So, we can go home now?'

'Oh, yes, absolutely. Though, can you let Alessia know when you tell her that she'll have to come back to Outpatients in a few days' time, to have a new dressing applied and so we can check that there's no sign of any infection. It's always better to be safe than sorry!'

'Have you not told Alessia?' Carl said, wondering why the nurse was saying all of this to him, as if she hadn't already recited it all to Alessia.

'Oh, I would have but her bed's been empty for ages. I just assumed she was in the loo, or here having a coffee with you,' the nurse said.

'She's not,' Carl said.

And Harriet and Amanda sensed it too. Something wasn't right.

'I'll check the main reception area,' Amanda said, hurrying off in one direction.

'I'll go and check the toilets,' Harriet said, seeing the flicker of panic spread across Carl's face, before she ran down along the adjacent corridor too.

'Alessia?' she called out as she pushed each cubicle door back, only to reveal that they were all empty.

A few minutes later, she walked back out to where Carl and the nurse stood. Just as Amanda reached them all, Harriet shook her head and confirmed what Carl had already suspected.

'Alessia is not here. She's gone.'

38

NOW

'Did she come back here?' Carl asked Andrew as soon as he entered the house, not bothering to close the front door behind him in his haste. He scanned the hallway and lounge for any signs of her coat or shoes, anything that would indicate that Alessia had made it home before him.

Alessia had taken their car. He'd made Harriet drive as fast as she possibly could through the London traffic to get home, praying the whole way that Alessia was okay, that she'd left the hospital in a hurry because she'd grown sick of waiting around for her X-ray results. Desperate to get back to Jacob. But she wouldn't just leave without him if that was the case. Or maybe she'd tried to find him and when she couldn't she'd made her own way home. Though there was no sign of the car outside in the street and he couldn't dismiss the rapidly growing bad feeling that he had in his gut right now that hadn't been the case at all. And Andrew quickly confirmed it.

'No, sorry. I haven't seen or heard a thing from her. I thought maybe you would have found her by now,' Andrew said, shaking his head and getting up from where he'd been sitting on the sofa. 'I'm sure she'll be fine, mate. She'll turn up soon.' He shot a look of sympathy to his friend just as Harriet and Amanda rushed in the house behind Carl.

'Anything?' Harriet asked, hopeful. Carl shook his head.

'Shit!'

'Look, I don't know what's going on, but I'm sure whatever's happened, Alessia will be fine,' Andrew said.

'It's a bit more complicated than that, mate,' Carl said, stopping himself mid-sentence as he realised that he couldn't even explain what was going on now, even if he wanted to. It was too complicated. Too messed up.

As far as Andrew knew he'd received a panicked phone call from Harriet earlier asking if he could mind Jacob while Carl took Alessia to the hospital because she'd hurt herself. And a second panicked call not so long ago from Harriet to say that Alessia had gone missing from the hospital. Ignoring the confused look on his friend's face, Carl paced the hallway distractedly, his eyes flicking back constantly to the door as he willed Alessia to walk through it.

'Sorry, I haven't even introduced you both,' Harriet said to Amanda and Andrew as she made her way into the lounge with Amanda following behind her.

'Andrew, this is Amanda. She's a social worker. Alessia used to be in her care.'

Andrew narrowed his eyes at this, about to say something else, before Harriet quickly intervened.

'Alessia isn't well, Andrew,' she said, her tone clipped as she made eyes at her husband and looked over towards Carl and nodded her head. Indicating to Andrew that she didn't want to do this now.

A silent look of understanding passed between them both as Andrew realised that Harriet hoped that he would take her words at face value and not quiz her any further on the matter. Not while Carl was in this state. Not when Carl was still in earshot. It might be too much for him, discussing what Alessia had been through.

'We need to find her because we think she may need some help.'

Andrew nodded to show he had got the hint.

'Seriously, mate, whatever is going on, I'm sure she'll be back before you know it. Hospitals are enough to creep anyone out.'

Carl had stopped pacing and stood in the doorway of the lounge, his body rigid as he leant against the doorframe, as if the structure was the only thing holding him upright. He wore the look of a defeated man on his face.

'Is Jacob asleep?' Carl asked, as if he hadn't been listening to Andrew at all. As if he'd only just noticed how quiet the house was. That his son's presence was missing from the room.

'Yep, he's currently conked out upstairs in his bed. Here, it's just as well you came back when you did, because that boy of yours has had me fit to collapse too.' Andrew laughed, feigning exhaustion. 'Christ knows where he gets his energy from. Or maybe I'm just getting old, eh! Didn't even stir when I had the hoover on. Had me playing dinosaurs with him for ages earlier,' Andrew said fondly, before quickly adding, 'thought I may as well have a hoover through for you while he kipped. I picked up all that glass too.'

Carl nodded in acknowledgement, because he knew by the state they'd left that room that Andrew was playing down the fact he'd no doubt spent the past half hour mopping up blood and cleaning up the shattered mirror upstairs.

'What time did he go down?' Carl asked, not wanting Jacob to sleep longer than usual. Because when Alessia came back – and she would come back – the last thing they needed was Jacob's routine to be messed up. If he slept too long, he'd be fractious late into the evening and bedtime would be a write-off. When Alessia got back, Carl wanted them both to sit down and talk properly. They already had enough to deal with, without adding a grisly, tired child into the mix.

'Oh, I don't know. About forty-five minutes ago I guess, the last time I checked...' Andrew moved his gaze to the baby monitor on the coffee table and his voice faltered as he saw it was no longer there. He looked on the floor nearby; it was face down on the carpet.

'Shit, I must have knocked it.' He picked it back up, and switched the power button on, hoping that the fall hadn't broken it, because the screen was black now. He pressed it again, before he followed the black cable with his eyes, considering if maybe the power was somehow out. It was only then that he spotted the plug had been pulled from the wall.

'Maybe I caught it with the hoover...'

And Carl noted how even he sounded unconvinced at his own theory. From what Andrew said, he would have been upstairs most of the time, cleaning. Though if he had quickly run the hoover around down here too, then maybe he had knocked the monitor off the table. It was possible. And maybe the hoover had caught itself on the monitor's cable. But that was a lot of maybes. Another thought popped into Carl's head.

'You don't think that Alessia...' he started. And as he looked over towards Harriet, he saw that she was already thinking the very same.

He ran, taking the stairs two at a time in his haste to reach Jacob's bedroom. He burst through the door and was relieved to find the room still in darkness from where the black-out blinds were drawn. He forced himself to breathe quietly, not wanting to startle the boy. But as he crept over towards Jacob's little cot-bed, he saw that the covers had been pulled back. Left in a heap at the bottom of the small bed. And the bed was empty.

'Jacob is gone!' Carl shouted, the panic in his voice catching even him by surprise. The sound lodged in his throat. Raw and urgent as if his words couldn't get out fast enough.

He ran to the spare room, searching frantically for his son. It was tidy now; the glass and blood had been cleaned away by Andrew. Then he noticed the stack of boxes on the floor by the wardrobe. Boxes he'd not seen before.

He knelt down and removed the lids before he looked through them. Recognising the things inside as Alessia's old things. From when he'd first met her. Things he thought that she'd thrown away. A photo of the beloved cat that she used to talk about. A navy scarf adorned with purple butterflies. Newspaper articles. Carl picked one up and stared at it.

Schoolgirl Faces Murder Charge

And he thought about what Amanda had said at the hospital. How Alessia believed that Sarah was doing these bad things to her. But Sarah didn't exist. And it might be Alessia who was really doing all these aggressive, threatening things. Unaware that she was actually doing them. That this was her survival mechanism kicking in.

Because she'd told him at the hospital that she was scared, hadn't she? She'd told him that she was worried Sarah might take Jacob. That something bad might happen to him.

Was that why she left? Because she believed that Jacob was in grave danger and she wanted to get to him first? Or had she fragmented into this Sarah again? Because Sarah was dangerous. Sarah was doing all of the bad things. And if she'd taken Jacob, would she do him harm? Carl recalled Alessia's words. *Bludgeoned to death by a hammer.*

All those years of lies and secrets. This woman that he'd married, a complete stranger. And now she had his son. The room started to spin and Carl felt as if the air had suddenly been expelled from his body. His lungs felt as if they were inflated so much they might burst, yet he couldn't seem to breathe in. He was going to suffocate. Blind panic engulfed him and took over. He heard the flurry of panic in the voices of the others behind him as they came into the room.

Then Harriet's voice.

'Carl?' she said softly, hoping that what she'd just heard him call out had been wrong. That he'd made a mistake. She needed to see for herself, and she did. Other than Carl, all the rooms upstairs were empty.

He stood there, the newspaper cutting gripped in his hand.

Tall and strong in the middle of the spare room, yet somehow now he seemed smaller. His shoulders curved as he shook his head. As if in shock. As if he couldn't believe it.

'Jacob is gone, Harriet. She's taken him.'

39

NOW

'Anything?' Harriet called out from the front door as she watched Amanda make her way back up the driveway, having just come back from her flat. She'd had a hunch that maybe Alessia might have gone back there. But her hunch had been wrong judging by the slump of her shoulders and the slow pace of her walk. And Harriet knew that Amanda would have called her right away if she had found Alessia.

'No. I don't know, I thought that she might want to speak to me again, after last night, but there was no sign of her,' Amanda said as she shook her head. She eyed the throng of police cars parked in the street. 'No luck here either, I take it?'

'Some of the officers have searched the house and the garden; a few others are doing a door to door. They are hoping to rule out if there were any sightings by the neighbours of Alessia coming back here and leaving with Jacob,' Harriet said, grateful now that calling in a favour with her sergeant had paid off. The fact that this case involved a mother and her own child wouldn't have warranted a search party in usual circumstances. But these weren't usual circumstances, as Harriet had been forced to explain to her boss. Having filled him in on Alessia's real identity and the murder she'd committed as a child, Harriet had told him her concerns about

Alessia's present state of mind. About the things that had been happening to Alessia recently. And the fact that she thought Jacob could be in real danger.

And she hoped that he was just as lenient with her and that he bore all of that in mind when they spoke about the fact that Harriet had lied today. That she'd feigned being sick so that she could look out for her friend.

And even if there were repercussions for her actions, she'd already justified to herself that she'd take them. That they'd be worth it. Especially now she knew the severity of Alessia's situation. And now that Jacob was missing too.

As much as Harriet had always believed that Alessia would never do anything to harm her child intentionally, she wasn't so certain of that any more. Alessia didn't seem like she was of sound mind right now. She wasn't thinking straight. And in Harriet's opinion, that was when people got hurt. Intentionally or not. Her boss had agreed, and immediately sent out a team of officers to help with the search. But so far, there was no sign of Alessia or Jacob.

'Carl's doing the rounds with the officers and going from door to door. I think he just needs something to do. Something to keep him from going mad, sitting around and waiting. Andrew is in with my colleague making his statement,' Harriet said as she nodded towards the lounge where Andrew and one her colleagues both sat. 'Though there's nothing that he can tell them that we don't already know. Andrew didn't see her. She must have snuck back here when he was busy hoovering up the glass in the bedroom. I just don't understand why she took him. Surely she'd know we'd all help her if there was someone out to get her. If she thought for a second Jacob was in danger, surely the safest place for him would be here, at home. Why take Jacob away from us all? And why be so secretive about it? Leaving the hospital, sneaking around here, so that Andrew wouldn't see her. It doesn't make sense.'

Amanda looked down at the floor. Her silence at Harriet's question spoke louder than any words.

'What?' Harriet asked, sensing that Amanda was purposely

holding something back. Whatever it was, now wasn't the time to do it. 'Is there something you want to say?'

'I don't know anything for sure. And I really don't want to worry you all, more than you already are. But what if this isn't about protection? What if that's not why Alessia took him?'

'I don't understand what you mean,' Harriet said, confused. 'She's scared that someone is out to get her. That they might hurt her or Jacob. Why else would she have taken him? She's scared that someone might hurt him.' Then seeing no reaction from Amanda at this, she continued defending her friend. 'Alessia loves Jacob. More than anything else in the world. That's a fact. I've seen her with him. How she adores him. She'd never let anything happen to him.'

'I don't doubt that one bit.' Amanda nodded, completely in agreement. Before taking a deep breath and finally sharing what was really on her mind. 'When Alessia killed her stepfather she had no memory of doing it. She used to talk about these dreams that she had, instead. Where she'd wake up, back there. In the doll's house. That's what she called the place where the abuse happened. A rickety abandoned workshop that was tucked away in derelict woodlands just behind her house. That place had become a fabrication of her mind too. Because when she'd first described it to me, she'd made it sound so far away, as if they'd walked for miles to find it. Another distortion of the truth to help her cope. It was the place that Alessia's stepfather used to take her when her mother was working nights. The place where he abused her.

'From what she eventually told me, about how she could barely lift her limbs up, or open her eyes, I'd say that her stepfather, Robert, had drugged her, so that she didn't have a memory of the things he did to her. And for a very long time she questioned her own mind. Her own sanity. Unable to peel apart the layers of what had been real and what had been imagined. What had been a dream and what had been reality. Because she'd made the doll's house a sanctuary of sorts in her mind. Pretending to herself that it was a play den that she and Sarah went to. That they were there alone. Two children, playing together and singing songs.

'But she'd created that illusion in her head, again, to get through the abuse. To survive. And slowly, very slowly we started to try and pick things apart. Until finally, one day, she did remember something. A vivid memory of standing there, in the doll's house, and looking down. Seeing the blood spattered across her dress, droplets up her arm. The red all over the hammer that was still clutched in her hand. And she could see his body sprawled on the floor, at her feet. And she knew that it wasn't a dream or a trick of the mind. It was a memory. A real memory of what had happened. She'd done it. She'd killed her stepfather.' Amanda winced at the painful memory of Alessia forcing herself to acknowledge a traumatic memory of what had happened that day. How painful it had been for her to absorb that she had committed the murder after all.

'And I remember how she told me that she'd felt as if she'd just woken up from a trance. That she wasn't properly coherent. That she had no idea what she'd done, or how she'd even got there. And part of her had been so sure, so certain that Sarah had been in the room with her. That she had been slumped in the corner of the room, crying. But when she looked down at the hammer in her hand, her stepfather on the floor, then back to Sarah, Sarah had gone. She'd disappeared as if she'd never been there at all. And Alessia never saw her again. And I think that was the first time that Alessia really accepted that maybe what everyone was telling her was true. That Sarah wasn't real. Don't get me wrong, she still fought it. She still tried to convince us that Sarah had been real. But something changed after that. It was as if she started questioning it too. As if sometimes she was almost trying to convince herself. That's how much she'd believed she had been real.' Amanda explained her theory slowly, because she knew that it would be a lot to take in.

'And I've been thinking, if her stepfather had drugged her,

then that would explain the confusion. The black outs. Maybe even the illusions. But what if it wasn't just the drugs that had clouded her head and made her incoherent?' Amanda said, gaining more certainty about what was going on the more she spoke.

'Last night she said that she'd found the article about her and the murder tucked away inside Jacob's book bag. She was convinced that Sarah had either been in her house or had been to Jacob's nursery. Either way, she'd got close. But Carl found the box of Alessia's things in her room, didn't he? There were articles in there. She must have put that article there, herself. Only she has no memory of doing it.' Amanda fell quiet. Allowing what she was getting at to sink in.

'So you think that the person Alessia is running from is herself?'

Amanda shook her head, her expression dark. 'No. What if Alessia isn't running at all? What if she isn't even aware that Jacob has been taken? What if she has no recollection of any of this happening at all? What if this is all Sarah? Alessia blamed Sarah for her own stepfather's murder. For throwing the brick through the window. For sending her the dead rat. What else is Sarah capable of? How far will she go? If Sarah is in control right now, then Alessia and Jacob are both in real danger.'

'Christ!' Harriet said as she finally understood the extent of how real Sarah could be. And the thought of anything happening to her friend, to Jacob, didn't even bear thinking about. She felt her tears as they threatened. Annoyed with herself for not remaining professional. For not staying focused. Because this was personal.

Alessia was her friend, and if Harriet wanted to help her then she needed to detach herself from that and stay focused. She needed to keep a clear head. She couldn't let her feelings and emotions get in the way of the job, not again. She needed to separate her friendship with Alessia and concentrate solely on finding her and Jacob and bringing them both home, safely.

'So that's the key then, to finding Alessia!' Harriet said,

focusing now. Fighting to keep her head back in work mode. 'We need to stop thinking like Alessia and start thinking like Sarah!'

Amanda nodded, agreeing with Harriet's reasoning. 'And the last place Alessia ever saw Sarah was at this doll's house place. Do you think it might still be there?' Harriet asked, hopeful that they might have a new lead. Something more solid to go on.

'I don't know. I guess it could be, yes,' Amanda said, trying to cast her mind back and be certain that the last time Alessia had been convinced that she'd seen Sarah had been there at the doll's house. It had been. Amanda recalled now how she'd described that last encounter so meticulously. So detailed and full of emotion for her 'friend' that even Amanda had questioned if perhaps Sarah could have possibly been real.

'It's been a long time. But from what I remember the woodlands behind her house had been a strip of wasteland tucked between the rows of properties. The workshop had stood derelict for years. The land may have been sold off since, it might have been torn down and replaced with a block of flats, for all I know...'

'But it might still be there?' Harriet said, determined as Amanda nodded her head in agreement, before she faltered.

'But I don't think Alessia would go back there. I don't think she would take Jacob there either. The doll's house wasn't just the last place Alessia had seen Sarah, it was also the place where the police found Alessia and her stepfather's body. It's the place where Alessia murdered him. It would be too much of a trigger for her to go back there. Especially when she's already so vulnerable.'

'A trigger for Alessia, but what about Sarah?' Harriet said, reminding Amanda that they might not be dealing with Alessia's persona here. If she was thinking like Sarah, and the doll's house was familiar to her, familiar to them both, maybe she had gone back there.

'And either way, I've got to take a look. It's not much to go on, but right now, it's pretty much all we've got,' Harriet said as she grabbed her keys. Happy to finally be of some use.

'I just hope whatever happens that when we do find her, she's okay.'

Amanda didn't reply. Because so far everything Alessia had done in the past twenty-four hours since she'd been back in Amanda's life had already proved to her that Alessia was anything but okay.

NOW

Her childhood home sat under complete darkness. The lights all off, and the curtains drawn. It had been almost a week since she was last there. The night of the anniversary. His anniversary.

He's dead. He can't hurt you any more.

She had been so annoyed at herself for coming back here. For finally giving in to her curiosity after all these years of blocking this place out. How she'd allowed herself to be wrenched back here. Still drawn by the pull the place had on her. Though it wasn't the house that had got the better of her. She knew that. It was what was in the woodlands behind it that had made her come back here.

The doll's house.

The house itself meant nothing to her. It held no real attachment to her. Though she had been shocked to see her childhood home's transformation. Because in her mind it had stood still in time. And she'd been expecting to see the same hovel of a place that she'd grown up in. Instead, the place had been almost unrecognisable.

And here she stood again, almost a week later, staring at the unfamiliar, new grey front door with the pretty stained-glass panels that ran down the middle. The two bay trees that stood tall in pots at each side. The garden neat and tidy. The grass recently cut and edged. The flowers and shrubs all in bloom, in the weed-free bed that ran underneath the front window.

The house looked as if was loved. Looked after. As if someone cared for it now.

She pursed her mouth, deep in thought. Last week. That had been the catalyst, hadn't it? Because that's when things had started to happen to her. Coming here again, had somehow opened up Pandora's box.

Because until then, she'd been doing just fine. Fully submerged in her new life. And she'd been happy. Genuinely. Probably for the very first time in her entire life.

But it was as if just coming here had triggered something that she'd thought she'd buried so deep inside of her that she'd never be able to reach again. Something so awful and frightening that she couldn't bear to face it. And now she was back here again for a second time. Only this time, she knew that she had no other choice. She needed to face her demons once and for all.

She shivered as she clutched Jacob tightly in her arms, knowing that she shouldn't have brought him here. But she hadn't been thinking straight. She hadn't been thinking at all, if she was honest. Because she wanted him near her. She wanted him close. She couldn't bear the thought of leaving him out of her sight. Not for even a second. Because Carl hadn't believed her when she told him that she thought she was in real danger. That Jacob might be in danger too.

It had only been the smallest of movements, a slight flicker of his eyes, the few seconds that he'd pulled his gaze from hers. And stared down at the floor. But she had seen it.

That trickle of doubt in his mind, it had shone out from his eyes. And she had known in that moment that Carl was just like the rest of them. That he didn't believe her. He didn't believe that Sarah was doing all of these things to her. He didn't believe in Sarah at all. And the only person he really thought that Alessia was in danger from was herself.

So, she had decided to take her fate into her own hands once again. She'd taken the car keys from where Carl had left them on the trolley inside the hospital cubicle, before she'd snuck outside into the carpark and had taken their car. Desperate to get to Jacob before they did. And Andrew had made it so easy for her. On his hands and knees in the spare room, with his back to the door. Too busy concentrating as he picked up the tiny specks of broken mirror that shone up at him from the carpet. The hoover still on, blaring loud, though it lay on the floor behind him. He hadn't heard a thing when Alessia had taken her chances and picked Jacob up from where he lay, out cold in his little bed. And she'd managed to sneak him out of the house before he woke up properly and made any real noise.

And now she was back here. And she was determined to face Sarah once and for all. Because Sarah would be here, Alessia was certain of it. She would be here waiting for her. And Alessia was finally ready to face her. Finally ready to face her demons.

She scanned the street and made sure that no one was watching her, as she held on to Jacob tightly and crept silently down the pathway that ran along the side of the house. Slowly, she pushed open the gate that led to the back garden, before she snuck inside. And once she was in, she kept to the shadows at the garden's edge. She prayed that if anyone was home, she wouldn't be seen. She eyed the netted trampoline and tricycle on the grass as she passed. Toys were scattered all over the patio. And she wondered if the young family that lived here now knew about the horrors that once happened here. She wondered what kind of family they were. And if they were happy here.

Her mother hadn't lived here for years. Alessia had found that out the hard way. That one time she'd come here when she'd finally been released from the mental health facility. She recalled how she'd geared herself up for an argument the whole way here on the bus. As she'd imagined her mother calling her names. Screaming and shouting and refusing to let her in. Or maybe she wouldn't react like that at all, she'd stupidly, naively thought. Maybe she'd be happy to see her again after all this time. A woman now, no longer a child. And maybe, finally, she'd feel something other than contempt for her, other than anger at Alessia tearing their family apart. Maybe just maybe, she'd finally take some of the blame. For the things she should have looked out for but claimed she hadn't seen. For the things she'd refused to believe had happened to her only daughter. But what had happened when she'd got here had been worse than any outcome Alessia could have envisaged.

The front door had been opened by a complete stranger, and she'd had to endure the humiliation of being told by someone she'd never met before that her mother no longer lived here. That she and her brother Bobby had both moved away. That they'd not left a forwarding address.

And Alessia didn't know why that had hurt so much. Seeing as she already knew how her mother felt. How she'd made that perfectly clear when she'd so publicly disowned her. When she'd called her a liar, and worse. When she'd insisted that Alessia go into foster care before the trial.

Alessia decided to change her name after that. On the bus on the way home. Deeply shaken at her mother's complete detachment from her. So brutal, so final. Alessia had known that day that she would have to make her own life for herself. And she had. And she wouldn't allow anyone to take that from her now.

Alessia reached the back fence and eyed the row of tall trees that lined the garden's border before she slipped inside the hedgerow. Soothing Jacob as she shielded his face and eyes with her hand as they felt the sharp, pointed branches poke and scratch at their limbs and faces.

'Ouch!' Jacob latched on a little tighter to her.

'It's okay, baby. Mummy's got you.' She was anxious as she swept her free hand along each crooked weathered panel, feeling her way for the gap in the fence. Worried all of a sudden that the gap in the fence might not be there any more. That the panels may have been replaced. That she might not be able to get through to the other side from here. And even if she did manage to get through, what if the doll house was gone? She didn't want to think about that. Because this was her only chance at seeing her again. Her only chance to end this. Her hand missed the next panel and fell through into the empty space. And she was almost relieved to have found it. Quick then, she squeezed through.

The woodland on the other side was dense and overgrown, and she winced in silence as she walked through the mass of brambles and stinging nettles that covered the ground beneath her trainers. The jagged thorns that scratched and tore at her skin. All the while she shielded Jacob with her arms, wrapping them tighter around him. She saw it then. In the distance ahead of her. The doll's house. So much smaller now than how she'd remembered. Or how her mind had painted it to her. A little cottage in the middle of the woods.

Now with clarity, she could see that it was nothing more than an old derelict workshop. With crumbling brickwork and boarded-up windows, the panes of glass missing. It stood in the middle of a large strip of wasteland nestled between the rows of streets.

'Mummy!' Jacob cried as he picked up on the tension from his mother. As he felt her body go rigid. As she'd unwittingly squeezed him to her even tighter.

'I want to go home,' he whimpered. Scared now.

'It's okay, baby. Mummy's here. It's going to be okay,' she said, though she had no intention of going home yet. Instead, she continued to walk. Her body shook as she made her way towards the abandoned building just ahead of her.

As she reached the doorway, she faltered. Her eyes on the greying brickwork and the mass of cobwebs spun across the door-way's entrance. She knew that once she stepped inside, there would be no going back. That she'd finally get her answers. She'd see Sarah. And she'd have her moment of reckoning. That this was the only way to stop her.

'Mummy!' Jacob cried out again as his little fingers dug into the flesh of her shoulders, as if he was trying to pull her away. Back from the house. To keep her from going inside. But it was already too late. She could hear her inside. She could hear that familiar sing-song voice of hers.

'It's raining. It's pouring. The old man is snoring. He bumped his head when he fell out of bed and he couldn't get up in the morning.'

The sound was faint. Very quiet. But it was her. She was sure of it.

'Can you hear her, Jacob? Can you hear Sarah singing?' Alessia asked as she searched Jacob's eyes through the darkness for some kind of recognition. Jacob shook his head, his mouth a stubborn pout.

And she was sure that he was just being wilful. That he could hear her really, but he was being difficult. Because he wanted her to take him home. Only she couldn't go back just yet.

'Sarah?' Alessia called out as she stepped inside the small building.

The floor creaked underfoot, and her eyes strained to focus through the pitch-black darkness. But she could just about make out the outline of the room from the small slither of light that followed her inside, from the open doorway behind her. Two small compact rooms. A workshop and a shed? Not a cottage at all? But it was the same place, wasn't it? It must be. And she recognised the narrow crumbling chimney breast on the back wall. And instantly she felt as if she'd been transported back to the day that Sarah had found the bird's nest. And then the doll. And the child's tooth that had sparkled from where it lay on the floor as the light had hit its shiny enamel. She remembered how she'd twiddled her own teeth afterwards to check that she hadn't lost one without realising it. It hadn't been one of hers, had it? And she couldn't remember what she had done with it. Where did she leave the doll? Her head felt fuzzy, her thoughts clouding.

'It's raining, it's pouring...'

None of it was real, Emma-Jayne. Sarah isn't real. It was your brain's way of protecting yourself.

Amanda's words came to the forefront of Alessia's mind. And

she shook them away. Because it all felt so real. Being here. With her.

Tiptoeing over to the fireplace she bent down and placed Jacob carefully on the edge of her knee as she balanced. Before she closed her eyes, for just a few seconds, so that she could shut the rest of the world out. She breathed in Jacob's smell as if for strength. As if to remind herself how far she'd come since then. Of how much she had to lose. And she willed herself then to remember what really happened on that fateful day. Allowing thoughts of him inside her head, she summoned him to her.

THEN

His face is a bright, puce red and it is just inches from hers now. A string of spittle trails from his lips, his spit landing on her face as he shouts at her.

Why is he so angry? She stares down at the floor. To where the doll lies between them. Her mother had mentioned it at dinner that evening. How she'd found the ugly doll, tucked down beside Emma-Jayne's bed. Though she hadn't mentioned the cuts and scratches all up Emma-Jayne's legs.

And Emma-Jayne had been grateful for that. And Robert hadn't reacted initially. He'd looked disinterested, as if he hadn't even heard her mother. Continuing to eat his dinner in silence. And she thought that she'd got away with it. Until he'd glanced up at her, just once, the look fleeting, just enough to tell her that he had heard. That he was paying attention. And that she would be made to pay for taking the doll later.

———

And later was now. Her mother left for work this evening, and he brought her out here, to the doll's house. The place where she'd found it. He tells her he is going to teach her a lesson. For taking things that don't belong to her. And she isn't sure what possesses her but she shouts back at him. That the doll doesn't belong to him either. That he can't just snatch it away from her.

'It's hers. The doll belongs to Sarah.'

And it startles her how shocked he looks. How she's rendered him completely speechless. As if her words are fists and she has just punched him. Making the air swiftly leave his body. How his eyes widen in shock at hearing Sarah's name. As if he wonders how she knew that. And she sees something else there, too, something that disappears as quickly as it flashed behind his eyes. Fear.

Though he tried to hide it. His panic, the way he starts acting frantic and crazy. Telling her that he's going to teach her a lesson for taking it, that it doesn't belong to her as he snatches the doll from where it lies between them, discarded on the floor like nothing more than rubbish. Grabbing it by its legs to throw it back inside the fireplace. A triumphant look in his eyes as he picks up a piece of wood and props it against the fireplace's opening. And Emma-Jayne watches him as he crouches down. And she understands what he intends to do. He's taking it from her, boarding it up inside the fireplace, as if attempting to keep the doll hidden from sight forever.

She eyes the hammer and small pile of nails on the floor beside him. And fuelled by the look of fear that spreads across his face. The injustice and the horror that she felt for Sarah. The hate she felt for him, she picks it up.

Crack!

The first hit floors him as the weighted head of the hammer smashes into his skull.

But it's the look of sheer surprise that flashes across his face that startles her the most. Because it's only then she realises the power that, for once, she possesses over him. Power in this one moment, these few seconds that she isn't going to waste. So she hits him again. Over and over, only she can't remember exactly how many times because it feels as if she must have blacked out.

And when she comes to, there are trails of blood splattered all over the floor, sprayed all up the wall, and his lifeless body is lying at her feet.

Emma-Jayne steps over him. Unfeeling. Uncaring. Glad that he is dead.

She bends down and picks up the doll.

NOW

Harriet glanced down at her phone as she made her way through the busy evening throng of London traffic, as she debated whether or not she should take the call as Rufus's name flashed up. It was the second time he'd called her in the space of five minutes. About to decline the call for the second time, she decided against it.

'Rufus! To what do I owe the pleasure?' she said smiling, her tone purposely laced with playful sarcasm. 'Don't tell me you're back on shift already?'

She glanced at the clock on her dash and realised how late it was. That her own shift, had she done it, would have finished over an hour ago. Which meant that a call from her colleague wasn't a good sign. It also meant that Alessia and Jacob had been gone for hours now too.

'Yeah, like you said, time flies when you're having fun. I managed a few hours' kip and a couple of games on the PlayStation,' Rufus said; his voice sounded full of regret that he'd been dragged away for something as mundane as actual work. 'Didn't manage to get myself that pizza though. Been craving it since I woke up. That's your fault. I might have to grab something when I'm out on patrol later. I take it you're still out looking for your friend?' he asked, having started his shift to be told about Harriet's friend going missing along with her young child. He knew that his colleague wouldn't be going anywhere until she found them.

'I'm just on my way to check something out... It could be nothing but...' Harriet said, before she paused. Not willing to divulge much more than that. Because she hadn't even told her superiors where she was going. On the off chance that Amanda was right and Harriet might find Alessia here, alone. She could talk to her. She could make her see sense. Make her bring Jacob home. And she was so close now.

She spotted the road sign ahead that only fifteen minutes earlier she'd tapped into her sat nav on her phone, having bypassed the patrol car's own one for fear of reprisals for coming here alone. The street name that Amanda had recited to her. The street where Alessia's childhood home stood.

'Well, I thought you'd want to know,' Rufus said, sensing Harriet's discomfort in her tone and not wanting her to think that he was calling her purposely to pry. 'That number plate you ran by me the other day, I know you said it would be a long shot, running the partial of the plate through the system to see if it throws anything up, but as it turns out, it has.'

'Go on,' Harriet said, not holding out much hope for it to come to much.

'Turns out that someone else reported an incident on the same day, involving a similar looking car driving recklessly. Only, they managed to get the full reg. So, I've managed to get a read on the plates and get some intel for you.'

'You did?' Harriet realised how doubtful she must have sounded. As if she almost hadn't believed that they'd get any result back from the plates. As if she'd half suspected that Alessia had made them up. Because in all honesty, she had begun to question if that car had even existed at all. And she had been worried that she was just wasting her colleagues' time, if everything that Amanda had told her about Alessia was true, that Alessia was doing all of this to herself. That she was channelling 'Sarah'. Which meant there wouldn't be another car. Except Rufus was saying that there was.

'It's hot. The plates belong to a white Vauxhall Mokka, and it was reported stolen by the registered keeper the same day that you asked me to run the plates through the system. In the morning.'

Harriet nodded her head at this information. Aware that Rufus couldn't hear her, but she knew if she tried to speak no sound would leave her mouth. The car chase had been real. Somebody really had tried to run Alessia off the road. But who?

'I also managed to pull some CCTV footage from a camera on West Park Road. The Vauxhall was tailing a blue Audi Q3, registered to Carl Hadley.'

Harriet bit down on her lip. Alessia had been telling the truth.

'The footage is a bit grainy but from what I could see the driver in the Vauxhall was all over the road. Driving erratically. Swerving. And it looks like they were intentionally tailing the Q3 for a while before they purposely tried to run it off the road.'

'Good work!' Harriet said. She was almost at the address now. Slowing her car as she made her way along the street, she could see the house number she was looking for just up ahead of her. Except now that she had this new information, she had no idea what to expect when she got there. Or who.

'Thanks for letting me know, Rufus,' Harriet said, grateful that her colleague was looking out for her, that he was trying to help.

'Do you want me to send the footage over to Tech Support and see if we can get an image of the Vauxhall driver? It's not the greatest of images and it might come to nothing, but it's always worth a shot.'

'Yes. Tell them to push it through. Tell them it's urgent,' Harriet agreed as she parked the car and stared at the blue Audi Q3 parked further up the road.

Amanda's hunch was right. Alessia was here.

'Shit!' She got out of her vehicle and saw another car further up.

A white Vauxhall Mokka. It looked as if had been abandoned

at the side of the road. One of the front wheels was up on the kerb, the back of the vehicle jutted out into the road.

'Rufus?' She made her way towards the car, so that she could get a better look at the number plate. 'That number plate that I asked you to run through the system, can you remind me of it again?'

'Sure. GU15...'

Harriet read the numbers of the plate silently inside her head, in time with him. His voice fading as he read the last few numbers out.

'It's here,' she muttered quietly, but not quietly enough.

'Harriet?' Rufus said as the line went silent. 'You still there?'

Harriet nodded again before she quicky replaced the gesture with her voice. A sense of urgency to her tone, laced with something else. A raw panic.

'Yes, I'm still here. And you're not going to believe this, Rufus, but I've just found the car. The white Vauxhall. I'm standing right next to it.'

'You are? No way! Bloody hell! What are the chances!' Rufus sounded impressed.

'Yeah, what are the chances?!' Harriet muttered to herself as she took in the crumpled bumper on the front of the car, the scrape of blue paint across it.

That was definitely the same car that had tried to run Alessia off the road. Which meant the person driving it must be somewhere around here too. Which wasn't a good sign at all.

'Rufus, I'm going to need you to put a call in to the sergeant and for you to give him my location. I'm going to need some backup here, and fast.' Harriet reeled off the same address that Amanda had given her. She couldn't do this alone. 'I'm going to be in the woodlands directly at the back of the property. I should be able to gain access from the back garden.'

'Can you wait until I can get a patrol car to you?' Rufus said, but Harriet was already running.

She ran as fast as she could, back up the street, towards the house. Bypassing the front door and the tenants inside to ask for permission to gain access through their garden. There was no time for that. And all she could feel was the sinking feeling of dread that formed inside her stomach.

'Harriet? Can you wait until I can get a unit to you?'

'No. I need to get to her. I think Alessia might be here, and I think whoever has been stalking her might be here too. I think she could be in real danger.'

NOW

Jacob was crying. His little sobs made his whole body shake against hers. Because he didn't want to be here. In this dark, damp, scary place. With her while she searched for a ghost that she knew no longer existed. All those awful, harrowing things that happened within these four walls. It was as if coming back here, being here now, had jolted something awake again inside of her. All those bad things that she'd pushed so far down, that she hadn't been able to reach. But she could reach them now. She could remember it all. Every single last detail.

She needed to get out of here. To get Jacob back home. She would speak to Amanda. She would tell her the truth, all of it this time. Finally. And Harriet, she would help her. She would believe her. Alessia was certain now.

'I'm sorry, baby! Mummy shouldn't have brought you here. Let's go home!' Alessia said as she kissed Jacob on his forehead and turned to leave. And it was only then that she saw the mound on the floor.

His body. And the sight of it physically floored her. No! How could he still be here now, after all these years? She sank down onto her knees as if she was in a trance. Before she placed Jacob down on the floor next to her. And she could hear him cry louder, but she couldn't comfort him. Because the room was spinning violently. The walls were closing in.

'You're not real. You're not here.' She felt physically sick as her mouth filled with a hot burning bile which she forced herself to swallow back down.

And when she looked again, she was instantly filled with relief. Almost euphoric with laughter as she realised the mound she saw in front of her was in fact a sleeping bag.

Stupid, stupid woman, she thought, mocking herself. How had she possibly thought that it might be him? Robert. Sprawled out on the floor. Dead. Right there in the very spot where she'd killed him. Only her relief was short-lived as her eyes went to a cup of water next to it. Nearby, a can of baked beans, half empty, with a plastic fork sticking out of it. As if whoever had been eating it had suddenly been disturbed.

Someone had been here. Sleeping here. Living in the damp, dark squalor. And she was overcome with a feeling, an overwhelming need to leave. The air suddenly electric, full of danger and malice. She turned to pick up Jacob. Realising then that his crying was quieter. And he was not there. No longer on the floor beside her.

And she felt the jolt of panic rip through her.

'Jacob?' she called out. 'Jacob!'

And then she heard the sudden noise in the other room. A clang, then footsteps. Bigger than Jacob's. And she realised that she wasn't alone.

NOW

He stepped forward.

In his arms he held a sobbing Jacob.

'Mummy!' Jacob called out.

And Alessia wanted to go to him. To grab him. But there was something about the strange man's stance that stopped her in her tracks. And she saw him as he gripped Jacob, holding on to him tighter. He was taunting her. Challenging her to dare step forward and claim her child. And at first, Alessia didn't recognise him. Not fully.

The green beanie hat he wore sat just above his eyebrows. Tufts of brown hair poked out from its edges. His facial hair was long and scruffy looking. Unkempt, just like the ragged, soiled clothes that he was wearing. But there was something about his eyes, something familiar about the way he looked at her. It couldn't be?

'Bobby? Is that you?' Alessia whispered. Her voice thick with emotion that until that very moment she hadn't thought she'd ever be capable of feeling. And yet her words crept out so quietly from her mouth, almost as if she couldn't quite believe he was really here. Standing in front of her. Almost as if she was frightened that if she said his name too loudly, she might break the spell and he might disappear.

'Mummy...' Jacob called out again, and she heard the fear in his voice at this stranger holding him. Keeping him from her.

'It's okay, Jacob,' Alessia said as she wondered if perhaps that was true – that it really might be all right. Because this was Bobby. Bobby, her baby brother. And she felt something like a connection as it swelled inside her stomach.

It was then that she saw the sneer on Bobby's face as his eyes flashed with something that looked a lot like hate.

'Hey mate, calm down. I'm your uncle Bobby. Or did Mummy not tell you about me? I guess she didn't!' Bobby spat the word *uncle* as if he was allergic to the taste of the word in his mouth. 'I guess I wouldn't fit the narrative of your fake as fuck new life, huh Emma-Jayne.'

Alessia held her breath, winded. Unable to speak. She wondered how much Bobby thought he knew about her life. And she realised that this wasn't a coincidence. Him being here. His sleeping bag strewn across the floor. He'd been staying here, yes. While he had tormented her.

It was Bobby. He had done all those things to her. He'd followed her, threatened her.

'It's okay, baby! Mummy is here.' Alessia directed her comment at Jacob as she fought the natural instinct inside to run to him. To claim her child. To protect him. Then she looked at Bobby. Those steely green eyes of his. His mouth twisted into a crooked grimace.

'It was you, wasn't it?' And she felt it. She was aware of Bobby's stance. Of something in his expression that told her not to step any closer. That she wasn't safe. Jacob was not safe. An air of danger crackled like electricity all around them.

'Please, Bobby. Jacob's scared. Give him to me.'

'Oh, I'm sorry. Are you scared, are you little buddy?' Bobby laughed bitterly before he nodded down at Jacob without any form of affection.

Yet he didn't make any attempt to do as she asked him, and she knew that this was what he wanted. To taunt her still. To use Jacob like a pawn, purposely just to get to her. And it was working.

'Please? He is your nephew, Bobby. His name is Jacob. Look at him, Bobby, he's frightened,' Alessia said quietly. Wanting to plant the connection in Bobby's mind, that he and Jacob were blood. That Jacob was innocent in all of this. But Bobby remained detached. Acting as if he didn't even hear her. Not interested in Jacob's fear.

His gaze was firmly fixed on her, and she could feel the malice shining out from his steely glare.

'I wouldn't have recognised you, Bobby. You've changed so much,' Alessia tried to pacify him. Tried to get through to him. To remind him of the people they used to be. Just kids. None of what had happened was either of their fault. And Bobby had been too young to know anything that had gone on back then. Except she felt the hate he had for her as it physically poured from him. They were nothing but strangers now. She needed to make him feel the connection. Make him realise she was not his enemy.

'My goofy little brother, who used to sit glued to his cartoons. Who used to ask me to read you all those bedtime stories...'

'But you didn't read to me!' Bobby scoffed. 'You didn't even like me!'

'No, Bobby, that's not true,' she said with thinly veiled hope that Bobby wouldn't have remembered any of that. He'd been too young.

He wouldn't know how she'd tried so hard to ignore him from the day he'd been born. How she'd always felt so insanely jealous of him. Because *he* hadn't touched Bobby. He'd left him alone. And deep down she had been wrong to hate Bobby, but she had been so confused and broken. Just a child herself. She had aimed all her hurt and anger at the wrong person. She knew that now. Blaming Bobby for coming along and ruining her family, when all the time it had only ever been Robert who had done that.

'She told you that, didn't she?' Alessia said. Guessing rightly when Bobby didn't answer. That their mother had done her best to poison him against her in their time apart. Just as she'd always expected she would. 'That wasn't what happened. It wasn't like that... There was more to it. It was never about you. Not really.'

'And you expect me to believe you? Ha! You were always good at making up stories, weren't you Emma-Jayne?' Bobby retorted, cutting her dead. 'You know, I thought that you'd figure it all out!' Bobby spat as he shook his head. His expression sad. Full of disappointment that she hadn't worked it out. That he clearly hadn't even crossed her mind.

'I thought you'd realise that it was me. But you still thought it was her, didn't you?!' Bobby laughed, but his twisted smirk didn't meet his eyes. 'I heard you call her name out. "Sarah, Oh, Sarah,"' he mimicked. 'You're still a mad bitch, Emma-Jayne! What are you? Thirty-two now and you're still searching for you imaginary friend? And what am I? Irrelevant? Insignificant? Because you had no clue, did you? I bet you haven't given me a single second's thought in all these years.'

Alessia didn't answer. Because she didn't trust herself to speak. Because he was right in a way. She hadn't thought of him. Not once. But not for the reasons he thought. She'd had no choice but to block him out. In order to move on. In order to make some kind of life from the charred ashes of what had been left of her old one. Like so many other things from her past, from her life, she'd had to leave him behind.

'Do you know how many times I thought of *you* over the years? I used to wonder what I would say to you, if I ever saw you again. I used to wonder if I'd even know what you looked like now. Only I recognised you right away. When I saw you last week. Pushing your kid in a pushchair, and standing so gormlessly out in the street, staring at our old house. A look on your face as if you were the victim. The house that you made us give up. The lives you ruined.'

Alessia held her breath. Caught off guard by his venom. By the raw hatred that he felt towards her. And now she knew how he'd found her. That night she had come here. On the anniversary. He had seen her. He had followed her home. That had been the night it had all started. The night the brick had been thrown through her window.

'I watched you as you bent down and kissed him,' Bobby said as he nodded down at Jacob as if he was contagious. 'You said something and he giggled.' Bobby shook his head. 'And in that moment, I've never hated you more. Because look at you? *Look at you*. You moved on. You made a new life. And you looked happy. Are you fucking happy, Emma-Jayne?'

She stared at Jacob as he started to cry. His arms outstretched as he reached for her. His terrified eyes boring into his mother's, as if he was silently pleading with her to take him. But Alessia knew she couldn't. Not yet.

'And here I was, hiding in the shadows. Like some weirdo not wanting to be seen. Watching you. This is where I've been living, here, Emma-Jayne. Like a tramp,' he shouted before he kicked the half-empty tin can across the room. 'Laying my head down to sleep each night on the same dirty bloodstained floor where my dad took his last breath. How sad is that? That I have nowhere to call home. That here, this place was the only place that I could think of where I could get my head down and be guaranteed to be left alone. Because do you know what they do to you if you sleep rough in some shop doorway, Emma-Jayne? Random groups of drunken lads. They dare each other to piss on you, and sometimes they beat the shit out of you, just because. For kicks. Imagine that. Beating the crap out of someone already down on their luck and who has lost everything. And the irony, huh, that I would choose staying here over that. That I actually deemed this place safer. This place!' Bobby shouted now. His voice shook, and a trail of snot dripped down from his nose, which he quickly wiped away with his sleeve.

And Alessia could see that Bobby was caught up with raw emotion, and that he didn't want to share that with her. How vulnerable he was. She watched as he looked down at the floor and tried to conceal the fact that he was crying openly.

'We've come full circle, haven't we? Because it was right here, in this room, we last saw each other. Do you remember, Emma-Jayne?' Bobby said as he took a long, deep breath.

Alessia nodded sadly. She did, of course she remembered. The last time she saw him would forever be imprinted on her brain. Bobby, just a little boy. Just a little older than Jacob was now.

How he'd looked so angelic. Little chubby cheeks. His piercing green eyes, wide. As he'd hovered just there in the doorway. Looking down at his father's bludgeoned face and body. As he tried to make sense of what he was seeing. A look of horror on his face as he realised what Alessia had done. It had been his screams that had woken her from her trancelike state.

'And the rats? You must remember the rats?' Bobby said, triumphant that he'd sent her such a personal gift. He held on to Jacob a little tighter in his arms as the child tried his hardest to squirm to get away.

And Alessia felt distraught that she couldn't get to her son when he needed her so badly. And she didn't want to talk about the rats, not here. And Bobby would know that: he was enjoying all of this, she realised.

'I've had nightmares about it for years, so you must have too.' Bobby's voice was thick with emotion. His eyes watering as he recalled the scene that had scarred him for life. 'Him lying there dead on the floor, the rats crawling over his body. And you just standing there with that stupid look on your face. Telling lies. Saying that you didn't do it, that it was Sarah!'

'Bobby... I wasn't lying, I was confused...'

'Oh you were confused, all right. Because my father didn't do any of those things, Emma-Jayne. He didn't do any of those disgusting things that you said he did. Because Mum told me, she told me that you were a liar. That you were jealous of them having me. That you made it all up. Like you used to make everything up.'

'I didn't, Bobby, please, you have to believe me. I was sick...'

'Sick in the head,' he spat.

Alessia nodded. 'Yes. I was exactly that. I had suffered years of abuse, Bobby. And I was unwell. Mentally unwell. But I didn't make things up. Not really. My reality was distorted because of the trauma. I was confused and I blocked things out in order to survive. And I know how hard it will be for you to understand any of that, because trust me, I went through it all and some of it I still don't understand. Not really. But I know that I buried things that had happened so deep inside of me that I couldn't reach them again. Until now. Until today. Until I finally came back here,' Alessia said. And she meant it. She was certain now that she finally knew the truth.

She remembered it all, clearly.

'Bobby, I know you won't believe me but I didn't mean to kill him. I just wanted to make it stop. I just wanted to make it all stop. The lies. The abuse. The hurt. I was just a child, Bobby. I was just twelve years old. And I was scared.'

Bobby shook his head.

'She said...'

'She's a liar, Bobby!'

'She's dead.'

They were both silent then. And it was Bobby who finally broke the silence and spoke first.

'Did you know that? She drank herself to death in the end,' Bobby added bluntly.

She knew that he was guessing by her reaction that she didn't know. That he wanted his words to cut through her like a knife. And they did. He saw it.

She remained silent. For a few seconds as she shifted awkwardly on her feet as if weighed down by the enormity of what he'd told her. To let it sink in. Her mother was dead. She had gone to her grave without ever making things right with her. Without ever acknowledging or believing what her own daughter had said had been true. And that was the only bit that hurt. Not the physical loss of her life. Because Alessia had grieved for the loss of her mother a long time ago.

'We moved around so much, but people still found out about us. About Dad. And as I got older, I became a target. The kids at school used to bully me. They said that I was just like him. The paedo's son, they called me. And they waited for me after school. They'd beat the shit out of me. Once, so badly that I had my arm broken in two places. And when I got home, she was so drunk that she couldn't even stand up. She couldn't even string a sentence together. I had to go to the hospital on my own. I gave up school shortly after that. What was the point? I gave up on everything. I sat at home and watched her rot. I watched her slowly turn to nothing. And now she's gone. And I was left with nothing.' Bobby paused, the memory too much for him.

'That was my life, Emma-Jayne. And you'd done that. You'd destroyed everything. And when I saw you that night, standing outside on the street, staring at our old house. With a child of your own. How you looked at him with such love. I wanted you to pay. I wanted you to suffer, just as I had. I wanted you to feel just a little how I had felt over the years. Scared. Unsafe. Not able to trust anyone.'

Alessia watched as Jacob squirmed again and kicked out this time. The force of the blows leaving Bobby no choice but to put him down. And Alessia could see that Bobby was done with holding her son. But he'd got no plans on giving him back to her yet either.

'Sit there and don't fucking move!' Bobby yelled at him, forcing Jacob into the corner, to huddle into the sleeping bag, before he pulled something out from where it was hidden underneath.

And it was only then that Alessia saw the hammer in Bobby's hand.

NOW

Bobby stood in the very same spot that he'd stood before. Back then. Standing right there as he blocked the doorway. And there was a glint in his eye that mirrored his father before him. And she felt it. The anger and rage he felt towards her, so pent up that it spilled over. The hammer hung loosely at his side, his fingers locked around it. And he stared at her, as he challenged her now, as he willed her to step forward. To try and claim Jacob.

This is Bobby, she thought. Her baby brother Bobby. He'd not been much older than Jacob when it had all happened, a year or so. Four or five years old.

And Jacob didn't understand what was going on. How could he? His cries grew louder as he shuffled forward and called out for Alessia to come to him. And Bobby screamed at him then.

'Don't you move. Don't you fucking move!' He held the hammer up above his head. Threatening Jacob, and Jacob, unable to stop himself, screamed out with fear.

And Alessia felt weightless suddenly. As Jacob cowered, oh so tiny, there in the corner of the room. As he pushed his little body up against the wall in a bid to get away from the bad man. And she felt as if she'd been here before. As if she'd seen this all before.

Her vision blurred. And Jacob's blond hair melted away and

for a few short seconds her son was replaced with what looked like a little girl. Her poker-straight brown hair. Her goofy crooked smile. But she wasn't smiling now. She was cowering in the corner. Sick all down her dress. All over the floor.

And as quickly as the vision came to her, it was gone. Alessia shook her head. She wasn't going to let that happen. She wasn't going to let anything happen to Jacob. Because she knew better than anyone how quickly these things could happen. How one strike, one hit could change everything. The butterfly effect. She ran. Without so much as another thought. Her mind was only on Jacob. She lunged at Bobby just as he realised what she was doing.

The hammer in his hand swung through the air towards her.

Smack!

The pain that radiated through her as it smashed against her bandaged arm was indescribable. Immobilising. The strike slammed her down onto the cold, concrete floor. She felt her ankle buckle under the pressure. And he was on her then. The weight of him pinned her there. She waited for another blow. Braced herself for the impact. As she imagined for a second how it would feel to be bludgeoned to death. Only Bobby loosened his grip on the hammer and dropped it down on the floor next to him. Before he wrapped his hands around her throat instead. So that he could throttle her.

And Alessia could hear the sound of Jacob as he sobbed nearby. The thought of him as he watched all of this. His mother having the air squeezed out of her, being murdered in front of him, willed her to fight back. She wouldn't let that happen. To her or to him. She needed to fight. She couldn't let Bobby win. She could not die here, not like this. She clawed wildly at Bobby's eyes, frantic then like a wild animal making its bid to escape. Digging her nails into his sockets. And in a bid to stop her, to protect his face, Bobby screamed out loudly, before he quickly rolled off her. Shielding his face.

And it was the few seconds that Alessia needed.

She pulled herself across the floor. Unable to stand, she

grabbed Jacob roughly by the arm and pushed him towards the doorway.

'Go, Jacob. GO, NOW!' Alessia instructed her son. But he faltered. As if he wondered why he had to go alone. Why she's wasn't going with him. Because he didn't understand that she was hurt and that there was no time. That she might not make it out of here, but she would do her damnedest to make sure that she saved him first. No matter what.

'Go!' she screamed. And Jacob did as she told him. He ran. Just making it out seconds before Bobby was back up on his feet.

He gathered himself as he slowly stood. His face distorted and twisted with rage. And she knew that she had no other choice but to stand and face him. She scampered to her feet. The heat of the pain radiated through her. But she couldn't just lie there like a dying dog on the floor.

Bobby didn't move. He didn't dare take a step. Because Alessia had the hammer now. She held it high above her head, aimed it at him: a warning. She'd done it once before and, if she needed to, she'd do it again. They both knew that.

Outside, Alessia heard a familiar voice. It was Harriet. She was comforting Jacob. She was telling him that everything was going to be okay. And Alessia wanted more than anything for her friend's words to be true. She wanted this all to stop, for good this time. But it had already gone too far and it wouldn't stop until she made it.

'I am not a bad person, Bobby. I killed him to protect myself. And if you take another step towards me, so help me God, I will kill you too. Because unlike her, our dear mother, I will do whatever it takes to protect my child.' Alessia was in tears. How had it come to this? Both her parents were dead, but their memory lived on. And it was slowly destroying what was left of them. Her and Bobby.

'She was a liar, Bobby. Our mother knew about the abuse. She made out that she didn't believe it, that she couldn't possibly believe it. And she took that to her grave. Because if she admitted she already knew, that I'd tried to tell her, then that would make her complicit.' Alessia saw Bobby falter as he registered what she was saying. But there was still an element of doubt to his expression as his face creased up. Or was that just pain? She wasn't sure. But she had to keep trying.

'She was the one who found the doll down beside my bed. It was the same day she'd caught me skiving off school. I couldn't face it. All of it. I had wanted to end my life. I wanted to end it all. And she'd pulled the covers back and seen what I'd done to my legs. How I'd sliced them to pieces with a jagged bit of glass I'd taken from here.' She opened her arms and indicated the room they both stood in. 'I don't think I really did ever want to die. I just wanted it to stop. It was all just a cry for help. And I saw the shock register on her face when I tried to tell her. About the bad things that *he* did to me. But it was so quick, so fleeting. It was as if her eyes just clouded over. She simply shut me down. She chose not to believe me.'

Alessia searched Bobby's face for empathy, for understanding. Yet still, she saw none.

'She tried to take the doll from me, but I pleaded with her. I begged her. I told her it belonged to Sarah and it was as if my words lit a fire of rage inside of her. She just lost it then. Snatching the doll from me. Screaming at me that I was a liar. That I made everything up. The abuse. Sarah. That none of it was real and that I was an attention seeker and I was trying to ruin her life. Ruin all of our lives.'

Alessia knew that her mother had taken these very thoughts to the grave with her. That these were the things she'd fed to Bobby all these years. It was no wonder he'd grown to despise her.

'She took the doll from me and threw it in the bin. And that was how Robert had found it. That's how he knew that I had taken it. From here. And he wanted to punish me.

'She knew that it was true, Bobby. She knew all along yet she had to stick to her story. And in doing so, she poisoned you against me, Bobby. She fed you her lies and made you believe that I made it all up too. But I promise you I didn't. He did those things to me.

She might have died from the drink, but it was the guilt that got to her in the end. Because she knew.'

And Bobby was crying then. Overcome with emotion, he sank down to the floor and sobbed loudly.

And Alessia knew that he believed her. That deep down he knew that she was telling him the truth. That his whole life he'd been used, caught up in this sick, disgusting lie simply to unburden his mother of her own guilt.

'Alessia?' Harriet's voice called out as she stepped into the rickety old workshop and shone her torch ahead of her, taking in the carnage of the room. A man crouched on the floor as he held his face, as if in pain. Alessia still holding the hammer high over her head.

'Alessia, put it down. Please,' Harriet instructed her.

'You don't need to ask me to do that, Harriet.' Alessia nodded, then she crouched down and placed the hammer down on the floor in front of her. Just like she was always going to do. Now she knew that Jacob was safe.

'I never wanted to hurt you, Bobby,' she said, sadly. 'And I wouldn't have unless you made me. I was just doing what any good mother would do, what our mother should have done for me. I was protecting my child.'

NOW

'The dogs haven't come back with anything and it's getting late,' one of the dedicated dog handlers said as they called the dogs back in before they walked them over to the Incident Response Vehicle and placed them inside the back of the van. It had been twenty-four hours since Alessia had told them that she believed a child had been murdered here at the old, abandoned workshop. So far, they'd searched the premises and the overgrown strip of woodland that stood between the rows of houses without any luck. And Harriet could sense that her colleagues' optimism on finding something here was fast wavering. Because all they had to go on at the moment was Alessia's word that a child had been killed here, where Robert Griffin had been murdered. And so far, Alessia's information wasn't paying off.

But Harriet believed her. She was convinced that Alessia was telling them the truth. She'd seen her distress. The way that she'd crumpled completely when she finally said it out loud. The one thing she'd known all this time. That Robert Griffin had brought another child here, and he had murdered her. Which had been why he'd reacted so badly to Alessia taking the doll in the first place. Because it was evidence that another child had been here. That another child existed. Evidence that linked Robert to her.

Alessia believed that she had woken up from what she was sure now must have been a drug-induced stupor. Barely coherent, she'd known that she wasn't the only child in the workshop. That another girl was crouched on the floor. And that she was sick. Really sick. And Robert was panicking. Because the child wouldn't stop crying and there had been sick everywhere. And Alessia had kept slipping in and out of consciousness after that. But when she awoke, the crying had stopped. And Alessia had told Harriet that had been the most frightening sound of all. That she knew then the child was gone.

And if it was true, if Robert had killed another child, then the likelihood was that he would have buried her body nearby. Wanting to hide all traces of his crime.

'What do you think, Sarge?' Harriet looked at her sergeant and took in the stony look on his face as she tried to read his thoughts. Because she knew that he had taken a risk here. Throwing in time, money and resources purely on her say-so. If he thought the search was futile, he could put a stop to the investigation at any minute.

'Maybe too much time has passed, and the dogs can't locate a scent. Let's try the ground-penetrating radar.'

Harriet nodded gratefully at his instruction, full of gratitude that he, like her, was not willing to give up so soon in the search for a missing child. If there was a makeshift gravesite somewhere here, then they both knew that GPR was their best chance at finding it. She stood in patient silence while her colleagues expertly set up. And she knew that they wouldn't have to wait long now. They'd get their answer soon. The vibration of her phone in her pocket pulled her from her trance, and she saw Rufus's name as it flashed up on the screen.

'This is becoming a habit, Rufus,' she said, full of hope that the reason he was calling her back so quickly was to give her some news. 'Don't tell me you've got something already?'

'I have indeed!' Rufus said, and Harriet could sense that he was smiling at her down the phone. 'We got the forensic results for that doll back. They rushed them through, just as you asked.'

'Already? One day has to be an all-time record!' Harriet said, impressed. Glad that something seemed to be going right today.

'I've emailed you the full detailed report. The pathologist said that the doll itself didn't contain much in the way of anything conclusive, but we struck gold with the child's tooth that had been concealed in the pocket of the doll's dress.'

Harriet held her breath. She needed this. She needed something conclusive. Something solid. So that her sergeant wouldn't give up. So that they'd have more time. And more than that, Alessia needed this too.

'We've got a match,' Rufus said, his tone quickly changing to something sounding almost sympathetic. Sad. 'The DNA that we've managed to collect from the tooth ties in completely with the information that Alessia gave you. The remains of the child we are looking for is ten-year-old, Sarah Benedict. She went missing from a park over in Barking in October 1997. There was an extensive search for her, but her body was never recovered. Her case remains to this day unsolved.'

Harriet felt the heaviness of her colleague's words. They hung in the silence between them for a few seconds as she let this news sink in. Sarah was real. She felt her tears fill her eyes. Because now they knew for certain that their search wasn't futile. They were no longer just trawling the woodlands searching through weeds and mud in the hope of finding something. They were searching for Sarah Benedict. A ten-year-old girl who was left buried in a shallow grave for over twenty years. They were searching on behalf of a family out there somewhere, a mother who never had the opportunity to grieve properly for her missing daughter. After all these years, the doll that Alessia had kept held all the answers.

'Thank you, Rufus. That's really helpful,' Harriet said as she ended the call and recited what she'd just been told to her sergeant.

They watched as the GPR continued searching, the mood sombre.

Until finally, half an hour later, the wait was over.

'We've got something!' one of her colleagues said.

'You're certain?'

'Well, you know, the GPR can never be one hundred per cent. But it's always as close to it as can be. The only way you'll know for sure now is to dig.'

So they did.

'We've found her!' someone finally said.

And Harriet felt a sudden jolt deep in her stomach. Anticipation mixed with utter dread. The discovery was bittersweet. But they'd found her. At long last.

They'd found Sarah.

NOW

'Come on in, the patient is just through here,' Carl joked as he led Harriet through into the lounge to where Alessia was sitting on the sofa. 'Careful where you tread though.' Harriet smiled down at Jacob, who was crouched on the floor as he played with all his toys.

'I keep telling him, I'm not a patient,' Alessia said, shaking her head despairingly at Harriet. 'Seriously, Harriet, you'd think I'd broken both my legs the way that he's fussing over me. Not just a twisted ankle and a mild fracture to my arm. He won't let me do a thing.' Alessia nodded playfully at the chaos of the lounge floor, as if to prove her point.

'Oh dear, Carl. Well, I'd say that you definitely make a better nurse than you do a cleaner!' Harriet laughed. She knew full well that Jacob would be running rings around his father. And from the grin on Carl's face, he knew it too.

'Hey, it's a work in progress!' Carl said defensively, picking up Jacob as he squealed in delight, before he threw him over his shoulder.

'And I'm up against it. Every time I put something away, Jacob drags it back out of the toy box. Don't you, buster.' Carl laughed, tickling his son while Jacob giggled loudly in hysterics. 'Right, this one is due his afternoon nap. And I'm going to make some tea. Have you got time for one?'

'I do, yes.' Harriet smiled as she picked the dinosaur toys off the seat and placed them down on the floor. But there was an undercurrent to her tone. 'I came to speak to both of you, actually. We've had a development.'

Carl glanced at Alessia. Because they both knew exactly why Harriet was here. They'd both been waiting for her. Having both braced themselves for the news that they knew was coming.

'I'll be back in five.'

'He hasn't left my side for a second,' Alessia said, changing the subject when they were on their own again.

'Well, he's just worried about you. That's all. You've been through so much, Alessia,' Harriet said, knowing how worried Carl had been. How worried they had all been. What Alessia had gone through in her life was horrendous and completely incomprehensible. More so the fact that she'd been made to go through it alone. On her own. Without any love or support from the people around her. Until now. 'Let him. You deserve someone to fuss over you for a while.'

'I know. I know,' Alessia said. 'And I feel grateful to have you all. Really I do.' Because she felt the support. From them all. Harriet, and Carl. And Amanda too. She couldn't have got through all of this again without them. Carl had insisted on taking some time off work, so that they could spend some proper time together. The three of them. So that they could talk, properly. And Alessia had talked. Once she'd started it was if she couldn't stop. She had told him everything. With Amanda there too, to help guide her back through her trauma and make sense of everything that had happened back then.

'How's Jacob doing?'

'Generally, amazing. Kids can be so resilient in some ways. But he woke a lot in the night. So it must have affected him. We're just going to take one day at a time, hoping that we can give him back some normality. The three of us here, spending proper time together while Carl is off. He's loving having us both at home.'

'Well, if he has even half of your strength and resilience, he'll be just fine, Alessia,' Harriet said as Carl came back into the room. Carrying three mugs of tea.

'He's out for the count already,' Carl said as he placed the drinks down on the coffee table, next to the baby monitor which was permanently switched on now. No matter what time of day, or where they were in the house. Carl had also booked a security company to come and install cameras around the property too.

Even though Bobby had been arrested and would be charged with harassment and stalking, and the violent attack against Alessia. Even though Harriet had assured them both that the chances were he'd be receiving a custodial sentence, and that he'd be going to prison for a long time. Carl had insisted on securing the house for Alessia's peace of mind. And his own, if he was honest.

'I wanted to speak to you both, first. Before we make the official announcement,' Harriet said softly as she got straight to the point of why she was here. 'We found her. We found Sarah.' She clasped Alessia's hand tightly. Knowing how raw this news would be for her. How much sadness it would bring her.

'Sarah Benedict was ten years old when she went missing from a park, just outside her home, where she lived in Barking. A year before your stepfather died.'

Harriet placed the photo down on the table of the little girl.

Alessia took in the image of the girl, with her poker-straight brown hair, and her goofy, crooked smile. She gasped, and felt tears start to flow down her face. It was her. It was the girl she'd seen at the doll's house. Sarah. Sarah who had comforted her when she'd been sick and disorientated. Confused from whatever drugs she'd been fed. Alessia could remember it all: her voice as she sang her song and ran her fingers through her hair. And then she was gone. Huge wracking sobs took her then, shaking her body with their intensity. And she felt Carl's arms as they wrapped themselves around her. The warmth of him. Harriet, holding her hand, at her side. And she stared down at Sarah's smiling face. Remembering the time that they'd spent together in the doll's house. And the tears rolled down Alessia's face. Her chest heavy, weighted with pain and loss. And the horror of all that had been done to this poor girl. That she'd been left there, in the ground, on her own for so long.

'Our team of specialists dug the site up throughout the night. We found her in a shallow grave, behind the workshop. The other side of the chimney. He'd buried her there. And I wanted to let you know first. Before the press got hold of it. I wanted you to hear it from me.'

Alessia nodded her head gratefully. She'd known from the second that she'd stepped back inside the doll's house, the night she'd found Bobby there. That her memory had been real. That Sarah had been real. It had taken her going back there to finally remember it all.

'It was hard to tell because of the deterioration to the skeleton, but early indications conclude that the cause of death was more than likely strangulation. Her hyoid bone is broken which suggests severe compressive force. The tooth that you'd kept in the dress pocket of the doll was a match. It belonged to Sarah.'

Alessia closed her eyes as she realised why the doll had always felt so important. So significant. It had been the key to unlocking it all. And she'd had it with her all this time.

'I should have said something sooner. I should have known.'

'Alessia, you were just a child too. And you couldn't have known. You were suffering from trauma. You'd been through enough,' Harriet said.

Because it was proof that Sarah had existed. That Sarah had been real. Only the truth had been too hard to process, and Alessia had shoved it down. So deep down inside her that even she couldn't reach it. But in the end, Carl, Harriet and Amanda had all believed her. And now they'd found her.

After all these years they'd finally found her.

NOW

Alessia knelt on the damp grass and unwrapped the blue scarf that was covered in pretty purple butterflies before she stared down at the doll for the very last time. It had started to rain, and at first she hadn't felt the droplets as they landed on her, as she crouched there, at Sarah's grave. This was the grave that Sarah deserved.

Adorned with huge bouquets of brightly coloured flowers, a pink fluffy teddy bear and a rainbow-coloured windmill that twisted around in circles as the wind caught its sails. And Alessia smiled at that as the windmill twirled so magnificently in the breeze.

She was certain that Sarah would have loved it.

A white spray of light shone from the newly polished headstone as the sun caught it from above. As if the golden ray of sunshine was letting her know that it was fighting its way through the rain and dense cloud above her. And she eyed the smiling photo of Sarah staring back at her. Those steel grey eyes, that dark poker-straight hair. That goofy, crooked smile. The very same photo that Harriet had placed down before her the day she'd told her that they'd found her body.

It was just how Alessia wanted to remember her. Happy and smiling.

She read the inscription on the headstone.

SARAH BENEDICT.

LOVING DAUGHTER, SISTER AND GRANDCHILD.

YOU WERE THE SUNSHINE OF OUR LIVES.

And Alessia liked to think of her that way. Because the Sarah she had known had been there for her on one of her darkest days. She had stood at Alessia's side and ran her warm sticky fingers through Alessia's hair, as Alessia had slipped in and out of consciousness. Her sweet songs floating inside her ears. Sarah had comforted her and given Alessia hope. She had made her feel less alone.

And maybe a lot of the memories of the doll's house had been fragments of Alessia's mind. Maybe she had closed her eyes and dreamt it all up about the bird's nest they had found together. About the games that they had played. About the times that they had collapsed in fits of laughter huddled together on the floor.

Either way, it comforted her to know that Sarah had been real after all. That she had been there with her. Even if it was for only the shortest of times. She'd been there for Alessia when Alessia had needed her the most. And Alessia would never forget that. Holding up the doll, one last time, she stared at the small worn face, the tatty dress. And then she kissed it on the head, twice. Once for her, and once for Sarah.

'Sleep tight, Sarah.'

She placed it carefully back down on Sarah's grave. Finally back with her, back where it belonged. And it sat amongst the pretty flowers, and the brightly coloured windmill as it twirled in the wind.

Alessia stood and looked up at the sky. Wiping away a stray tear just as a rainbow managed to break out from beneath the darkened clouds. And the sun beamed down on her, shining brightly. She smiled. Sarah had brought the sunshine for her that one last time. And Alessia vowed to do the same. To keep Sarah in her dreams. In her heart.

Forever her best friend.

A LETTER FROM CASEY

Dear reader,

I want to say a huge thank you for choosing to read *I'll Never Tell*. This is my second psychological thriller, and I have to say I thoroughly enjoyed the dark, twisted turns that this book took as I started to write Alessia's story. As always with my books, I started the writing process with such a small seed of an idea, but *I'll Never Tell* very quickly evolved, almost as if it had a mind of its own.

For those readers who have followed me from the gritty gangland reads, thank you! I hope you enjoyed the change of pace, and that you still got your fix of darkness.

If you did enjoy this book, and you would like to keep up to date with all my latest releases, just sign up at the following link. Your email address will never be shared and you can unsubscribe at any time.

www.bookouture.com/casey-kelleher

I'd love to hear what you thought of *I'll Never Tell*, so if you have the time, and you'd like to leave me a review on Amazon it's always appreciated. (I do make a point of reading every single one.)

I also love hearing from you, my readers – your messages and photos of the books that you tag me in on social media always make my day! And trust me, some days us authors really need that to spur us on with that dreaded daily word-count.

So, please feel free to get in touch on my Facebook page, or through Instagram, Twitter or my website.

Thank you,

Casey Kelleher

www.caseykelleher.co.uk

 facebook.com/officialcaseykelleher

twitter.com/CaseyKelleher

instagram.com/caseykelleher

ACKNOWLEDGEMENTS

Many thanks to my brilliant editor Therese Keating. It's been an absolute pleasure working alongside you for a fourth time on this dark and twisted psych thriller. As always you really helped me pull the story together so perfectly. Wishing you the best of luck with your next venture. Thank you also to Janette Currie for the fantastic job with the copy-edits. All I can say is that thank God you don't have to trawl through some of my earlier drafts! Thanks for doing such a great job! Special thanks as always to the amazing Noelle Holten – PR extraordinaire! And to all of the Bookouture team. You guys really are the best!

Special mention to Emma Graham Tallon, one of the most genuinely loveliest, supportive people I've met since I started writing. I'm so lucky to have you as such a good friend. Also, my lovely friend, Emma Kennedy, also known as Alex Kane, who I was lucky to meet so early on in my writing career. So happy to see your books doing so well, you deserve it! Thanks also to Angela Marsons, Helen Phifer, Susie Lynes, Barbara Copperthwaite, Victoria Jenkins, and Pete Sortwell. For so many reasons, but mostly for all the giggles along the way (and for keeping me sane).

Huge thanks also to Colin Scott and for the Savvys for all your fantastic advice and support. And to all the lovely NotRights.

Special mention to the real-life Lucy Murphy, my bestie! Who has always been so super supportive of everything I do. And to The Party People! HA! You know who you are!

Thank you to Graham Bartlett and Neil Lancaster for all your help and advice when it came to police procedures. As always, creative licence does come into play when writing fiction, so any discrepancies will, of course, be mine.

As always I'd like to thank my extremely supportive friends and family for all the encouragement that they give me along the way – the Coopers, the Kellehers, the Ellises.

Finally, a big thank you to my husband Danny. My rock! Much love to my sons Ben, Danny and Kyle. Not forgetting our two little fur-babies/writer's assistants Sassy and Miska.

And to you, my lovely reader. This book is my fourteenth book, and marks the ten-year anniversary of my writing career. And what an incredible journey it has been so far. I say this often, because it's true. I truly have the best, most supportive readers. You are the very reason I write. Without you, none of this would have been possible.

Casey x